MURDER ON THE NILE

BOOKS BY VERITY BRIGHT

THE LADY ELEANOR SWIFT MYSTERY SERIES

1. *A Very English Murder*

2. *Death at the Dance*

3. *A Witness to Murder*

4. *Murder in the Snow*

5. *Mystery by the Sea*

6. *Murder at the Fair*

7. *A Lesson in Murder*

8. *Death on a Winter's Day*

9. *A Royal Murder*

10. *The French for Murder*

11. *Death Down the Aisle*

12. *Murder in an Irish Castle*

13. *Death on Deck*

14. *Murder in Manhattan*

15. *Murder by Invitation*

16. *Murder on the Cornish Cliffs*

17. *A Death in Venice*

18. *Murder in Mayfair*

MURDER ON THE NILE

VERITY BRIGHT

bookouture

Published by Bookouture in 2024

An imprint of Storyfire Ltd.
Carmelite House
50 Victoria Embankment
London EC4Y 0DZ

www.bookouture.com

Storyfire Ltd's authorised representative in the EEA is Hachette Ireland
8 Castlecourt Centre
Castleknock Road
Castleknock
Dublin 15 D15 YF6A
Ireland

ISBN: 978-1-83525-587-2
eBook ISBN: 978-1-83525-586-5

Three may keep a secret, if two of them are dead.

~ Benjamin Franklin, *Poor Richard's Almanack*

PROLOGUE

ENGLAND, 26 JULY 1924

The port town of Southampton was clothed in a cheerless blanket of drizzle as the ship docked. But Lady Eleanor Swift was just relieved to be back on dry land. Although as the Rolls splashed onwards through the sodden town, there was little 'dry' about it.

It had taken a week to travel back to Alexandria where they'd waited five days for a ship sailing to England. And now, nine days later still, they were here, three thousand miles from where it had all started. It had taken several hours to disembark, go through customs and reclaim the Rolls, by which time she would have heartily loved to book into the nearest hotel, fall into a hot bath, and forget about everything. But she was only a few hundred miles from the end of her promise. A promise she'd made a month ago, in a foreign land, to a dead man she hardly knew or liked...

1

EGYPT, 30 JUNE 1924 (A MONTH BEFORE)

Lady Eleanor Swift flicked a cloying red curl from her forehead and shielded her eyes against the fierce afternoon sun. Swarms of flowing robes, coloured headscarves, fezzes and skullcaps jostled along the palm tree dotted walkway down to the line of jetties on the banks of the Nile. She shook her head at the domestic livestock milling amongst the crowd, thinking such disorder would not be tolerated back home in prim and proper England. Twirling her ivory parasol, she turned to her butler.

'It's simply too... oh, what's the word, Clifford?'

'Chaotic? Crowded?' He sniffed, flicking a pristine handkerchief over the travelling cases at his feet. Whipping off his bowler hat, he flapped it admonishingly at a lop-eared goat nibbling on his jacket hem. 'Cacophonous, perhaps?'

The hem-nibbler dealt with, he passed Eleanor a flask of water. She took it gratefully, her throat parched.

'Yes, all those things. Clearly, however, this blistering Cairo heat is too much for you in a heavy English suit. I tried to get you to admit as much while we were in Alexandria the first week. And I implored you throughout our subsequent week here in Cairo to change into something cooler.' She shook her head, trying to look serious. 'But now, you're so overheated you're fighting with goats! Hardly befitting a butler, Clifford?'

His eyes twinkled with amusement. 'Whereas squabbling with one's mistress *is*, my lady?'

Before she could reply, the throng in front of them parted. Six Egyptian soldiers marched into view, their tightly grasped rifles leaving no doubt they were on patrol. Before they reached her, the two rear soldiers broke rank. Grabbing a man from the crowd, they dragged him in front of the other four. After a quick-fire exchange between the arrested man, the onlookers, and the soldiers, he was taken away, hands pinned behind his back. The whole incident had only taken a matter of minutes.

As the spectators dispersed, Clifford lowered his voice. 'If I might once more counsel vigilance, given these are rather turbulent times in this part of the world?'

She nodded, knowing he was referring to the aftermath of the Anglo-Egyptian war and Egyptian independence. It had, in theory, ended four decades of British occupation. The problem was, two years on and the British Army was still in force in the country. Ostensibly to protect Britain's interests, including the all-important Suez Canal. Eleanor had the feeling, however, most of the population held the view that they were actually there to make sure Egypt stayed firmly under the Empire's control.

She sighed with sympathy for the uncertainty the local people must be facing. Fortunately, the distrust and dislike of the British military didn't seem to extend to civilian travellers, and so far she and her entourage had been treated with nothing other than courtesy and kindness.

She waved an arm across the scene of teeming bustle towards the jetties. 'Our boat's boarding point might not be in quite the smartest quarter of Cairo as we expected, but at least we're here now.'

'*We* expected?' Clifford murmured.

She shook off the testy feeling the inescapable searing heat was bringing on. 'Go on, Clifford. Get it off your chest, I insist. You've been dying to since this morning.'

'Ahem. It merely strikes, my lady, that our three-day Nile cruise is the only part of our Egyptian sojourn not... *properly scrutinised*, if you will forgive the observation.'

'Meaning I chose it, not you?' she said, searching through her sage linen jacket's pockets with her one free hand. 'Clifford, the River Nile is the crowning gem of Egypt's exquisite wonders. A swathe of romantic mystique threading her way the entire length of the country and more.' She pointed down the slope at the wide expanse of blue-green water. 'Just imagine what that has seen on its near four-thousand-mile journey from the heart of the African continent to here.'

'If I might respectfully decline,' Clifford said with a shudder.

She tutted in mock disapproval. 'Stop fussing, do. Look! The magic of Egypt is perfectly encapsulated in the cruise offered in the brochure. I'm so pleased I had the foresight to collect it from the travel stand at the British Empire Exhibition in London. It must be. It says so. But now I can't find the blessed thing, dash it!'

An artfully folded set of two illustrated pages appeared in her eyeline, held between the thumb and forefinger of her butler's gloved hand. 'This one, perchance?'

'It might be.' She took it with a good-natured huff. 'You know, it has struck me as more and more odd during our time in Egypt so far.'

'What has, my lady?'

'That when Uncle Byron so kindly left me Henley Hall in his will, he didn't include a manual on how to survive the razor-sharp wit and unparalleled sniffiness of his long-standing butler and confidant!'

He bowed from the shoulders. 'Neither,' he said teasingly,

'did his late lordship leave his staff one on how to survive the lack of social etiquette and sensibility of their new mistress.'

She laughed. 'Touché! You and I are going to have so much fun squabbling until we catch up with the ladies in... What town was it?'

'Bawaaba. By which time they should be well settled into the rented townhouse. However, since nothing even remotely resembling the paddle steamer, SS *Cleopatra*, seems to be moored at the grand pier from which she supposedly departs in' – he examined his pocket watch – 'in a matter of minutes...?'

Eleanor looked along the jetties filled with a mixture of small cargo and ferryboats, quietly admitting he had a point.

'I know. It seems unlikely she'll leave on time. Granted. But our floating home for the next few days will make an even more regal entrance when she does finally arrive.'

'Hmm.' He scanned the river through a set of pocket field glasses, his six-foot frame helpfully setting him head and shoulders above most of the surging crowd.

She caught his brow flinch. 'What is it?'

'Hopefully only the debilitating effects of excessive heat. Because I have just spotted that the visible part of the name of the boat moored at the furthest jetty is "SS C-l-e-"—'

They both turned at a wheezy laugh from behind. A man with a worn leather bag from which poked an official-looking register looked between them, his black eyes dancing with humour.

'Sir?' Clifford said. 'You wish to say something?'

'Most certainly. It is not the sun playing tricks on you. That is the SS *Cleopatra*.'

Clifford tapped the brochure he was carrying. 'Well, it certainly does not resemble the boat portrayed in this illustration.'

Before the man could reply, Eleanor's attention was

diverted by a strident voice cutting across the surrounding hubbub with a series of barked commands.

'Get out of my way, people! Move aside! Now!'

She frowned at the man striding up the slope sporting a pale woven helmet, belted khaki jacket, and calf-length trousers with long socks. Realising that he was also imperiously waving a walking cane, she turned to Clifford.

'Thank goodness he's evidently just left one of the boats, rather than about to sour ours with his arrogant presence!'

Her butler nodded hesitantly. 'Indeed. Though, with a voice that carries so clearly I would conjecture it has been instilled from days of military service in some capacity.'

'That's no excuse. He's not in the barracks now. When you and Uncle Byron were in the army together, you would never have spoken to the local population like that.'

'Quite, my lady. As the gentleman seems to be English, it would be wise for him to moderate his behaviour if he wishes to avoid trouble in the current climate of unrest. And, in the process, lose his pith helmet!' He glanced at his pocket watch. 'Not wishing to change the subject, but perhaps we should board our boat before it leaves without us?'

He lunged for the luggage and retrieved it from the danger area as a wizened old man paused to let his equally long in the tooth donkey relieve itself. Eleanor hid a smile as Clifford followed her at a respectful distance, keeping a wary eye out for patrolling soldiers, arrogant Englishmen and incontinent donkeys.

2

Eleanor avoided Clifford's gaze. There was no denying the scrolling white lettering along the front bow spelled out 'Cleopatra'. The name, however, was the only similarity with the boat she'd booked in the brochure. The foredeck was open to the elements, rather than enclosed in an elegant conservatory-style superstructure as advertised. And, instead of two decks of highly varnished teak, there was one of sun-faded, black panelled wood. Cane chairs along the side decks, however, did add an old-fashioned charm, even if they were a little careworn. The rest of the boat looked much more promising, however.

'Oh, Clifford! Look at the row of darling cabins. The pretty oyster-grey panels, proper brass portholes and canvas sunscreens suspended between the rail and upper deck are just gorgeous.'

He sniffed loudly. 'Which is roofed by nothing more than what I suspect is stiffened sailcloth. Plus, the portholes are not all of the same design or size. To say nothing of the significant absence of a steam funnel and paddle wheel as also shown in the brochure.' He winced. 'And the engines sound as if they are on their last legs! Not to mention the clatter of the bilge pumps adding to the general cacophony.'

She sighed. 'Clifford, I can go alone, you know? Or I'll bail out of our booking altogether if you wish? This is your holiday too.'

He bowed his head, then looked up with a rare smile. 'I think not. The former would leave my mistress unrestrained to commit endless faux pas. While the latter would deprive her of the romantic mystique a trip on the Nile clearly conjures up, for some inexplicable reason. But sentiment noted and appreciated.'

'You are a sport, Clifford. Thank you.'

His lips pursed. 'However, the captain of this vessel has some serious explaining to do.'

She shifted her parasol to one side to look up at the wheelhouse. It had the air of an afterthought, being a boxy affair plonked between the fore and aft sections of the second deck. Behind the glass, a flash of mahogany curls below a navy-blue captain's hat made her wince in anticipation of the verbal roasting the man would soon receive from her butler.

'I say,' Clifford called, holding up their boarding tickets to a tall, slimly built man with fine features set in silken-looking, almost black skin who had appeared on the lower front deck. Dressed in a fulsome, ankle-length white robe, tied at the waist with a red sash which matched his tasselled fez, he cut a dashing figure.

Having leaped down onto the jetty with the nimbleness of a mountain goat, he put his hands together and shook his head. 'Sorry, sir. I am Deckhand Farah. No English.' Joined by another slimly built, but slightly shorter man dressed in a similar robe, he gestured between them with a broad smile. 'This, Deckhand Ali. Also no English. A thousand apologies.'

'A delightful welcome, nonetheless, gentlemen,' Clifford said equably. And pointlessly, it seemed, given the deckhands' mystified shrug. They flapped away his tickets, picked up the bags, and led the way up the steep gangway.

She set off after them, murmuring to Clifford, 'Gracious, how do they manage any kind of deck duties in those beautiful white robes without looking like they've just rolled in a muddy gutter?'

'I believe it is simply a case of taking care and not charging at everything as if one were a rhinoceros, my lady,' Clifford said drily.

She laughed. 'Very droll, you terror.'

As she stepped off the gangway onto the deck, she was met with a disembodied, 'One moment, please.'

Peering through the open French doors, she blinked in the darkness of the inside. After a moment, a square-built man in his forties with copper-brown skin and penetrating dark eyes topped by a navy skullcap swam into view as her vision adjusted. He seemed devoid of hair except for a short, but full black beard, which shook as he spoke.

'A good afternoon to you. I am First Mate Jabir. Welcome aboard the SS *Cleopatra*.'

His monotone revealed the lethargy behind his guttural Arabic accent, as if he'd regurgitated his introductory speech a few too many times before.

She smiled, taking in the striking cool blue of his partially buttoned jacket worn above white, blouson-bottomed trousers. Clifford offered their tickets again.

'This is Lady Swift. And I wish to speak to the captain immediately.'

Jabir remained unmoved. 'You may. But when he is free. Which is not now.' He turned to Eleanor. 'Your cabin, Lady Swift, is' – he took the tickets – 'the stateroom. At the end of this passageway to my right.' He nodded at Clifford. 'And you will find yours on the left.'

'And the captain?'

'Will happen along sometime.'

With that, he bowed to Eleanor and strode away.

'Stateroom, Clifford? How wonderful!' she said quickly to distract him from the outrage he would be feeling over her not being escorted personally to her quarters.

'Naturally, my lady. This booking could not have been countenanced if suitably generous accommodation for yourself had not been listed in the brochure.'

'I only really looked at the pictures,' she confessed, following him along the oak-lined passageway. 'They alone hooked me in.'

'Like a fish after bait. As it is now obvious was the intention,' her sharp hearing caught him murmur.

At the door marked with a slightly tarnished brass plaque bearing the word 'State', Clifford tutted. 'Clearly, the engraver charged by the letter.' He pushed it open and turned his back.

'Oh no you don't.' She nudged him over the threshold. 'I'm not setting sail until you've checked it over and given it your seal of approval. Although, as you know perfectly well, I inelegantly pedalled my way across the world on my bicycle alone not so long ago, so I've stayed in some—'

'Indeed you did, and have, my lady,' he interrupted hurriedly. 'But that was before you inherited your title.' He hesitated. 'Might you at least check first that your, ahem, sleeping and ablution areas are concealed?'

She slid past him. 'Quite safe, my ever-chivalrous knight.'

He stepped reluctantly in beside her. 'My lady!'

'Not concealed enough, hmm?' she said innocently. 'Well, you're in here now. And as I'm not rolling about on top of the sheets in my under-frillies or splashing about naked—'

He clapped his hands over his ears.

'—you might as well check it out with me. Look, there's a quite enormous bed with a brass bedstead set with sumptuous red pillows and exquisite silk covers with gold banded edging. And two bedside stands. All up these two steps on a raised dais.' She ducked under a small arch. 'And there's a miniature chaise longue in matching red, cream and gold accents in this little alcove area. Along with a dainty writing table and cane chair. Hanging space, with padded hangers too. And behind this screen which must slide out... look! Porcelain wash facilities generously proportioned enough that I won't sink the boat by flinging water everywhere. And that large porthole I could almost climb out of gives the suite plenty of light.'

Clifford, who had averted his eyes, now ran the tip of his gloved finger along the wood panelling of the wall. He then tapped the nearest lamp fitting, cocking his head to hear the tone it made. Stepping to the porthole, he inspected the cream curtains.

She crossed her fingers behind her back. 'What do you say?'

He pursed his lips. 'If the lady absolutely insists, it might just be deemed serviceable. Though it is far from the suite suggested.'

'Stateroom,' a smooth English voice with a hint of the exotic said.

They both turned to see a man in a jauntily tied red neckerchief, white shirt, trousers and peaked navy-blue cap leaning on the doorframe. A matching brass-buttoned jacket hung from his shoulders.

Clifford strode up to him. 'You are the captain of this craft, I presume?'

'Owner and captain, yes. Captain Anders. And you are the lady's man, I presume?'

Eleanor winced, recognising that glib response was probably the final straw for her butler's usually unshakeable sangfroid. She also couldn't help thinking that the captain had something of the rakishly attractive pirate about him. Those dark hazel eyes glinting in a suntanned face, framed by untamed mahogany curls! His resemblance to her own fiancé was unmistakable, although Hugh was always dressed in a suit and leaner-cheeked from overwork.

'This craft' – Clifford whipped the brochure from his pocket – 'is not at all as illustrated.'

Anders glanced at the images Clifford was pointing at. 'This purpose-built cruiser is the SS *Cleopatra*, her name being clearly printed here in the header.' He pointed to it. 'Those images at the bottom of the page are—'

'Of an entirely different craft!' Clifford said sharply. 'Being it is a paddle steamer. Of perhaps twice the size of this one. And what is more, "SS" is a universally accepted maritime abbreviation for "steamship" or "steam screw", which this boat is patently not, nor has ever been.' He regarded the captain sternly. 'I suggest, sir, that you have deliberately misled her ladyship, not to mention the other passengers.'

Anders' smile didn't falter. 'Well, this boat is the same one I started ferrying passengers up and down the Nile on fifteen years ago. And "SS" in this case is a maritime abbreviation for "Sebastian's Ship".' He tapped his chest. 'That's me. And if that's not acceptable, the lady is welcome to buy me a newer, bigger paddle steamer and I'll give her first choice on the largest suite aboard. Happy sailing, folks.' With a smart salute and another charming smile to Eleanor, he walked away.

'Good try, Clifford,' she said. 'You're absolutely right. But we can't actually refute his words, can we?'

He took a deep breath. 'Not without indicting him on a charge of criminally mangling semantics before a judge, no, my lady. Thus, shall we conclude what's done is done and make the best of it?'

She clapped her hands. 'That's the spirit! Nothing is going to spoil this trip.'

'Get out of my ruddy way, people!'

She rolled her eyes as more barked commands filtered through the porthole from the jetty outside. 'Nothing. And definitely not that bore. Goodness, I pity whoever's boat he's getting on!'

3

Twenty minutes later, at the prolonged blast of a whistle, indicating they were about to leave port, Eleanor yanked open her stateroom door, only to run slap into her butler. One hand raised to knock, he carried a small leather case.

'Ah, Clifford! Race you up onto the second deck for our last views of Cairo?'

He tutted. 'Might we remember the concession you made to adhere to at least a modicum of decorum on this cruise, my lady?'

'You mean, me not letting on that I have yet to master all the intricacies of being a titled lady? Or that I have, on occasion, got caught up in unladylike endeavours? Or both?' She smiled impishly. 'While I'm at it, I'll also pretend my butler isn't a total scallywag with all manner of dubious skills up his impeccable sleeves. How's that?'

He rolled his eyes. 'Too gracious. Please give my regards to Cairo. With your permission, I will finish unpacking to avert the inevitable aftermath of a certain lady unpacking for herself.'

Still smiling at his reply, her natural exuberance propelled her up the curving steps, taking them two at a time. At the top, she paused below the canopy roof among the sporadic cane chairs. She wasn't the first up there, however. A solidly built man in grey flannel trousers and a burgundy jacket was leaning over the starboard rail. As she approached, she called out, 'Good afternoon.'

The man spun around, hand to his chest, as if he'd received an electric shock rather than a cordial greeting.

'Gracious! Apologies if I made you jump.' She noted the man's square jaw and pale-blue eyes. The deep curving creases running from his nose to his chin highlighted his small pinched mouth, which was gripping a cigar, the falling ash not entirely missing his maroon bow tie.

'Afternoon,' he mumbled as he turned back too brusquely for her to place his accent.

'No wonder you are devouring the view,' she said. 'Just look at all those minarets, domes and exotic sandstone buildings. What a pity we can't join Captain Anders in the wheelhouse so we can see the whole intoxicating panorama in one unbroken vista.' She paused, but the man stayed silent. Shrugging at his lack of response, she ploughed on. 'I'm Lady Eleanor Swift, by the way. Forgive me. I probably should have started with that.'

The man sighed and turned to face her. She held out her hand. Not that he seemed at all inclined to take it. Instead, he removed his cigar and tilted his head, making his swept-back greying hair flutter in the breeze.

'I am Herr Ernst Piltz,' he said in a throaty voice.

She withdrew her hand.

Ah! German, I think, Ellie.

'Delighted.' She was genuinely always keen to meet people from different cultures. 'Holidaying too?'

'Business.'

She waited for more, but the man failed to elaborate. The prospect of being in confined proximity with this chap for the next three days didn't fill her with joy. 'I confess I'm pretty much a novice to Egypt. But I'm already convinced a lifetime would be too short to devour all the wonders she has to offer. I've seen some amazing sights since I arrived. Have you?'

'I live in Cairo,' he said with a cursory tone, leaning on the rail. 'I am a dealer of art. Modern art.' He blew out a plume of smoke. 'Is there anything else you feel the need to know?'

She smiled, taking the hint.

Not everyone wants to make new acquaintances, Ellie.

As the boat bumped the end of the jetty as it left the port, she turned away. 'I shall leave you to enjoy the view, Herr Piltz.'

Before she could, however, a man and woman stepped onto the deck. The first thing she noticed was how tall they were. All the more noticeable, given their matching khaki-belted jackets, although the man wore his with the sleeves rolled up to his suntanned forearms. He also sported loose trousers with long pockets, while the woman wore a stiff low-calf skirt with buttons up the front. Eleanor forced herself to stop marvelling that the man's shoulder-length shock of straw-blond hair was as untamed as his thick beard, while the woman's hair was tourniqueted into a high-top bun.

'Well, hello and good afternoon,' the woman said with only a slight nuance of an accent. She pointed at the view.

'And goodbye, Cairo.' The man's voice had a delightfully rhythmic cadence, stressing every other syllable. It seemed Eleanor's face had given her away, as he added, 'We are Dutch. But I am the one who sounds it most.'

Eleanor smiled at them. 'And yet, like Herr Piltz here, you speak superb English.'

Piltz offered only a wave of his cigar to the pair by way of greeting.

The woman nodded. 'Naturally, we are both fluent. No one speaks Dutch outside of Holland.'

'Which puts me to great shame,' Eleanor said. 'I'm afraid I couldn't say a word in either Dutch or German. My butler, however, probably can. Infuriatingly, he tends to trump me at most things.'

The Dutch couple laughed while Herr Piltz merely puffed on his cigar, seeming to have abandoned any pretence of polite interest.

'I am Ludo de Groot,' the Dutch man said. 'And this is Frederika.'

'Also, "de Groot",' the woman added quickly. 'We are wife and husband.'

Eleanor hid a smile. Such a perfect command of English suggested Frederika had reversed that everyday idiom on purpose.

Looks like she's the one who wears the trousers in their marriage, Ellie.

'And you?' Ludo asked.

'Happily engaged.' She was unable to stop her shoulders rising with glee as her fiancé's face swam into her mind. 'Wedding date not set quite yet, though. He's a detective chief inspector back in England, so it's hard enough for him to get the time off to eat properly, let alone get married!'

Ludo shook his head with an easy smile. 'I meant your name?'

'Ah, didn't I say? It's Eleanor.' She remembered her pledge to Clifford regarding decorum and etiquette. 'Lady Eleanor Swift.'

Frederika stared at her, then exchanged a glance with Ludo. 'Lovely to meet you, Lady... er, Swift. We haven't met many English ladies here. I have been to Egypt before, but for Ludo, it is his first time. We are archaeologists.'

'Really?' Eleanor said, genuinely fascinated. 'I imagine since the discovery of Tutankhamun's tomb, you are in high demand!'

Frederika nodded. 'There are digs everywhere. We are on our way to Aswan to join one of the most prestigious. There are around two dozen archaeologists there. It will be the pinnacle of our careers to date.'

'How exciting. I know a man who will be ecstatic to make your acquaintance later. And I hope you don't mind my saying, but your marriage seems a match truly made in heaven as you both share such an unusual passion.'

'It is.' Frederika turned the shiny gold wedding band on her finger, then slipped her arm through her husband's, which seemed to catch him by surprise. 'I doubt many women have been proposed to in a thirty-foot pit in central Greece, over a nine-thousand-year-old skeleton.'

Eleanor laughed. 'I daren't ask what delights you booked for your honeymoon, though part of me is dying to.'

Watching Frederika still toy with her wedding ring made her heart skip back to her own fiancé's fairy-tale proposal. They still had so many wonderful things to plan, she thought excitedly. Not least of which was the wedding date itself. And where they'd go on their honeymoon. A blissful smile lit her face at the idea of her being wife to the man who had made her feel whole for the first time in her life. She turned to Piltz.

'Are you interested in Egypt's ancient history?'

'No!'

She bit her lip, keen to hang on to the more convivial tone the conversation had taken since the de Groots arrived. She turned back to them. 'Herr Piltz lives in Cairo. You see, the poor fellow has already played twenty questions with me.'

'Who won?' Ludo said in a jocular tone.

'Lady Swift,' Herr Piltz gruffed, holding Eleanor's gaze.

Frederika nodded. 'Naturally. But tell me, as you live here, what is your opinion of the Egyptian government trying to close down the torrent of artefacts leaving the country?'

Herr Piltz threw the last of his cigar into the river. 'I have no opinion, Mrs de Groot. Since I do not care either way. I have interest only in my business. Which is to deal in art. Modern art. Now, please, you will all excuse me?'

He strode away across the deck, pausing begrudgingly at the top of the stairs to let a gracefully built Egyptian man in a crisp olive-green suit pass. Frederika pulled a disparaging face at Piltz's disappearing form.

'Ridiculous basis for a business. Whoever heard of modern Egyptian art!'

The new arrival paused. With a slight frown, he ran a hand over his wide black moustache, then turned and walked the other way.

Eleanor winced. And then grimaced as she caught a strident voice barking more haughty commands to the world at large.

The Englishman with the pith helmet, Ellie. We must just have passed the jetty or boat he's on.

Before she could hear what he was saying, Ludo spoke.

'Nervous, Lady Swift?'

She shook her head. 'Gracious, no. I'm actually too excited for words now we're underway.'

'Progress finally then, is it?' a melancholic voice said from behind.

Along with the Dutch couple, she turned around. A short, russet-haired man stood in front of them, tugging on the collar of his obviously over-warm brown tweed suit jacket. Framing his narrow face, his slicked back hair unflatteringly emphasised his large ears, which gave him the appearance of a wide-handled urn. She decided to do the introductions.

'This is Mr and Mrs de Groot. And I'm Lady Swift. Do please join us, Mr...?'

'Wesley Merrick. I'm travelling to Aswan.'

'Ah! A Welshman, perhaps?' Eleanor said, having caught the giveaway singsong in his intonation.

'From the valleys, as we say, yes.' His chest swelled enough for the neat row of matching silver pens adorning his breast pocket to glint in the sun. It didn't, however, seem to brighten his mood. 'Not that this is my first trip to Egypt, of course. No, no.'

Frederika shrugged dismissively. 'What an insatiable tourist you must be.'

Ludo's genial expression flinched as he glanced at her.

'Not a bit, Mrs de Groot,' Merrick said defensively. 'I reside here at present. I am on important company business. As I always am, wherever I am. Men of my busy ilk do not have time for the fripperies of sightseeing.'

Eleanor bit her lip. She was determined not to let anything or anyone's mood spoil her trip.

Let's put any irritability down to the oppressive heat, Ellie. Even normally easy-going people are bound to feel a little... testy. Or maybe there's more to it than that?

'Perhaps we've heard of your company, Mr Merrick? What line of business are you in?' she said brightly.

He snorted. 'Doubt you've heard of us. And, anyway, hardly matters nowadays, does it? It's twice as hard to get anything done! I tell you, we British should never have given this country so much as a sniff of independence!'

Oh dear, Ellie! Is there any safe topic of conversation?

She looked around, relieved that at least the Egyptian man seemed to have melted away. Hopefully far enough away not to have heard.

'Yes, yes, it's a terrible pity. For them,' Merrick continued firmly, adopting a straddled pose as if now fully mounted on his hobby horse. 'This country has never been better off than when we British were at the helm.'

Before Eleanor could offer a rather different view, Ludo waved a hand. 'But the early days of Egypt's glory, Mr Merrick? You don't see that in the magnificent ancient architecture? Even the British cannot claim the majesty of the pyramids. Or the grandeur of the Sphinx.'

Merrick sniffed. 'I haven't noticed. But why would I? That was then. This is now.' He waggled a finger. 'Take the pyramids, as you mentioned them. What use are they? Just occupying space where something industrious could be built. Like the Aswan Dam. Largest in the world when it was finished in 1902, you know. Why? Because it was built by—'

'The English,' Frederika said caustically. 'Not the Welsh.'

Merrick's pale face suffused red.

'But none of this matters,' Ludo said hurriedly. 'Not to new and... good friends.' He smiled broadly at Eleanor. 'We are each here for our own reason. What does it matter if the four of those are different?'

Frederika grabbed his arm. 'Three, Ludo, dear.'

Eleanor dug deep for something they might all agree on.

'We're definitely on the way now,' she said with extra gusto. 'Cairo is behind us. Adventure ahoy! And just look at those lush, thick-stemmed grasses growing along the bank. Is that papyrus, does anyone know?'

The others stared over the rail as a dark shape slithered through the clump she had pointed out and hit the water with a splash.

'Aagh!' Merrick whimpered, leaping back from the handrail.

Frederika threw him a scornful look. 'Really. It's only a crocodile.'

He scowled. 'There is nothing "only" about a beast who could bite any of us in two, madam!' Without so much as a backward glance, he stomped off to the stairs.

'Frederika, must you?' Ludo muttered.

'Talk? Yes, why shouldn't I?'

'I mean, can't you talk *nice*?'

Eleanor felt every inch the uncomfortable gooseberry as Frederika folded her arms. 'Except when it suits you that I don't, of course?'

'That again! Frederika, you know I'm thankful you agreed—'

'Ludo, dear,' his other half interrupted, suddenly all sweetness. 'Poor Lady Swift doesn't want to listen to us pretending to argue with each other.' She spun him smartly around, calling over her shoulder to Eleanor, 'We must go and unpack now. See you at dinner.'

Left alone, Eleanor stared out at the riverbank gliding by, trying to soak up the peaceful sound of water passing. After a minute, she gave in. The conversations had been so strained, she needed a little time with her infallible rock of good humour. Her butler.

As she stepped away from the rail, another sudden splash made her jump. She stared over the rail at the foaming water. A moment later, and the surface returned to its calm state.

She grimaced.

It will soon be your dinner time too, Ellie.

4

Finding her stateroom door ajar, Eleanor stepped in and glanced around.

'Gracious, Clifford, you wizard!'

Not only were all her clothes hanging in colour-coordinated ensembles, an occasional table had magically appeared. Purely, it seemed, to display a vase of graceful white lilies, their divine scent wafting through the cabin. A slim leather folio case lay open on her writing bureau, revealing a set of ivory vellum notepaper and envelopes, while a plump silk cushion sat on the cane chair. On one bedside stand was a silver tray with a small decanter of brandy and a balloon glass. On the other, a generous bowl of the tiger nuts she'd fallen in love with on day one in Egypt. And nestled on an extra pillow, a tantalisingly book-shaped parcel in emerald-green tissue paper awaited. She shook her head in affection.

'Thank you. But I want you to take these few days as a holiday, too.'

He bowed. 'Thank you, my lady.'

'Which means "no", you stubborn donkey!'

'Might a sherry assist the lady in navigating the dilemma of choosing her dinner attire?'

She shook her head again. At his stubbornness this time. 'Yes, please. A small snifter will serve as a welcome toast that our cruise has begun. Only, it's bad luck to toast alone, you know?'

He permitted himself a quiet sigh. 'My lady, I have already committed a gross number of infractions against the rules between butler and mistress.'

'A shockingly fearful amount, yes. But you've bigger ones to break yet. Because I'll need you at dinner, so no wriggling out of it. Or the snifter.'

With both of them sipping a fine Oloroso sherry she knew had been her beloved late uncle's favourite, she settled into the cane chair.

'Did you meet all the other passengers on deck, my lady?' Clifford said, moving onto unpacking the leather case he'd been carrying earlier.

'I don't think I can have. There were only four. Oh, and a fifth chap I didn't get a chance to talk to. How many cabins does the SS *Cleopatra* have?'

'I counted nine.'

'An odd number?'

'I believe there were ten, but your suite, the only one onboard, was fashioned from number one and two. Hence the cabin next to this one being number three.'

'Well, let's hope there are more passengers.'

He arched a questioning brow.

She shrugged. 'Conversation was tricky... to hideous, actually.'

'Ah!'

'"Ah!" is all very well, but we're trapped with these people for several days, so let's cross our fingers the other cabins are occupied.'

'Choppy sailing ahead then. But hopefully cool nights at least.' Clifford clipped an intriguing contraption with a fold-out fan to her bed's headrest.

'Something you've designed yourself, you clever bean?' She examined the slender pendulum set below an egg-shaped disc, weighted at each tip and bearing a central spindle wound with fine twine. From behind that, a slim brass rod extended upwards, ending at a stout hinged clip of crocodile-worthy teeth which held the fan.

'An adaptation, my lady. It is a perpetual-motion fan. It can be started by simply unlatching this small hook, like so. And paused by re-latching it, thus. Though I doubt the Father of Pneumatics, Hero of Alexandria, would recognise much of his inimitable genius in it.'

'It's perfectly wonderful, thank you. And "Hero of Alexandria"? I say, what a fantastically romantic name. If you'd said, I would have treated your love of scientific faddle with a visit to his workshop when we were in Alexandria.'

'Too kind. Though, it would have been a challenge without time travel apparatus. The gentleman passed away almost two thousand years ago. In seventy AD, if memory serves. Now, I shall leave you to unpack the, ahem, last case.'

'My underfrillies, perchance?' She laughed. 'I wondered why that case had a scarlet ribbon attached.'

'Courtesy of your housekeeper. Until dinner, my lady.'

'Earlier!' she called as he closed the door. 'Don't leave me to pre-dinner drinks alone, you rascal.'

A short while later, she stopped twirling in front of the mirror and nodded, her glossy red curls bouncing on her forehead. Her fern silk gown felt elegant and cool, which, given the stifling heat even at this late hour, was a blessing. The pearl beads of its organza-capped sleeves were echoed among the delicate embroidery around the gown's sash, which flattered her slim hips. And gave a demure suggestion of the feminine curves she always felt she lacked.

As she left her cabin, Clifford stepped from his. Number nine was opposite hers as the numbers ran down one side and up the other. He nodded approvingly at her attire, only to pinch the bridge of his nose at her wolf whistle.

'Titled ladies never whistle, my lady. Particularly not in such a... licentious manner.'

She tutted. 'Says the man looking even more handsome and distinguished than ever in his dapper dinner togs. I've never seen you wear a white evening jacket and black bow tie before. Nor a kerchief in your breast pocket. But rotten luck, Clifford. The only females aboard are me and a married woman, in case you were planning on having the decks covered in swooning ladies!'

Despite his chiding tut, his lips quirked. 'Shall we, my lady?'

Located amidships, the lounge was home to an eclectic selection of seating and coffee tables. The cherry wood panelled walls held a similarly diverse range of art, from framed scenes of boats to dancing couples. Dominating the centre of the room was a striking figurine of Cleopatra, sporting an elaborate head-dress. Eleanor thought it all romantically bohemian. Her butler's sniff told her he categorically didn't.

First Mate Jabir appeared with a tray of mosaic-patterned ceramic goblets. 'Good evening. I have flavoured sodas, fruit mixes, hop beer or Egyptian wine. Red or white.' He held the tray out to her. 'Which will you have?'

'The tall one with the reed straw, please.' Anything long and cold would be welcome. She caught Clifford's imperceptible shudder as he declined, asking that a carafe of water and two glasses be brought to their table instead.

'Oh look, there's Herr Piltz,' she said, spotting the solidly built German perusing several shelves of rather tatty books.

'He's a modern Egyptian art dealer. Let's go and... oh!' Piltz, having noticed her heading towards him, had grabbed the nearest book and strode out through the open side door to the deck.

She shrugged. 'Alright, let's not.' Selecting a wingback chair, she settled into it. Noticing her butler hovering, she whispered, 'Clifford, I know sitting with me goes against your ever-respectful approach, but how's it going to look if I have to physically wrestle you into a seat every time?'

'Distressingly, not that far from the norm, my lady.' He pinched the tops of his suit trousers and perched reluctantly on the opposite chair.

She sucked on the straw, which made the malty liquid splash back up her throat into her nose. 'It's delicious,' she wheezed.

'Hello again, Lady Swift.' The slightly downbeat tone of the words from behind her needed no further introduction.

'Mr Merrick, how delightful. This is Mr Clifford. Won't you join us?'

His short frame appeared at her elbow, his previously slicked russet hair now so thickly oiled, it seemed almost mahogany. His clothes were different, too. Gone was his over-warm tweed suit, but the midnight velvet jacket he now sported looked hotter still. He dropped into the wingback Clifford slid over.

'Well...' he said hesitantly. 'Here we are then?'

Eleanor hid her smile, her worries she would be the passenger least versed in social chit-chat banished.

'I know. And keen for dinner.' She flapped a discreet hand at Clifford's evident dismay at her stomach gurgling in unladylike assent. 'I believe, Mr Merrick, that you will be on board for longer than me as you are going all the way to Aswan, aren't you?'

He huffed loudly. 'Unfortunately, yes. If only Aswan wasn't so wretchedly far down this infernal waterway.'

'Mr Merrick is travelling there on business,' she said to Clifford, before turning back to Merrick. 'Do remind me, what line did you say your company is in again?'

'I don't think I did, as it happens.' Merrick eyed Jabir's tray as he stopped in front of them. 'I'll have white wine.'

'And our water, if you please,' Clifford said, taking the carafe and two glasses.

Before she could pick up the conversation, a barked command interrupted her.

'Well, sort it, man! And produce some gin, for pity's sake.'

Eleanor groaned to herself, hoping it wasn't who she feared it was. Catching Clifford's eye, he arched a brow in confirmation. The overbearing Englishman she'd thought was sailing on another boat was actually a fellow passenger.

'You were saying, Mr Merrick?' Clifford said smoothly.

The businessman busied himself inspecting his drink. 'Was I? Oh, yes. About at home in Wales being where I'd rather be.'

She frowned. No, he wasn't, Ellie.

As Clifford went to reply, the Englishman marched up to them, waving his cane impatiently at Deckhand Ali to bring another chair.

'Evening, people. Shocking show on this primitive canoe, of course. But what could we expect?'

He at least had the courtesy to nod to Eleanor before plumping down into his seat, but her hackles were still bristling from his superior attitude.

She smiled sweetly. 'I think the SS *Cleopatra* is wonderful, Mr...?'

He looked at her as if she had been recently dropped on her head. 'Alton Baxter. Lieutenant.'

'May I present Lady Swift?' Clifford said firmly. 'And Mr Merrick.'

Looking marginally abashed by her title, Baxter's gaze flicked away from scrutinising her face. 'Hmm,' he grunted. 'Not old hands in Africa though, any of you, I can tell.'

Eleanor bit her tongue in deference to her promise to Clifford not to let on about her adventurous past. However, the rigid set of her butler's shoulders betrayed that he himself was itching to deflate the puffed-up newcomer by regaling him with her exploits in Africa and further afield.

'Thought so,' Baxter continued. 'Myself, I've been protecting British interests abroad most of my career. And a goodly amount of that time guarding the Suez Canal and other strategic points in this damnable country. Really, the stories I could tell!'

Eleanor hoped he wouldn't. 'As you aren't in uniform, Lieutenant Baxter, is it impolite to ask if you are no longer in military service? Or perhaps you're on leave?'

That seemed to catch him off guard. 'Uniform, what? Oh, no, Lady Swift, I don't wear it. Not on leave. Now, where's my dratted drink!' he added, frowning around the lounge.

On following his gaze, Eleanor noticed the Egyptian man entering. She waved in the hope he would join their party. He did.

'Good evening,' he said in a soft-spoken voice as he came over. 'Please forgive my intruding.'

She shook her head. 'Not at all. We're all just getting acquainted. Do take the seat Mr Clifford has pulled up for you while I do the introductions.'

He listened intently as she did so, nodding to each of them in turn. 'It is my pleasure to be travelling with you all. My name is Yakub Sharaf.'

Eleanor went to speak again but realised she wasn't sure how to address him.

'Our collective pleasure also, Sayyid Yakub,' Clifford said, clearly having read her mind.

He nodded appreciatively, his smile broadening. 'Thank you for your politeness. For ease though, "mister" is better for everyone, I think. Or even Yakub, if anyone prefers just first name terms?'

'From Cairo, are you, Sharaf?' Baxter barked, using none of Sharaf's suggested forms of address.

'Actually, I am from a small town far from here,' he said amiably. 'I am travelling only as far as Bawaaba.'

That's where we're meeting the ladies, Ellie.

She gestured between her and Clifford. 'We've so much to see along the way. Like the tomb tour tomorrow. Who else is booked on that?'

'Total waste of time!' Merrick declared fervently.

She groaned, wishing she hadn't asked.

'Frankly,' he continued, 'I'd rather sit here and stare at the wainscotting.'

'You'll have trouble, in my experience,' Eleanor said. 'I don't think there is any. It's far from a common feature on boats.'

She caught Sharaf hiding a smile.

'About time!' Baxter grumbled as he took a drink from Jabir's tray. He waved it at Merrick. 'With you on that. Who's interested in a crumbling hole in the ground? Or the piles of old rubble masquerading as tourist sites in this blasted country?'

Eleanor turned apologetically to Sharaf, but he laughed, a soft musical chuckle that made her smile. 'Lady Swift, I confess, I also have visited enough of my country's ancient monuments to last me for a good while!'

'Does that mean you won't be joining our tour tomorrow, then, Lieutenant Baxter?' she asked innocently, hoping fervently his answer would be yes.

He downed the rest of his drink and rose. 'I wouldn't be seen dead there!'

As he strode off, she shook her head to herself.

Dash it, Ellie, Clifford was right. Why did you have to pick this cruise?

5

The strains of a reedy trumpet cut across the SS *Cleopatra*'s lounge. Eleanor caught her butler shudder as it tailed off in a discordant whimper.

'Dinner is ready!' First Mate Jabir announced.

She hid a smile. 'Makes a change from being called by a gong, doesn't it?'

'As would fingernails scraped down a blackboard, my lady,' Clifford said drily. 'With equal disincentive to one's digestion, however. Though one amongst us will no doubt prove me wrong,' he added mischievously.

She laughed. Keen to start the charge towards the dining room, she paused as he beckoned Jabir over.

'I trust Captain Anders is on his way?'

Jabir's black beard twitched dismissively. 'He is not. Too busy.'

'To join his guests for dinner on the first evening?' Clifford tutted. 'Neither her ladyship nor I have seen him since we left Cairo. Beyond the pale, frankly.'

Jabir shrugged. 'But I think you wish the *Cleopatra* to arrive safely to your destination? So does he.'

'Lady Swift, if it is not inappropriate of me to ask?' Sharaf's soft-spoken words made her spin around. He bobbed his head apologetically as he put his hands behind his back. 'Maybe I can accompany you to the table?'

She mirrored his stance to let him know she understood his religious reasons for not offering her his arm. 'I would be delighted.' She glanced around. 'Have Mr and Mrs de Groot heard the trumpet summons to eat?'

Jabir shrugged again. 'Probably. But not with pleasure.'

'Why do you say that? I'm sure they're hungry like the rest of us.'

'Headache. So, no dinner wanted.'

'Oh! Shame one of them will miss it. Which one, by the way?'

'Both.'

'A double pity. Still, more for us then,' she said, forgetting she was trying to be the polite society lady. Sharaf's quiet musical chuckle not having quite drowned out her butler's weary sigh, she added, 'I meant, er, I'm sure it will be delicious.'

Jabir flapped them all forwards. 'Of course. I am also the chef!'

On entering the dining room, Eleanor decided that any failings the SS *Cleopatra* might have had up to that point were more than made up for by the exquisite backdrop. The setting sun filled the wide span of arched windows, bathing the entire space in a burnished glow. The main table was dressed in tasselled gold linen, which shimmered in the light of the lamps dotted along its length. At each of the seven place settings, crimson-stemmed glasses matched the pyramid-folded napkins, flanked by golden cruet sets and cutlery. The crowning centrepiece was an enormous glass bowl ringed with soft-fringed palm fronds framing vibrant indigo lotus blossoms. Two woven reed bladed fans turned slowly above it all.

Sharaf led her to the central lattice-backed chair which had the best view of the sunset and pulled it out for her.

'Goodness, how special,' she said breathlessly, overcome with the romance of it all. 'The serving cutlery is resting on exquisite ceramic-painted fish, too. And even the lighted salver braziers are as intricately patterned as the wall panelling.'

Clifford gave her a reassuring nod to show he was considerably appeased on her behalf at the crew's efforts.

Once the men's ritual undoing of jacket buttons, tugging on waistcoat hems and pinching trouser tops saw them all seated, he took his place. He half rose again as a man in his early thirties with champagne-fair hair and deep-lagoon blue eyes ambled in. The new arrival waved cheerily.

'Hello, all. I'm Trott. Felix Trott. Sorry if I'm late. I got totally caught up scouting for specimens.'

She noticed Merrick was fussing with the silver pen clips adorning the breast pocket of his velvet dinner jacket. Given how intently he was fiddling to align them exactly spaced, she felt a wave of sympathy for him. Perhaps they were more of a crutch for anxiety in social situations than the much-needed tools of the busy businessman he'd insisted he was.

'Park yourself on the double, if you will! Trott, was it?' Baxter huffed. 'The natives have likely been holding back on serving rations until you joined the fray.'

She was about to tut to herself at the lieutenant's lack of manners when she registered the tone of his voice. Despite his gruff words, he'd sounded less... sure of himself than before? She glanced at him again, noticing him tapping his fingers on his arm.

Is our fearless lieutenant nervous, Ellie?

Before Trott could oblige and 'park himself on the double', all gazes swung towards the door at the sound of voices. Voices speaking something akin to the Afrikaans Eleanor had always delighted in hearing during her years in South Africa.

'Ah, Mr and Mrs de Groot. How wonderful you're feeling bright enough to eat after all,' she said as the Dutch couple appeared in the doorway.

'It was nothing. We are recovered,' Frederika said, switching seamlessly to English over the sound of the men's chairs sliding back as they all rose. She cleared the floor to the table first, leaving a resigned-looking Ludo to catch her up.

'Good evening, everyone.' She scanned the faces of the other diners. As her gaze fell on Clifford, her cheeks flushed, and she slid quickly into the empty seat beside him. As everyone sat down again, Ludo slid resignedly into the chair opposite him.

Deckhand Farah stepped in, dressed in an enchanting red ochre robe and yellow sash. 'Excuse, please.' He smiled, hurrying to set out two more place settings.

'Yes, alright. All present now. Hasten the food, would you, man?' Baxter huffed. Turning to the other diners, he snorted. 'Whoever heard of the first mate being the chef, I ask you!'

Again, Eleanor noticed a slight waver in Baxter's voice. He also seemed to be scrutinising everyone's faces so intently, she wondered what he was looking for.

She looked around the table, intrigued. On her left was Sharaf, then Trott. On her right, Piltz, then Ludo, who had the air of a man already on his last effort to elicit more than a monosyllabic response from the German. On the other side of the table, opposite Sharaf, was Merrick, who was fussing with his napkin. And next to him was Frederika holding court over the politely nodding Clifford. Eleanor turned to Trott.

'Would some introductions be helpful?'

His face broke into a boyish grin. 'Do you know, there's not a face here that means a thing to me.'

As the introductions were completed, Farah re-entered with his colleague Ali, carrying a pot-bellied cauldron between them. Jabir followed, balancing a tower of bowls and baskets against his green and yellow splashed apron. He passed the first to Eleanor, indicating she should pass it on down to the other diners. Once all the bowls were distributed and the baskets of bread placed on the table, the crew left.

Eleanor looked up from her bowl of potage. 'What an exquisite green colour. Almost like melted jade.'

Merrick tentatively poked his spoon at it. 'Looks like they've dredged the bottom of the Nile!'

Eleanor tried not to look at Sharaf as she winced.

'Can't be,' Trott said jovially, 'because there's no crocodile lurking in mine. Or did I simply miss out on one?'

The whole table laughed, including Sharaf. But not Merrick, who pushed his untouched bowl away.

Waiting no longer, she dived in to taste it. 'It's genuinely delicious. Do you know its name, Mr Sharaf?'

He nodded. 'It is called *molokhia*. Its main ingredient and source of colour is mallow plant leaves which are most nutritious.'

'It's sublime. As are the baskets of fresh breads.'

Amid more sporadic efforts at general chit-chat, Farah and Ali reappeared and set a series of long platters along the braziers running down the centre of the table. The new offerings looked so enticing, Eleanor hurried through her last few spoonfuls of *molokhia*.

Bowls cleared, the platters were passed around. Eleanor turned to Sharaf questioningly. He inclined his head.

'These are *maluf mashi*, cabbage rolls filled with rice and beef. Those are *tameya*, chickpea falafels, I think you would say. That is *kofta*, lamb on skewers. And these are *kibbeh*, bulgur wheat and minced beef parcels. The spicy sauce is *harissa*. And to dip your oiled bread in is *dukkah*, a mix of spices, nuts and herbs.'

Eleanor clapped her hands. 'I never realised this cruise down the Nile was going to be such a culinary odyssey!' She caught Clifford's eye playfully. 'Reason enough alone to have come. But, of course, it is already a cultural odyssey as well.'

'Everyone is here for their own reasons,' Piltz said, as if he'd suddenly found his voice. Eleanor's neck prickled. Not only had he all but echoed Ludo's earlier words, but his tone had been positively... she searched for a word other than 'ominous' or 'foreboding', but came up empty. Glancing at Baxter, she was surprised to see he was polishing his wine glass with his napkin. Long-standing military men in her experience were usually less fussy, having eaten and drunk goodness only knew what in the cause of duty. Except for her still ever-meticulous butler, who'd served as her beloved uncle's batman. She shook her head in amusement as Baxter surreptitiously sniffed his now full glass.

Has he suddenly become paranoid, Ellie? He's acting as if he thinks someone's trying to poison him!

Ludo waved down the table to Trott. 'On the reasons for travelling here, we are archaeologists.'

'And married,' Frederika added, frowning at him.

'Married archaeologists, eh?' Trott said. 'Well, I'm a single herpetologist.'

Baxter frowned. 'Not surprised. A word of advice, mind. Wouldn't go around advertising that in these parts if I were you! Not the single part. The other one.'

Eleanor bit back a smile. She didn't know what a herpetologist was, but given Clifford's disconcerted twitch at Baxter's pronouncement, she doubted it had anything to do with the unmentionable medical condition it sounded like.

'A herpetologist, Mr Trott? An expert on reptiles,' Clifford said smoothly. 'How interesting Egypt must be for you.'

Trott nodded. 'Rather! I'm here to study the Nile crocodile. Grows up to twenty feet, you know. They're cold-blooded killers. Fascinating habits. Once they have you in their sights' – he grimaced theatrically – 'a truly gruesome end awaits.'

Merrick's fork clattered on the floor. 'Clumsy of me,' he muttered, ducking under the table.

Trott continued unabashed. 'They are unimaginably clever. Many reach fifty years in age so they've seen, beaten and eaten everything in their time!'

Merrick reappeared and perched on the edge of his seat. 'I'm sure everyone's heard enough, thank you.'

Trott grinned at him. 'Just offering useful advice, old man. Because really, they kill hundreds, if not thousands, of people every year. They're even more deadly than the Egyptian cobra whose venom can kill an adult elephant in three hours. The cobra only attacks if threatened, you see, while the Nile croc—'

Merrick scraped his chair back and stalked out. As he did, she saw a look of triumph flicker across Trott's face. Eleanor's brow furrowed. Surely she'd misread it? Trott had insisted he knew no one at the table, so he couldn't have known the Welshman was terrified of crocodiles?

'Maybe our Egyptian spices are not agreeing with Mr Merrick?' Sharaf said mildly.

Ludo shook his head. 'It was Mr Trott's rather... colourful description, I think,' he said, voicing Eleanor's thoughts. And Clifford's, his coded glance her way told her.

'I can't see why you would think so, Ludo,' Frederika scoffed.

'Because I was uncomfortable myself to hear it with ladies here at the table,' he said stiffly.

His wife tutted. 'Nonsense! You know that I am not a wilting flower. And Lady Swift most definitely isn't one, according to...' She cleared her throat loudly, avoiding Eleanor's gaze.

Eleanor fought to keep a frown off her face. She'd kept her word to Clifford and given no hint of her previous unladylike exploits. Nor of her more recent ones solving several murders.

'Ah! Sounds like the main course arriving,' Ludo said.

Everyone turned towards the door. Except Baxter, Eleanor noticed. He was staring fixedly at Frederika.

Sharaf gestured at the dish of rich, sun-ripened tomato stew now in front of her. '*Bamya*. Okra with beef.'

Her taste buds tingled at the wafts of garlic, cardamom and coriander swirling up from the pointed green vegetable halves which looked as succulent as the meat rings.

'Oxtail, my lady. Stewed and served on the bone.' Clifford gestured discreetly at the empty side dish they had all been given for the debris.

Trott speared a meat ring from his stew. 'See now, with a crocodile amongst us, we could just throw all these bones his way. Their stomach juices are so acidic they dissolve their victim entirely. Including the bones, you know, so no trace remains.'

Although Eleanor was not squeamish, his words brought on a rash of goosebumps.

Gracious, how macabre, Ellie! If it was a case of murder, all the evidence, including the body, would simply disappear!

'They are the perfect killer,' Piltz said, breaking his silence again. That he had echoed Eleanor's unspoken thought unnerved her all the more.

'You're right. Truly deadly,' Frederika said.

Ludo sighed. 'Surely enough now, everyone?'

'Hear, hear!' Baxter muttered into his stew. He glanced up. 'They're nothing but bigger than average fish with a poor attitude.'

Given his mood swings over dinner, she wondered if she'd misjudged him. Maybe his gruff military exterior was more a defensive front? Long-gone days of former glory could do that, she thought.

Farah and Ali brought in dessert; nougat with honeyed nuts. Trott, Ludo and Baxter, however, rose and excused themselves almost as a man.

'More for us, Lady Swift,' Sharaf said quietly, making her smile that at least someone else seemed keen on enjoying the trip.

Later, in her cabin, the hypnotic swish of Clifford's ingenious fan and her surprisingly comfortable bed brought on a welcome drowsiness. She nestled into her pillows and slid into the arms of deep sleep.

Her next barely conscious thought was that the gargantuan crocodile she was balancing on wasn't being helpful. How could she hope to referee the boxing match that had erupted between the other passengers if the reptilian beast was going to bump into things like that?

She forced herself to open one eye and blinked blearily around her suite. Had she been dreaming, or had that been an actual bump? She dragged her head off her pillow to listen questioningly, but only the fan's rhythmic swish answered. Putting it down to the effects of the heady spices and wine at dinner, she drifted back to sleep. And a more obliging crocodile.

6

'What better way to spend the morning than a delightful donkey ride across the shimmering sands, Clifford?' Eleanor waved her hand at the desert landscape as her butler's soft-grey steed joined hers at the head of the party.

He eyed her sideways. 'Heartening news that one of us finds the indignity such, my lady.'

She waggled a finger. 'No use you playing the stuffed goose. Not after letting slip that you and Uncle Byron lived like cowboys when you were in the wilds of America. No doubt, on highly dubious business.'

He sniffed. 'On thoroughbred Quarter Horses, actually, my lady. Of impeccable grace and speed, if you will forgive the correction. But never with vultures circling low enough to see the rapacious intent in their eyes!'

She squinted up into the blinding white flare of the midday sun, gaping at the ring of leviathan birds wheeling slowly overhead. 'Oh my! I haven't seen any since I left South Africa. I say, Clifford, this trip is turning out to be... ah, yes.' She put on a prim face. 'That thing that we titled ladies would never engage in, of course.'

His lips quirked. 'Good effort. But clearly still nothing calls the lady's spirit more than adventure.'

'Or her butler's,' she half teased.

The burnished dune dipped dramatically without warning. The two local donkey handlers leading their party disappeared over the edge. Behind them, one of their party inhaled sharply. But as surefooted as mountain goats, the other donkeys followed, picking their way down the loose slope as if merely on a ramble.

On the sand-rippled plateau, the handlers dismounted at a handful of abandoned walls seemingly randomly erected amid the endless miles of desert.

She stood up in her stirrups and peered to where they were unpacking the donkeys' slim saddlebags.

'A picnic in the shade, do you suppose, Clifford?' she said eagerly.

'Only for those of us keen to devour the history of an ancient culture, rather than more of the local cuisine so soon after breakfast.'

She tutted. 'It wasn't my fault that the poached eggs were served in that divine paprika-spiced sauce. And with tomatoes and sweetened onions. So moreish! I just had to have a second helping.'

'The moreishness, or otherwise, of the *shakshuka* notwithstanding, I believe we have arrived at our tomb, my lady.'

She eased her mount to a stop and glanced around. 'Mmm. Not quite what I imagined.'

Ludo brought his donkey alongside hers and stretched his long legs out stiffly. 'The most interesting finds are always underground, Lady Swift.'

She laughed. 'Not that you're biased as an archaeologist, I suppose?'

'Hmm, maybe a little,' he called back cheerfully as his donkey plodded on ahead.

'My husband is right.' Frederika appeared at Eleanor's elbow. 'We have never found anything worthwhile lying in ready view. If you want to uncover the secrets of the past, you must be prepared to dig for them!'

Eleanor nodded. In her experience, however, unearthing secrets from the past could be dangerous. If not deadly. 'Out of curiosity, what particular aspect of archaeology do you specialise in?'

Frederika's eyes shone. 'The remains of human life! Here in Egypt, mostly represented by mummies, Lady Swift.'

'Bit of a macabre reply, Clifford,' she muttered, gesturing at Frederika as the woman rode on ahead of them.

He nodded. 'On paper, perhaps, my lady. However, to the anthropological branch of archaeology, the ahem, deceased, can offer the prize of previously unknown knowledge. Opening a window, as it were, onto lost civilisations.'

'Move, beast!' a gruff voice urged from the rear of their group. Baxter's donkey laid its ears back and stayed where it was.

Trott chuckled, leaning on his mount's neck to catch Eleanor's eye. 'Unpredictable creatures these. You know where you are with crocodiles.'

'As you described in great detail again over breakfast, Mr Trott,' Clifford said pointedly.

'Always keen to share, my friend,' Trott replied genially. 'I so hope there's a raft of mummified ones in there. The ancient Egyptians worshipped them, you know.'

She said nothing, watching the handlers assist Frederika, Ludo and Trott down from their mounts to join the impatiently pacing Baxter, who had given up on his donkey. Oddly, his eyes darted left and right as he walked, and he was wringing his hands.

Piltz, meanwhile, looked offended that both men offered to help him down, though he didn't protest as his heavyset build was finally heaved out of the saddle.

Eleanor smiled and shook her head as they then offered to help her. She slid lithely down in unison with Clifford, then slipped around to his side.

'Baxter seems very keen, doesn't he?' she whispered. 'Odd, as he was very definite in his disparaging opinion of Egypt's historic sites. He must have told First Mate Jabir last night he'd changed his mind for there to be an extra donkey on hand.' She busied herself with her hat as Baxter caught her looking at him.

'And Piltz, Clifford?' she continued. 'What interest can an ancient burial chamber have for a dealer of modern art?'

He shook his head. 'I do not have an answer to either, my lady. Perhaps I might instead note that this marvel was created close to four and a half thousand years ago?'

'Fascinating. Genuinely.' She waved him forward. 'Come on, my favourite historical boffin. Let's go be overawed.'

The forty-foot-high walls of the tomb's entrance were built of sizable clay bricks. Pink inside, the sun had bleached their exterior to ghost grey. But it was the remnants of a leviathan sculpture, set on a weathered plinth, that caught her eye. She walked around three of its sides, the fourth built into the tomb wall itself.

'Gracious, it's a pair of giant legs, Clifford!'

The others drifted over like curious sheep.

'Indeed,' Clifford said. 'Possibly once those of Anubis. Often depicted as half-man, half-jackal. Widely considered to be the ancient Egyptian deity responsible for, amongst other associated tasks, protecting graves and ushering the deceased into the afterlife.'

'Do not any of you wish to hurry inside, out of the sun!' Jabir grumbled.

'Frankly, even less now,' Eleanor's sharp hearing caught Baxter mutter as he dragged his gaze away from the statue's remains.

Ignoring him, Jabir ushered everyone into the tomb.

Inside, as her eyes adjusted to the dim interior lit only by flaming torches, Eleanor's breath caught. Pleased all the others, except her ever-respectful butler, had surged on ahead, she stepped forward reverently, running her hand down the first of the elephantine columns. The atmosphere felt charged with an inexplicable sense of suspense.

'Clifford. I feel like I'm standing on the very threshold of time,' she whispered.

He nodded. 'I concur, my lady.' He slipped out his slim, leather pocket book and opened it at two crisp new pages.

They walked on slowly, equally entranced by the monolithic, yet intricate, architecture and the expansive wall carvings disappearing into the lofty shadows. She willed her footsteps not to echo on the gargantuan stone slabs of the floor. Spirits were resting there. She could feel them. And she felt every inch a guilty intruder.

'A regardful visitor warrants no comparison with a grave robber, my lady,' Clifford said, seemingly having read her mind. She glanced at his notebook, the pages already filling with meticulously inked symbols, sketched figures, and cross-section diagrams.

The second great hall was flanked on either side by eleven formidable statues, each thirty feet high, and all wearing elaborate headdresses.

She caught the voices of the de Groots and Trott receding ahead, out of sight, then the tap of Baxter's cane. She followed Clifford as he criss-crossed to each statue, pen poised over his page. Having overtaken him, she continued into the next chamber.

She stopped dead, her hand flying to her heart.

'Goodness, Lieutenant Baxter! You made me jump, lurking like that.'

'Lurking! What a suggestion, Lady Swift!' he blustered. 'I merely came to check you were not lost, since you've not been with the rest of our party from the off.' He glanced around nervously as if expecting to see one of them leap out at him.

She shook herself. 'Oh, thank you. Then my apologies. But I'm simply too entranced to go any faster. And Mr Clifford is with me, just over there.'

His gaze felt a little too intense to be comfortable. 'I hadn't imagined you as a devotee of times long gone?'

Nor you, she thought. 'What have you been imagining me as, then?' she said out loud.

He traced the carving in the doorway with his finger. 'Perhaps, umm, a lady, equally fierce in intellect as determination?'

'A most astute estimation, Lieutenant.' Clifford's firm tone filtered over. He cleared the gap in two long strides and regarded Baxter coolly. 'Though a somewhat questionable statement for a gentleman barely acquainted with her ladyship?'

With a quiet growl, Baxter spun on his heel and marched away. As he went, she noticed his eyes darting around again.

'What was that about?'

Clifford half bowed. 'Apologies, my lady. I should, perhaps, not have spoken out of turn.'

She tutted. 'Not *your* behaviour, my ever-chivalrous knight. I meant *his*. He's acting quite differently from yesterday. He seems more' – she shrugged – '*anxious*? And less, I don't know, less of an oaf?' She smiled at his chastising look. 'Mr Sniffy, this tomb is too magical for us to squabble in.'

'Shame,' he quipped, gesturing for her to lead on.

The doorways to each of the next four halls shrank in size until they were barely wide enough to pass through. In each chamber Clifford pointed out the deep curved recesses, which he suggested had been used to house embalming oils, mummification linens and other items he declined to list.

In the last chamber, she stopped short and pointed at the walls. 'Look, Clifford! The carvings are all of cats. Even the pillars are sculpted as cats.' She bit her lip. 'You know Mr Trott has been harping on about mummified crocodiles. The ancient Egyptians didn't...?'

'Yes, my lady. Cats were also embalmed. What a double blessing your own ginger menace of a tomcat went on ahead with the ladies to our rented townhouse.'

She see-sawed her head. 'Oh, I don't know. Even Tomkins wouldn't be able to cause too much trouble down here.'

He arched his brow in dissent. 'In cahoots with your wilful bulldog?'

'Ah, the terrible two!' She smiled, wishing she could give each of her beloved pets a cuddle.

'Onwards, my lady?'

'Yes. But where? This seems to be a dead end. Although' – she frowned – 'the others haven't passed us again, have they?'

'No. I imagine they took the right-hand passage earlier.'

They followed the tunnel to the last of the great halls and turned right. She jerked to a stop.

'Oh! It's a positively gargantuan sculpture of a... beetle!'

'Indeed, it is. A stone scarab.' He paced around it. 'Sixteen feet in circumference.' He added a series of measurements to his sketch. 'And through here, I believe, yes, this is an offering table.' The immense slab and its intricate carving were swiftly immortalised on a new double page of his notebook.

At the next doorway, she fancied there was a slight cooling of the air. Before she could comment, Trott's distant voice reached her ears. 'Here, folks. Mummified crocs aplenty!'

She rolled her eyes. 'That will make him happy. But that sounded like it came from below?'

Clifford nodded. 'Beyond the lengthy slope down to the burial chamber itself, my lady.'

The passageway to the lower level was breathtakingly steep. There was no handrail or steps to assist the descent, just a hand-hewn incline, made even more slippery by the wash of sand, brought in on curious footsteps over who knew how many years. Little wider than her arms stretched out, it made her feel claustrophobic. Especially as the low roof forced Clifford to stoop, reminding her of the terrifying time they had both been trapped underground by a rock fall in an old mine workings.

At the bottom of the passageway, the air was noticeably chillier. Even the flames from the torches seemed to exude cold, not heat. She frowned in disapproval as she caught the sound of fractious voices ahead.

This is still a resting place for the dead, Ellie.

'Leave the wretched crocodiles, Trott!' Baxter was commanding as they approached the rest of the party.

'Just stomp on ahead, old timer,' the usually jocular Trott replied testily. 'We've no need to hold hands on this tour, for Pete's sake!'

'Disgraceful,' Clifford muttered, joining her.

'I'm going to explore through here on the left, Ludo. You go right!' Frederika's forthright tone came from what Eleanor could now make out was a bell-shaped cavern.

'No dithering, Lieutenant Baxter,' Trott jeered. 'You military types are supposed to be fearless!'

'Caught you all up at last,' she said in a pointedly quiet voice. 'What a dramatic resting place for a deceased soul.'

'No need to whisper,' Trott said with a grin, brushing past Baxter. 'Dead men can't hear. Any more than they can tell tales. Besides, those crocs likely got to eat his ears off first.' With a boyish laugh, he bounded off, calling, 'Frederika, where have you gone?'

Turning to face Baxter, Eleanor felt a wash of sympathy. He looked ashen, his gaze darting between her and Clifford.

Poor fellow, maybe he suffers from fear of confined spaces, Ellie?

Something she hadn't empathised with until that cave episode.

She discreetly flapped Clifford on to join the others. 'It's rather... oppressive, isn't it, Lieutenant Baxter?' she said in a kindly tone once they were alone.

His sudden barked laugh made her jump. 'Oppressive, Lady Swift? Of course it's oppressive. It's a tomb!'

Her hackles bristled. 'I know perfectly well what it is, Lieutenant Baxter. However, I remain unwaveringly respectful of what it was built for.'

She turned to go after Clifford.

'But do you, Lady Swift?'

It was so softly spoken, it compelled her to turn back.

She pursed her lips. 'Naturally. To bury the dead.'

He nodded slowly. 'True. Or' – his eyes darted around the room, his voice dropping to a cracked whisper – 'to bury the secrets of the dead!'

Unnerved by his words and manner, she hurried out, calling back, 'I believe First Mate Jabir is waiting with the donkeys by the main entrance, since you've clearly seen enough.'

As she rejoined Clifford, he scrutinised her face, raising a questioning eyebrow.

She smoothed down her dress. 'It's nothing, just Baxter being... Baxter! Let's go. I think I've had enough of tombs for today.'

Outside the tomb, the blinding brightness of the sun stung her eyes. Turning away, she shook her head, blinking rapidly. A movement on the horizon caught her attention. On a distant sand dune, two horsemen in white robes were staring at the tomb party. One seemed to point at her, then say something to the other. As they turned and rode off, she caught sight of the rifles slung over their backs.

For some reason, Baxter's strange remark came back to her. She shrugged it off, and with another glance at the now empty sand dune, climbed back on her donkey.

7

Back on the SS *Cleopatra*, Eleanor sat in the deserted dining room staring out the window at the setting sun. Unlike her fellow diners, she'd been in no hurry to leave after the last course.

'Perhaps a wheeled chair might offer some alleviation, my lady?'

She turned around. 'Very droll, Clifford. But I'm not too full to move, you terror! Although that aromatic baked fish, with its sublime cumin and sweet paprika seasoning, was too delicious to resist a second helping of.'

He tutted. 'Nor a third, evidently. *Tilapia* is the local name for the fish. On this evening's menu courtesy of Deckhand Farah, who caught them off the starboard bow whilst we were at the tomb, I learned.'

'Then I shall ferret him out to say thank you.' She waved a dreamy hand at the sunset. 'Once, that is, I've watched the very last romantic band of violet-blue tinged with fingers of fired-gold fade completely.'

'Ahem, in that case, Euclidean geometry may help you. If you will forgive the suggestion so soon after eating?'

She rolled her eyes good-naturedly. 'Forgiven, Clifford. And the intelligible version is?'

'The view of the sunset would last an estimated six and a half minutes longer with the greater angle of elevation from the second deck. Although, admittedly in a lengthy silk evening gown and heels, a significant portion of that would be lost walking in a ladylike manner—'

'Brilliant!' she called back, already speeding along the passageway with her gown hitched high.

As she bounded up the steps, all thoughts of sunsets evaporated when she heard a raised voice. Turning the corner, she saw Captain Anders' peaked cap shaking as he berated someone in Arabic. He tailed off at the sight of her.

'Ah! Captain Anders,' she said. 'And Deckhand Farah. Beautiful evening, isn't it, gentlemen?'

'Lady Swift, good evening,' Anders said, smiling the sort of piratical smile that had made women swoon for centuries.

He dismissed the deckhand with a curt jerk of his thumb. Once the man's black tasselled fez had disappeared down the steps, he swept off his cap with a flourish, which made his collar-length mahogany curls flutter. His resemblance to her handsome fiancé was distressingly striking, she thought again.

'I hope my crew has been treating you well, Lady Swift?'

She nodded. 'Absolutely. Their behaviour has been exemplary. In fact, I came up here to thank Deckhand Farah for providing this evening's delicious fish.' She glanced down the steps. 'I trust he isn't in too much trouble?'

Anders shook his head. 'No... not at all. He has lost the keys to cabin number five, that's all.'

She kept her face neutral, even though his smile seemed forced. She tried to picture whose cabin that was, but realised she'd taken no notice of who was where.

'If it's the de Groots' cabin, I'll be happy to lend Frederika anything necessary until you can find the keys. And Clifford will too, for Ludo, unquestionably.'

Anders waved her offer away. 'Very generous spirited, but unnecessary, thank you. Cabin five is unoccupied. It's Farah's job to keep the keys safe until the cabins have been allocated to each passenger. Unfortunately, there is too much petty thieving when boats dock.' He let out a long breath. 'However, there are more cabins than passengers, so it is a minor inconvenience. I can get a new key sorted in Aswan. I hope you enjoy the rest of your evening, Lady Swift. Please excuse me.'

He strode away, the rigid set of his shoulders suggesting to her he was more annoyed about the matter than he was letting on. She wondered where he could have been on such a modestly sized boat to have only just discovered the keys missing?

She shook her head. It was none of her business. She was there on holiday, cruising along the mystical Nile. She glanced down at her shoes as a wave of childhood memories washed over her. Carefree, barefoot days aboard her parents' sailboat before they had inexplicably vanished one night. Silently apologising to Clifford, she slipped them off and padded on towards the second deck, hoping to catch the last minute of sunset.

Again, however, she was pulled up short by the sound of a raised voice. Only this time it was Ludo's. And he'd just mentioned her name. Not wanting to appear to be eavesdropping, she started to turn back, only for Ludo to appear with Baxter.

'Lady Swift *is*, I tell you. Sounds too fantastic, I know, but it is true. She not only—'

They both leaped like startled deer on seeing her, then glanced at each other with a guilty look.

'Evening, chaps. Been discussing the cricket scores?' she said brightly, pointing to the copy of the *Egyptian Gazette* in Baxter's hand. Feigning she hadn't heard a word of their conversation, she continued. 'Or the financial markets, perhaps? It's a bonus Captain Anders provides the English language newspaper, isn't it?'

Ludo's lips broke into a relieved smile. 'Yes, umm, yes, it is.'

'Well, don't let me interrupt you. I'm only here for the sunset.'

'You've just missed it.' Frederika appeared at the top of the stairs. 'As you have your shoes, Lady Swift. Come, Ludo!' She hooked her arm through his and dragged him away.

She sighed to herself. Being alone with Baxter was definitely not on her list of treats for the evening. He was staring at her fixedly.

She opted for a fictitious shiver. 'You know, it's quite chilly now the sun's gone in. I think I shall retire to my cabin, it's getting late. I'll leave you to read your newspaper in peace, Lieutenant Baxter.'

He held up a halting hand. 'Lady Swift. It is never too late to uncover the secrets of the dead. Especially for someone equally fierce in intellect as determination.'

With an awkward cough, he spun on his heel and, as fast as his cane would allow him, hurried down the stairs.

She leaned over the rail and watched him go, shaking her head in puzzlement.

His behaviour seems to be getting odder by the hour, Ellie. I've no idea what he meant by 'uncover the secrets of the dead'? And why he repeated himself about me being so 'fierce and determined'? Her frown deepened. From her position above, she saw him turn as if heading to the cabins and then furtively glance around. Instinctively, she stepped back out of sight. Waiting as short a period as she dared, she peered over the rail again to see a shadowy form disappearing down the roped-off lower deck stairs.

Before she could wonder what on earth Baxter was up to, another figure emerged from the shadows and ducked under the rope. As it disappeared down the stairs, she stepped back out of view again and shook her head.

Why on earth is Piltz following Baxter down there at this hour?

She shivered. Ironically, she realised she was actually cold. Her cashmere wrap was needed. At the top of the stairs, however, she realised it wasn't just the breeze giving her the chills. It was the eerie feeling of being watched herself.

Using the cover of putting her shoes back on, she bent over and peered around the deck. Nothing. Had she been wrong? Her growing goosebumps told her otherwise. She discreetly dropped her lace handkerchief and started down the stairs, quickly turning around to retrieve it.

There, Ellie! Someone moved in the shadows.

At the bottom of the only stairs off the second deck, she slid into one of four colonial rattan chairs set in a circle, its high back hiding her. A minute later, she heard tentative footsteps. A neatly suited figure stealthily descended and silently crossed the lower deck, disappearing through the door into the corridor to the cabins.

She rose from her seat, a little shaken.

Why on earth would Sharaf be lurking in the dark eavesdropping, Ellie? Has everyone on this boat gone mad?

Unable to come up with a solution, she returned to her cabin, brooding.

Not wanting to interrupt her butler's uncharacteristic disappearance to enjoy some long overdue solitude, she spent the next half hour attempting to write to her fiancé. Unfortunately, her thoughts were too full of questions from the last two days' conversations and events to detail any of the wonders she'd seen. Or, unusually, describe the food. Nor the mischief the four ladies of her staff had got up to before they had parted ways. Finally she gave up trying to express just how much she wished he could be there, and scrunched the ink-splattered vellum sheets into one big ball and dropped them in the wastebasket.

After reading for an hour or so, she started Clifford's thoughtfully improvised fan and flopped onto the bed, her mind returning to the strange behaviour of Sharaf. She frowned. In truth, all the passengers had something a little... odd about them. Much as she sympathised with the Welshman, Wesley Merrick, his nervous overreactions struck her as peculiar for an international businessman. And he'd repeatedly evaded stating what exactly his line of business was. Herr Piltz's refusal to be drawn into conversation wasn't so odd in comparison. Maybe he was more garrulous with his clients? But his shadowing of Baxter was most suspicious. And Felix Trott, the herpetologist? Now, there was a queer fish! On the surface, he appeared amiability personified. But he seemed to have been goading Merrick, a perfect stranger, from the night of the first dinner. And there was something a little... incongruous about the de Groots, too. She shook her head. Were they just having a hiccup in their marriage or was there more behind their distinct lack of togetherness? And what had Ludo been muttering to Lieutenant Baxter about her? And why? As for Baxter's increasingly strange utterances, she wondered if the poor man was unhinged? Strangely, the only straightforward one among them all *had* been Sharaf. But tonight, she'd caught him skulking in the shadows, eavesdropping. Why?

A voice in the corridor broke into her thoughts. Captain Anders. Her frown deepened. Where had he really been since they'd left Cairo? And why was he so annoyed at the loss of a set of keys for an empty cabin he confessed they didn't need and could easily get replaced in Aswan?

Rolling onto her front, her eyes fell on her bedside clock. Almost midnight. She groaned. She ought to turn in if she was going to feel fresh enough to enjoy tomorrow's planned activities. But her mind was too full for sleep. What she needed was a quick breath of air. Slipping her velvet slippers on, she headed out.

On the front deck, the exotic scents of the Nile assailed her nose and the magical symphony of cicadas in the thick rushes along the riverbank her ears. But most pleasing was the sight of her butler.

'My lady.' He consulted his pocket watch. 'Good morning. Almost.'

She laughed. 'Hello, Clifford. I don't want to interrupt your very rare chance of not being saddled with me. I just—'

'Felt the need of' – he stepped sideways to reveal a tray waiting on the table behind him – 'a flask of warmed milk, with a dash of slumber-inducing brandy? And that which I have heard described as the lady's "favourite sounding board"?' He gestured at himself.

She fought the urge to squeeze his arm. 'Thank you, my mind-reading wizard. Please tell me though, you haven't been waiting out here for ages in case I—'

She sniffed the air, then glanced up at the wheelhouse. Leaning forward, she lowered her voice. 'Clifford, if First Mate Jabir and deckhands Farah and Ali are up there, who's smoking around the corner?'

'I believe it is Mr Sharaf.'

'Ah, good!' She beckoned him closer. 'There's something not right about him. I need your flair for unobtrusive observation, please.'

He nodded and followed unquestioningly.

'Good evening again, Mr Sharaf. And so soon.'

He rose swiftly from his chair, running a hand over his thick moustache as he hastily stubbed out his cigarette. 'So soon, Lady Swift?'

'Of course. We chatted throughout dinner. But I don't think either of us explained what draw the town of Bawaaba has for us? After all, we are the only passengers to be disembarking, I believe?' At his silence, she continued. 'I've rented a townhouse there.'

He smiled thinly. 'An unusual place to holiday, if I may say so, Lady Swift? It is very rare for a foreigner, particularly an English one, to rent in such an unknown place. And, forgive me saying so, but particularly a lady travelling un—'

'Unmarried? Perhaps. But I have my ferocious chaperone, Mr Clifford, with me. And the rest of my staff are waiting there already.'

'Her ladyship rented the property,' Clifford said smoothly, 'to provide a brief respite from travelling through your wonderful country.'

'Egypt can be very overwhelming, I agree.' Sharaf scrutinised Clifford's face. 'But Bawaaba is also less expensive than the popular tourist areas. Which, perhaps, appealed to you as the guardian of the accounts of the house? A task you carry out fiercely, I imagine? Like your duty as a chaperone to Lady Swift? A task you carry out one might even imagine as a soldier would?'

Has he been eavesdropping all along, Ellie? Or is he just astute?

'What a lucky guess, Mr Sharaf,' she said. 'Clifford spent many years in the army, serving with my late uncle. But on that note, I wanted to apologise. There have been a few insensitive comments from some of the other passengers. And I want you to know I don't share those views at all. Neither of us do. Nor, necessarily, every action of our country in the last few years.'

He bowed his head. 'Thank you. But an apology is not needed. Britain has been acting to protect her interests. Egypt does the same. It is the way of the world.' He shrugged. 'I admit, like most Egyptians, to feeling some mistrust of British authorities. But not of individuals.'

She held his gaze. 'Ones acting honestly, of course?'

He hesitated, then shook his head. 'Lady Swift, you are

even more sharp-witted than I suspected. Please accept that every act of mine on this boat is with the most honourable of intentions.'

'That's comforting to hear,' she said, not in the least comforted. 'And since it's probably morning now, I'll leave you to enjoy your—'

A sharp crack split the night air.

For a second, they stared at each other. Then, as a man, the three of them ran towards the direction of the sound.

8

'It seemed to come from this direction, my lady.' Clifford rattled the double doors into the dining room. 'Locked!'

'Lounge!' As she ran in, she collided with Merrick coming out. Looking pale and shaken, his eyes darted between the three of them. 'Tell me that wasn't a... a shot?'

'We believe it may have been,' Sharaf said calmly.

'Where do you think it came from?' she urged. 'If not from in here?'

Merrick stared at her like a frightened rabbit. 'Oh, heavens! It came from the rear of this floating nightmare, I think.'

With Clifford and Sharaf on her heels, she sent the lounge chairs scattering as she ran back out and down to the cabin corridor. There, she stopped, staring around.

Where is everyone, Ellie?

Feet pounding down from the upper deck brought First Mate Jabir and the two deckhands. A second later, Anders appeared through the door to the rear deck.

'The shot didn't come from back there or down below,' he said in a taut voice.

Sharaf nodded. 'Nor the front deck, dining room or lounge.'

'Not the wheelhouse either, Captain,' Jabir said.

Anders took a deep breath. 'Then it had to have come from one of the cabins. Split up. We'll take one each.'

'And quickly,' Eleanor couldn't help adding, her war nurse's training kicking in. 'Someone might be badly injured.'

Anders nodded. 'Nine doors, but four of you passengers are here.'

'Which leaves five.'

'Four. Number five is empty.' Jabir slapped a heavy hand on the door. It swung open. He and Anders exchanged a confused look.

Anders said it was empty, Ellie. But—

Her attention was distracted by Piltz stumbling out of his cabin half dressed.

'What is this madness happening at this hour?' He glared at Anders, ineffectually holding his hands in front of the voluminous shorts cladding his stocky legs when Frederika stormed out of the de Groots' cabin.

Swathed in an ankle-length nightgown and a high-collared robe, she frowned at the crowd staring back at her.

'What is going on? This is unacceptable!' she said stiffly.

'Frederika, hush, can't you?' An agitated-looking Ludo came out behind her, his dishevelled bush of straw-blond hair incongruous with his pyjama top tightly buttoned up past his Adam's apple. 'Oh! Everyone's here.'

'Not everyone,' Sharaf said. 'Two are still unaccounted for.'

Eleanor felt an icy prickle in her stomach. 'Mr Trott and Lieutenant Baxter!'

Jabir raised his fist and hammered on the door of cabin number six. The door opened and Trott ambled out, pyjama top open, the strings of his bottoms sliding undone as he stretched languidly.

'Looks like a case of man the lifeboats!' he said with a yawn. 'Sinking, are we, folks?'

Ignoring him, Eleanor ran to the last unopened door. Cabin four. Before she could knock, she felt Clifford's respectful tap on her shoulder.

'Captain Anders should, my lady.'

With a brief nod to her butler, Anders stepped over and rapped on the door. Eleanor's insides clenched at the silence that answered. He tried the handle.

'Locked.'

'Break it down!' she blurted out.

'No need.' He beckoned to Farah. 'Quickly. The spare key.'

Farah fished out a bunch on a large iron ring. Swiftly choosing one, he tried to insert it in the lock, but failed. Anders squatted down to the keyhole.

'The key's in the other side. We'll have to break it down.'

With the help of Jabir, he shouldered the door open. Eleanor hurried forward, praying they weren't too late.

It was dark inside. Too dark for her eyes to adjust quickly, with only a hint of light shining in from the corridor. Clifford's arm brushed hers as he flicked on the switch, the yellow glow spotlighting Baxter stretched out on his bed, a crimson spray of blood glistening on his pillow.

'Oh gracious!' Eleanor breathed, knowing that those lifeless eyes staring up at the ceiling left no doubt he was beyond help.

'Well, now we know where the shot came from,' Anders said grimly. 'Jabir! Where are you?'

'Here, Captain.'

'Get the passengers into their cabins immediately. Then post Ali and Farah in the corridor to make sure they stay there.'

Eleanor turned away from the tragic sight of the dead man as Sharaf stepped into the room.

'Captain!' Jabir reappeared, hesitating at seeing Sharaf. 'You are needed. *Most urgently.*' He jerked his head behind him.

Anders hesitated, then nodded and strode out, slamming

the door shut. Sharaf tutted as he dragged his gaze from the dead man and followed the captain, closing the door quietly.

Eleanor hardly registered him leaving. Rooted to the spot, her head was ringing with the last words Baxter had said to her in the tomb. "*To bury the secrets of the dead!*"

And now he's dead, Ellie!

'There really is nothing that can be done for the gentleman,' Clifford said gently. 'And Captain Anders has asked that all passengers return to their cabins.'

'I know,' she murmured. 'But something he said to me...' She wrung her hands. 'Oh, Clifford! I think I misjudged him dreadfully. Only now, I can never make amends.'

Her butler sighed quietly. 'Which will trouble you forever unless you can make peace with what happened. However, please, at least, allow me.'

He stepped around her. Bending close to the barrel of the gun, he sniffed. 'Cordite. This revolver was recently discharged. By the lieutenant's own hand, one can surmise, since his forefinger is still hooked through the trigger guard.' He scanned the dead man's face, then straightened up. 'Perhaps at least solace might be drawn that, with the accurate aim to his temple, the gentleman would not have suffered, my lady?'

'Y-e-s, in a way, I suppose. But if he took his own life, it can only have been to end the suffering consuming him every day.' She pressed her hand to her chest. 'Such a decision can never be one taken lightly.'

'I don't think there is any doubt about that, my lady.'

She didn't reply, an odd feeling she couldn't place muddling her thoughts.

The sound of voices in the corridor penetrated the door, but no one came in.

'He was very neat, wasn't he?' she said quietly, looking around the cabin, hoping to glimpse one hint that the lieutenant's last days hadn't been entirely dark. But on the writing desk there was no framed memory of a happy time immortalised in a photograph. Only the neatly folded newspaper she'd seen him with earlier. The only clothes hanging on the rail were two practical belted khaki jackets and three matching calf-length trousers, his pith helmet sat on the shelf above. No well-thumbed, favourite book awaited on the two-seater settle, its one cushion highlighting he'd had no caller among the other passengers aboard to sit with him.

She forced herself to look past his head to the bedside table. Empty except for a glass of water. No notebook filled with his hopes and dreams lay next to it to bid him restful slumbers. In fact, the only non-functional item in the cabin was a small figurine on an otherwise empty shelf. She shook her head. 'It's all so... bare. As if to ensure he left no one the trouble of picking up so much as a scrap of paper in case he suddenly—'

'Orderliness is invariably a habit among long-serving military men,' Clifford said quickly.

Looking across at the writing desk again, she was taken with the unexpected impulse to brush her fingers over the newspaper, maybe that being the last thing he'd held.

No, Ellie. That was the gun.

But her brow furrowed as that odd feeling washed over her again. She stepped over to the desk. Only then did she see the single sheet of white paper. Despite not wanting to pry, her eyes couldn't help reading:

Dear World,

Tonight, we are done together, for good. And thanks be. For a worst friend you could not have been.

'Clifford, there's a note,' she said breathlessly.

He joined her, scanning the first few lines. 'It is a suicide note, my lady, as I'm sure you guessed.' He read on down. 'At least he is at peace now.'

She sighed heavily. 'Perhaps. But I have the most ridiculous feeling. Especially as I'd only just met him. The best way I can explain it, is one of wanting... Oh, it's too muddled to express sensibly!'

'Of wanting to commune with him?' Clifford shook his head. 'A selfless and kind-hearted wish can never be ridiculous, my lady.'

She nodded, swallowing hard. 'I want... I want to let him know I'm sorry that I didn't realise he needed help.' As her head fell to her chest, something under the desk caught her eye. She knelt and picked it up. It was a broken pen clip. Trodden on, she assumed.

Still kneeling, she closed her eyes and sent a silent prayer heavenward that Baxter's soul be eternally free of anguish.

The door opened abruptly. Anders strode in, slowing as he looked between them with a frown.

'Her ladyship stayed to pay her respects,' Clifford said smoothly.

She nodded as she rose. 'There's a... a note on the desk.'

Anders walked over, scanned the first few lines, then folded it roughly before slipping it into his pocket. She gasped at his casual manner.

'You will make your way to the lounge, please. Now.'

'After the distressing scene her ladyship has witnessed, I think not,' Clifford said sternly. 'I distinctly heard you tell your crew to ensure all passengers returned to their quarters. Which is what I shall do with Lady Swift. Whatever it is you require can wait.'

Anders raised his hand. 'No, Mr Clifford, it cannot. Except ourselves, all passengers and crew are already assembled in the lounge. And not at my orders!'

9

Stepping into the SS *Cleopatra*'s lounge, Eleanor sighed. The other passengers were sitting so far apart, one would think an influenza outbreak had just been declared. Even the de Groots had chosen wingbacks with an empty one between them. Piltz had commandeered an armchair and dragged it around by the bookshelves though he didn't seem to be perusing them. Merrick was perched on an upright chair as far as possible from Trott, who was sprawled on one of the settees, while First Mate Jabir was pacing by the door through to the dining room. Only the deckhands, Farah and Ali, seemed at ease, whispering to each other by the window.

'Of all the times some unity would be welcomed,' she muttered to Clifford, 'it's now after the tragedy that's happened.'

He nodded. 'Indeed, my lady. Although, given that the passengers were immediately relegated to their cabins, and then presumably herded straight into here moments ago, one wonders if they are aware of what has occurred?'

'Good point. Especially since we can't be sure ourselves,' she murmured.

Selecting a chair at the front of the room, she didn't miss that Clifford perched on the one beside her unbidden. His repeated glances gave away his concern for her over the disturbing scene she'd just witnessed. Although, as he knew, she'd seen far worse as a nurse in the war. Looking down, she realised she still had the broken pen clip in her hand. She absent-mindedly placed it in her pocket and turned to Clifford.

'Sharaf isn't here. Surely Anders would have rustled him out from wherever he's snuck off to?'

'As he did us. In a disgracefully inappropriate manner where you were concerned, my lady. I shall have stern words the moment this meeting concludes.'

'I'd rather you didn't, Clifford. Just this once. Much as I truly appreciate your ever-devoted sense of duty, it hardly matters compared to our finding poor Baxter like that.'

'If you insist, my lady. Then perhaps Mr Sharaf's absence explains Captain Anders' as well? If the latter is searching for the former?'

She shook her head, pointing to Jabir opening the dining-room door for the very two men they'd been discussing. 'Here they are now. And I have a feeling we're about to learn why something's been bothering me about our Mr Sharaf.'

Anders stepped into the middle of the room and stopped by the Cleopatra figurine. He looked at Eleanor and Clifford in front of him, then surveyed the others. 'Can the rest of you sit nearer, please? This is very important,' he added testily at the grumbling that followed.

Jabir barked something at the two deckhands. In a trice, chairs had been fanned out at the front of the room. This galvanised the other passengers to move forward, except for one.

'Mr Trott!' Clifford called with uncharacteristic force. 'I believe it would be collectively appreciated if this takes no longer than necessary. Particularly given the extremely early hour.'

'Why not, friend?' the herpetologist said cheerily, ambling over. 'Though you should try the settees. More comfortable than my berth, I can tell you.'

'When you are ready, Mr Trott,' Anders gruffed. 'Right, I have something to say. To announce, actually. Regarding the passenger not among you. Most of you heard the shot, I know. Well, we found Lieutenant Baxter dead in his cabin shortly afterwards. He left a suicide note.'

Eleanor's stomach twisted at his words. She discreetly watched the others' reactions. Merrick looked shocked, then... relieved? Piltz's eye twitched, but a moment later he stared back at the captain dispassionately, while Frederika and Ludo shared a look, then quickly glanced away. Only Trott seemed completely unperturbed.

'I say, what would the old stick have done that for?'

'To finish his days, obviously,' Piltz said irritably.

'I didn't mean... oh, forget it!' Trott drummed his fingers on his legs.

Behind Anders, she noticed Sharaf scrutinising each passenger. As his gaze reached her, he inclined his head slightly.

Anders raised his hands. 'I appreciate this is unpleasant news. And, believe me, it is as unwelcome as it is unexpected to have your cruise blighted on the SS *Cleopatra* by such a happening. I can only apologise. That said, however, I need to ask if any of you knew Lieutenant Baxter?'

Everyone shook their heads, except Eleanor.

'We can all say we've known him since we left Cairo, given that the poor chap was a fellow passenger.'

Merrick bobbed out of his seat. 'But he... well, he didn't say much.'

'He said too much, to my ears,' Piltz retorted coolly.

Merrick scowled. 'About himself, I mean.'

Trott leaned forward. 'You want to be clearer, old man. People want to get back to bed, you know.'

Eleanor fought the urge to bang their heads together, given the lack of respect anyone was showing for Baxter's tragic death.

'Gentlemen, please! I understand you're all tired, but Captain Anders is asking for our help.'

'Thank you, Lady Swift,' Anders said. 'But I doubted there would be much any of you would know about the lieutenant.' He held his hands up as half the passengers rose. 'We're not finished yet. Mr Sharaf would like a word with you all.'

Ludo seemed to have reached the end of his tether. 'It is a marvellous idea, I am sure. But I do not wish to hear consoling words of wisdom right now.'

'Then you will be happy to stay,' Sharaf said in an authoritative tone, so far removed from his previously soft-spoken manner, Eleanor leaned forward. 'All of you.' He stepped closer to their arc of chairs. 'Because I am not here to dispense words of consolation. Nor wisdom. I am here to tell you that I am on board the SS *Cleopatra* in order to take up my new position as chief of police in Bawaaba. However, it is now necessary to begin my duties early. With the arrangements for the deceased Lieutenant Baxter.'

As he waited, hands behind his back for the passengers to hush and stop fidgeting, she assessed this information. Now she understood his odd behaviour. He'd obviously kept quiet about his occupation to enjoy a few peaceful days of holiday before he took up his post. After all, Hugh, her own fiancé, rarely mentioned he was a detective chief inspector on the few occasions he grabbed even half a day away from his burgeoning case files.

She frowned. *But that doesn't explain Sharaf eavesdropping, Ellie. Unless, being a policeman, he couldn't help himself?*

She tuned in to the fact that everyone was finally giving Sharaf their full attention.

'Thank you. Now, we will dock in Bawaaba later this morning, and Lieutenant Baxter's body will be taken ashore. Then, after the necessary procedures and formalities have been completed, you will be able to continue on with your journey. But' – his gaze turned steelier – 'not until full permission is granted from the Cairo Police Bureau.'

Frederika leapt up. 'Well, how long will that take?'

'I cannot say. Hopefully you will not have too much of a delay.'

Merrick snorted. 'That's not on, I tell you! I have to arrive in Aswan as planned. I have an important business meeting.'

'No doubt,' Sharaf said blandly. 'Any other questions?' He looked around the room. 'Very well. You may go now. Thank you for your attention.'

He gestured to Anders, and the two of them disappeared back into the dining room and closed the door.

She glanced at her watch.

One o'clock, Ellie.

'You should slide off to your cabin for some rest, Clifford,' she said casually, trying to hide that the last thing she wanted was to be alone.

'Categorically not, thank you.' He scanned her face. 'As I have oft had cause to repeat, shock is never to be taken lightly. Even by a lady determined that irrepressible and indomitable are the same as invincible.'

She smiled gratefully. 'Alright, I shan't argue this time. But I can't face going to my cabin. What do you propose?'

His answer couldn't have been more perfect. He escorted her to the otherwise deserted upper rear deck.

'Thank you,' she breathed, nestling into a soft wool travelling blanket as she sat down.

He held up a still-glowing brazier from the dinner table and set it down in front of her, the waves of heat warming the chilly night air. Producing a glass of brandy, he passed it to her. She cocked her head questioningly as he then pulled a tiny brown bottle with a green rubber stopper from one of his pockets.

'*Ignatia amara*, my lady. Extract of the St Ignatius bean. A highly effective remedy against sudden emotional distress. Or grief. Two drops under the tongue. With no arguments, please.'

'Understood, Doctor Clifford.' She managed a wan smile and did as he'd prescribed. 'Though how you could conjure up this comprehensive mistress repair kit from the one small valise you brought on the cruise, I can't imagine.'

He arched a brow. 'My mistress happening upon deceased persons is a distressingly regular occurrence.'

'I know, inexplicably. And you've been with me every time. So, please join me in a brandy. Seeing poor Lieutenant Baxter like that was yet another hideous sight for you, too.'

'Perhaps one might be countenanced on this occasion, as we obviously have much to talk about.' He halted her stilted protestation with a respectful hand. 'My lady, your concern at Captain Anders' announcement that Lieutenant Baxter committed suicide was palpable. But only to my familiar eye.'

'Oh, Clifford, I wasn't going to say it to you tonight, well this morning, because Baxter's death is just as raw for you, too. And it will sound improbable, I'm sure.' Her chest constricted. 'However, you are right. My heart won't believe it was suicide.'

'As I feared,' he muttered. 'But, my lady, the gentleman's cabin door was locked from the inside. We saw ourselves it needed to be shouldered open. His gun, which was still in his hand, had been recently discharged. And you found his suicide note.'

'But did I?' her lips let fly, before she'd even formulated the thought.

Clifford folded his hands in his lap, his sign that he was listening patiently. And would for as long as she needed.

'What I mean is,' she said, feeling a wash of trepidation mixed with sadness, 'that, yes, it appears to have been suicide. But I can't shake off two niggling worries. First, his change of demeanour, which started at dinner on Monday night, and then accelerated until he seemed to morph into a completely different person. One anxious and fretful. That doesn't fit with the image of a long-serving military man, now does it?'

'Mostly, no. However, due to their extreme experiences, some regrettably develop the mental condition known as "battle fatigue", as I am sure you yourself observed as a nurse. Unpredictable behaviour and reactions are the highly lamentable, but often noted, symptoms in such cases.'

She nodded sadly. 'Those poor men. You're right. I saw a fair bit of that during the war. But I never saw a case where they were perfectly lucid and self-confident one day, and so markedly opposite the next. Like Baxter's vehemence before Monday's dinner he would never consider wasting his time visiting a "crumbling hole in the ground", as he referred to the ancient tomb. Yet within an hour or so he must have had a dramatic change of mind as there was a donkey booked and ready for him the very next morning. And the same again in the tomb. When he first boarded the *Cleopatra*, he acted like a... well, not meaning to speak ill of the dead, like a bombastic barrack-room brigadier! But in the tomb, he acted like a man terrified of... well, I don't know what.' She held his gaze. 'Does that fit with your diagnosis of battle fatigue?'

'Hmm, no, I concur.'

'Precisely.'

'And your second reservation?'

'The peculiar things he said when we were alone in the tomb yesterday. And then again up here on this very deck earlier this evening.'

His brow flinched. 'Utterances of what nature?'

'That's just it!' She leaned forward. 'They made no sense at the time. But he said them as if it was imperative that I heard him.'

'Forgive my asking, but why did you not mention this before, my lady?'

She groaned. 'Because I didn't think it was important. Now, it feels like, like…'

'The gentleman is talking to you from the other side?' he said softly.

'Pleading with me, I'd say.'

'What exactly did he say on both occasions?'

She thought back. 'When we were alone in the tomb he asked me if I knew what it was for? The tomb, that is. And then he said' – she frowned, trying to make sure she got the exact words – '"To bury the secrets of the dead!" Then tonight, he said, "It is never too late to uncover the secrets of the dead."' She shook her head. 'It's not just me, is it? Doesn't it sound horribly like he'd had a premonition of his own death?'

'In truth, yes. However, my lady, that would be the case if he had reached the point of contemplating suicide.'

She nodded grimly. 'Or if he knew he was going to be murdered!'

10

At the washbasin in her suite, Eleanor buried her face in a towel, the tragic image of Baxter's glassy eyes fixed on the afterlife still haunting her. And worse, the shocking crimson stain framing his head. She groaned. It was an unearthly early hour, but sleep was out of the question.

She stared in the mirror, willing the whole thing to have been just a fitful nightmare. But it hadn't, her reflection told her. If Baxter had taken his own life, the suffering he must have been enduring was too awful. Why hadn't she realised in time to help? On the other hand, if his life had been taken by another, then evil stalked the SS *Cleopatra*. A murderer, in fact!

But which was it?

Clifford's coded knock on her door made her breath catch. At least they might now learn which of the two unbearable answers was the truth.

'My lady, all the other passengers have finally retired,' he whispered. 'Also, Lieutenant Baxter's body has been moved and is ensconced below deck. I checked personally.'

'Thank you,' she murmured back. 'And for sparing me the details that the poor fellow has been dumped between the spare ropes and the canned provisions, I imagine. Since there can be little room below, given the crew sleep there as well.'

He shook his head. 'Rest assured. I overheard Captain Anders tell the deckhands Farah and Ali to make sure Lieutenant Baxter's body was shrouded in clean linen and placed in a cleared-out cabin.'

She looked up sharply. 'I hope that's the only cabin they've cleared!'

Clifford's brow flinched. 'If I may beg one last time that I be permitted to search Lieutenant Baxter's cabin alone?'

She shook her head. 'No. Not because I don't sincerely appreciate your solicitude, though. But because it will take the two of us to work out this puzzle. Including your flair for infallible logic.'

He nodded resignedly. 'And your uncanny faculty for the irrational.'

She smiled weakly. 'I'll take that as the compliment intended. Now, it's time to go.'

A moment later, she stood guard outside Baxter's door. As the lock had been broken when Anders and Jabir had shouldered it open, a padlock on a chain had been fixed across. It was, however, no match for her butler's picklocks and they were soon inside.

'Thank goodness you have such dubious skills hidden beneath your impeccably turned-out togs, Clifford,' she whispered. 'I wish I could match them in other ways.'

'Such as?' he asked, as he slipped his picklocks back into his jacket.

'By working out what Baxter meant by those two cryptic remarks. But I haven't a clue.' She bit her lip, gazing around the cabin, still as tidy as a few hours before. More so, she thought with a shiver, given the absence of a body. 'It seems terribly wrong to rip his last resting place apart. But I can't see any other option if we're to glean anything. Let's hope Anders or Sharaf don't suddenly appear.'

Clifford eyed her sideways. 'Surely, therefore, grounds for employing the swifter method of deduction, instead of desecration? Perhaps by starting with the reason the lieutenant uttered such puzzling remarks to you?'

She nodded. 'Excellent point. Well, we're agreed most likely he wanted me to do something about his murder.'

'Ahem.'

She groaned. 'Your respectful way of saying you're still not convinced it was murder? And that he simply had two moments of impaired lucidity because of battle fatigue or similar, when I happened to be alone with him, yes?'

'In regard to the latter, categorically not,' he replied, sidestepping the first part of her question. 'I am certain the gentleman approached you specifically. And for a good reason. Possibly because he had noted your remarkable intellect.' He fiddled with his jacket cuff. 'For which I regrettably reproached him for articulating to you in the tomb.'

'Don't worry. It didn't stop him approaching me again.' Her eyes widened. 'Of course! Do you remember, at dinner the first night afloat? Trott was regaling us with his unpleasant facts about the Nile crocodile? And Frederika told Ludo that he was fussing unnecessarily?'

'Because neither she nor yourself were shrinking violets, my lady? Yes, I remember.' He stroked his chin. 'Hmm. It appears the de Groots know something of your former exploits. Despite neither of us breathing a hint of such.'

'Then how can they?'

'I suspect from either a mutual acquaintance of which you are unaware, or from having recognised your name from one or more of the newspaper reports which featured your solo bicycling adventures across the world. Or, a more recent one regarding yet another murder you solved.'

'*We* solved. We're a team. Even when we disagree there might have been a murder, like now.'

'Notwithstanding, I concede, my lady, it follows that the lieutenant approached Mr de Groot to find out more about you after hearing Mrs de Groot's comment at dinner.'

'Exactly. So Baxter asked Ludo what his wife had meant, and I overheard a fragment of the conversation. But why would that make Baxter act the way he did?'

Clifford tapped his fingertips together. 'Very possibly because he wanted you to help him with something, as you have surmised? But help with what, exactly, eludes me. Though the obscureness of his remarks suggests he could not risk them being understood if he was overheard.'

She shrugged. 'I'm flattered by his faith in me, really. But it seems rather misguided.'

'Yet here you are here, in his cabin,' Clifford said sagely.

She winced as she gazed around again. 'Well, I am here, Lieutenant Baxter,' she murmured. 'But I need you to tell me more. And fast before we're interrupted.' She clicked her fingers. 'Clifford, wait. He was there at the pre-dinner drinks when I told Sharaf we were only going part way on this cruise. So, he must have realised I'd only have a short time to work out what he wanted me to do.'

Clifford's brow creased. 'Whatever other impression Lieutenant Baxter made on me, it was not one of stupidity. So let's tackle each remark in turn. The first was, I believe, "To bury the secrets of the dead!" Which does, on reflection, suggest he was hinting that he had a secret someone might consider it worth killing him for. While his second remark, "It is never too late to uncover the secrets of the dead," suggests, perhaps, he was asking for the reason for his murder to be uncovered. And, one assumes, the murderer brought to justice.' His frown deepened. 'But for that to happen, he would have needed to pass on to you something significantly more concrete than just his two, somewhat cryptic, utterances.'

She nodded again, this time with more vigour. 'Something else written, perhaps? And artfully hidden, lest it be found by his killer?'

They split up, Clifford stepping smartly over to search the bed for propriety's sake and hers, as Baxter had so recently died in it. That left the clothes rail, writing bureau, wooden settle and a modest travelling trunk she assumed wasn't part of the cabin furnishings, but Baxter's. Plus a washstand with a white bowl set on a spindle-legged wood tripod. There were no pictures on the wall and only one ornament, the small figurine on the shelf she'd noticed before.

She quickly assessed the clothes rail as the last place to look. Searching the pockets of the dead man's clothing would be the most obvious first move for whoever the lieutenant had been trying to keep his own secrets safe from. And, therefore, the last place Baxter would have secreted anything. As would the trunk.

She opted to start with the writing bureau instead. It was rather a generous description, as it did not have any drawers and only a modest leather insert graced the top. She quickly checked every leftover paper but found nothing hidden. Even the neatly folded newspaper was devoid of scribbled notes on any of the pages.

She turned to the settle and inspected the cushion. Nothing. Next, she checked the seat. A frisson of hope tingled down her back as she lifted it. The storage space inside was, however, disappointingly empty. She moved on to the trunk, which was similarly empty except for the lieutenant's cane. That struck her as odd. She'd never seen him without it, so to tuck it away like that seemed unnecessary. She took it out and examined it.

'Merely an ordinary walking aid, I imagine, my lady,' Clifford said, appearing at her side. He tapped it and nodded. 'Formed of Irish blackwood, I believe. This brass ring part way down is a repair, not an embellishment. Likewise, the hardened metal ferrule, or sleeved pointed tip, here at the end, is purely to add durability and additional grip on looser surfaces. And this stitched leather pommel handle is to protect the palm, suggesting the lieutenant's injury caused him to lean heavily on it.'

'I never saw him actually limp though, did you?'

'Now you mention it, no. Hmm, then maybe...'

She held her breath as he pulled and twisted various parts of the stick, checking for a removable tip or handle, or lever that might reveal a secret compartment. With a consoling shrug, he gave it back to her.

'Nothing, regrettably. Despite the item perhaps having called to you?'

'It really did.' She frowned, turning it in her hand. 'It sort of embodies my whole impression of him, as he was when we first met him. Striding about, waving this at everyone, blustering out his contentious views.'

'I fear we are on a fruitless mission.' His tone was tinged with urgency. 'We should leave before being discovered. However, I shall swiftly check the gentleman's pockets on our way out as our last—'

'Don't bother!' she said excitedly, bent over the trunk. 'I think I've found what we're looking for!'

11

'Your torch, quick.'

Clicking it on, Clifford shone the beam into the trunk.

'Look, there's something written on the wood here where the cane was resting.'

'Bravo, my lady! Would that we could take it away to peruse somewhere safer, however.' He held the torch for her as she read aloud in a whisper,

'"*We aren't no thin red heroes, nor we aren't no blackguards too,*

But single men in barracks, most remarkable like you;

And if sometimes our conduct isn't all your fancy paints,

Why, single men in barracks don't grow into plaster saints"'

She stared at Clifford with a groan. 'Another unfathomable riddle!'

'Not entirely, my lady,' he said thoughtfully. 'Those lines of verse are from *Barrack-Room Ballads* by Rudyard Kipling. '

'Which I remember you reading. Recently, in fact?'

'Rereading, if you will forgive the correction. In fact, the copy I had came from his lordship's library. That collection of poems has been a stalwart, shared among soldiers since it was published in 1890.'

She was stunned. 'Gracious, I never imagined tough military men sitting around devouring poems together.'

He shook his head. 'They do not as a rule. But in these particular poems Mr Kipling expressed his heartfelt respect for soldiers of any rank. Hence the lines are from the poem "Tommy", that being a generic name for an English soldier.'

'But why would Baxter have left that inscription hurriedly scrawled in ink as a clue for me? I knew he was a soldier. We all did. He publicly declared so.'

'Yet that particular stanza out of all the other verses and indeed poems was chosen. Ah! Perhaps as a reference to himself?'

'Why? To say that some of his conduct I might not have approved of? He knew that. I'd made it clear to him in no uncertain terms.' She ran her hands down her arms. 'I still feel he was trying to tell me something about his death. Dash it, what am I missing?' She dropped to her knees to reread the inscription. 'He didn't believe he was a hero. Nor a blackguard, maybe. Nor a saint. Hang on. Plaster...' She leaped up and darted over to the figurine. 'This chap with a shield? He isn't a saint, I suppose?'

Clifford nodded, eyes bright. 'He most certainly is, my lady! St George. One of the patron saints of... soldiers,' he ended in a whisper, gesturing for her to turn it over.

Holding her breath, she prised out the barely noticeable small white rubber cap in the base and shook the figurine. A tightly rolled piece of notepaper dropped into her hand. She unfurled the top with trembling fingers and scanned the first line.

'Clifford, it's a letter. We've found it!'

'Indeed, my lady. But I fear we've been here too long already.' He hastily replaced the cap and then the figurine.

They left Baxter's cabin, relocked the padlock, and hurried along to hers. Once inside and the door locked, she unrolled the paper.

'Here goes,' she said breathlessly.

Dear Lady Swift,

If you are reading this, I'm already dead. And you will have worked out, dead by the hand of another. One who acted swiftly once they realised I would leave this boat earlier than I had stated publicly. But my death is inconsequential. I did not write this to ask you to bring my killer to justice.

Eleanor frowned.

Then what on earth has he written it for, Ellie?

I wrote this to ask you to finish what I have started!

I confess, I have struggled with my conscience ever since that terrible day. At first, I told myself it was not my fault. And in some regard, that is true. I fooled my conscience into agreeing that it was not my responsibility to act. So I waited, hating myself for my cowardice.

And then it seemed a miracle happened. I congratulated myself on keeping quiet. On doing the 'smart' thing. But the miracle failed to materialise, and I had to face my conscience anew. And this time it brooked no lies or excuses.

I had little time left to put right the great injustice I am responsible for, if only in part. And if you are reading this, I have failed to do even that.

So I am begging you to finish what I started. As I cannot be there, you must take alternative proof in my place and present it by the 16th of this month or it will forever be too late. You will find this proo

She turned the paper over. 'That's it! He must have been interrupted.'

By his killer, Ellie.

She took a deep breath. 'At the very least, this shows that he believed someone was trying to kill him. Which means it's unlikely he then committed suicide, isn't it?'

Clifford nodded slowly. 'I must agree. Not impossible. But unlikely.'

Her frown deepened. 'Something doesn't quite add up though. He must have known who would try and murder him, otherwise how did he know they were on the boat?'

'Fool, man!' Clifford hit his fist against his forehead.

'What have you got?'

'A confession. Of unforgivable stupidity.'

'Of which you are incapable, so I shan't accept that. What you meant to say was, in hindsight, you've realised what?'

He stopped pacing. 'At the time, I thought it unimportant. It was during pre-dinner drinks Monday evening. I passed the lieutenant's cabin on the way to mine to collect something, and heard him utter an, ahem, expletive.'

'Go on.'

'Thinking he might need assistance, I knocked. To which he responded by opening the door only enough to insist he was fine. I could not fail to notice, however, that his cabin was in disarray. Realising I had noticed, he dismissed the mess by explaining he had misplaced something and was looking for it.'

'Not that unusual. I often turn my room upside down looking for something.'

Clifford shuddered. 'Repeatedly. However, I now recall having passed Lieutenant Baxter in the corridor only a few minutes before. It is highly improbable, therefore, he would have had time to reach his cabin and disarrange it so thoroughly. I believe now he must have returned—'

She gasped. 'And found someone had ransacked it! That's how he knew the murderer was on the boat! Which explains his dramatic change of behaviour. He must have thought of me as his only hope.'

She felt a sudden wash of responsibility.

But to put right what 'great injustice', Ellie? And exactly how?

As usual, it seemed her face had given her away as Clifford tapped the paper. 'Whatever it is, it was enough for the lieutenant to be murdered over, my lady. Which begs the chilling question of the likely fate of one who takes up his mantle where he left off, does it not?'

'I suppose,' she murmured, her thoughts already having run on too far down a different track to register his words. 'Well, at least we can go to Sharaf. This letter confirms Baxter didn't commit suicide.'

He held up a finger. 'If we take it as genuine, yes. Then the suicide note must be false. However, there is no evidence it could not be the other way around. Or at least, Chief Sharaf might see it that way. So, the question is, how can we persuade Chief Sharaf to investigate what seems to be an obvious suicide?'

She rolled her shoulders back. 'I don't know yet, is all I can say. Any more than I have any inkling how we'll take up Baxter's mantle and finish his quest in time to put right this "great injustice" without even knowing what it is.'

'Nor whether the murderer now has this "proof" Lieutenant Baxter mentions? One can only assume it was the killer who ransacked his cabin. And that they did so to get hold of the "proof", whatever it may be.'

She grimaced. 'Whether or not Baxter's killer found it, we've only got until the sixteenth to take it to goodness knows where. And show it to goodness knows who!' Her jaw tightened. 'Despite what Baxter said at the beginning of this letter, we have only one option; to catch his killer which will also, hopefully, lead us to the other answers we are looking for.'

Clifford's expression turned graver. 'While somehow ensuring both of us do not end up in a similarly tragic manner to the late lieutenant!'

12

Breakfast seemed a hideously protracted affair to Eleanor. Normally it was her favourite meal of the day. But this morning, after no sleep, and with no sign of the one passenger she was desperate to speak to, it felt interminable. And that was before First Mate Jabir appeared with yet more food: baskets of fresh bread, extra fried eggs and a pot of hot creamy beans topped with fragrant parsley, all bubbling below a hint of oil and lemon juice.

She shook her head apologetically at the bowl Jabir presented to her. Delicious though it looked and smelt, her stomach was too tense. She rose and joined Clifford at the buffet table, which was set with a surprisingly generous selection of cakes, bowls of exotic fruits, and a range of juices.

'An unprecedented effort this morning, my lady,' he murmured, holding only a cup of coffee. 'Perhaps Captain Anders is trying to appease the passengers? Not that we have seen him since the early hours.'

'Nor Sharaf, more importantly,' she muttered back.

'As I mentioned earlier, he cannot have left the SS

Cleopatra without us having docked, which we did not.' He poured her a coffee. 'My lady, patience will—'

'Get a punch up her snout if she's mentioned again, Clifford!'

'Hardly Queensberry Rules,' he said mischievously.

She knew he was just trying to ease the tension, as he was by also inching the nearest plate of cake closer to her. He raised a brow as she brushed the offer aside.

'I stand to be corrected, but I believe no battle of wills was ever won by grinding one's teeth enamel alone?'

Her stomach gurgled. She laughed. 'Alright, you win.'

He half bowed. 'Naturally. But only in the nick of time. Your quarry has just arrived.'

Not wanting to let the other passengers know she'd been waiting to pounce on Sharaf, she busied herself with her plate.

'Can I pour for you, Chief Sharaf?' Clifford said as the Egyptian stepped towards the table, rubbing his hands over his clearly sleep-deprived face.

'Thank you, Mr Clifford.' He nodded to Eleanor. 'But I only announced my profession and title last night to explain how it was I would take charge of Lieutenant Baxter's arrangements. So, we can return to being informal.'

She shook her head and lowered her voice. 'Not this morning. We need to talk to you in your official capacity. Urgently.'

His brow furrowed as he held her gaze. 'Very well. Breakfast can wait. In the captain's office?'

'If I might suggest instead...?' Clifford gestured discreetly towards the door out to the deck.

A moment later, Eleanor left through the opposite door to find Sharaf on the side deck, hidden from those taking breakfast inside. He was staring at Clifford, who was standing by a table covered in a smart linen cloth. It was set with a large coffee pot, cups, and a selection from the buffet.

'Don't ask,' Eleanor said at Sharaf's questioning look. 'He's actually a wizard. That's the only explanation I can come up with.'

'As can I.' Sharaf waited for her to get settled in one of the two chairs before taking the other. 'So, Lady Swift. I am here. Though I am puzzled why it is you do not want anyone else to know we are talking? Including Captain Anders. If that is the reason we are not in his office?'

She nodded. 'It is. Because we have no clue as to who did it.'

'Did what?'

'I'll get to that. You must eat first, though, as I whisked you away from your breakfast. I shall sit quietly while you do.'

With an appreciative nod, Sharaf placed his hands together, palms open and facing him. '*Bismillahi wa barakatillah.*'

The breeze stirred the papyrus along the bank. A soft salmon-pink heron rose languidly from the Nile. The three of them watched it glide silently away.

'I am listening.' Sharaf accepted a coffee from Clifford.

She nodded. 'Thank you. It's... it's something troubling. About Lieutenant Baxter. And... and his apparent suicide. I only wish I'd realised straight away when we found him in his cabin.'

She repeated the first of the dead man's cryptic remarks.

Sharaf shrugged, his matter-of-fact expression making his words unnecessary. 'Wholly insignificant to his suicide. Forgive me for noting so plainly, but the lieutenant is dead. By his own hand. If it is salvation for his soul you are hoping to achieve, I am not the man to beseech.'

'It's not that. Please bear with me. You see, only the following evening he approached me a second time.' She repeated the second of the lieutenant's cryptic remarks.

Sharaf looked back at her dismissively. 'Again, what of his words? Whatever meaning you find in them, I have to say, I do not.' He bit into a cake hungrily.

'His meaning was that he knew he was going to be murdered,' she said evenly.

Sharaf slowly stopped chewing. 'Murdered?' His gaze swung from her to her butler. 'Mr Clifford, what is this?'

'Deeply concerning, Chief Sharaf. But not a delusional aberration of her ladyship's from the effects of heat and lack of sleep, in case the thought had occurred.'

Sharaf folded his arms. 'Well, of course it did.' He turned his gaze back to her. 'No offence, Lady Swift.'

'None taken,' she said genuinely.

'My apologies again, nevertheless.' He thought for a moment, then shook his head. 'It does not make sense. The lieutenant would not whisper puzzling statements to you if he believed his life was in danger. Why did he not confide in you clearly? In fact, why did he tell you and not Captain Anders?'

'We believe it was because he did not know who on the boat would try to murder him.' She realised how unconvincing that sounded in the bright light of morning, compared to standing only inches from Baxter's deathbed.

Sharaf put his hands together. 'Lady Swift, I am concerned.'

'Thank goodness,' she said in relief.

'Not about a murder. Because there was not one. I am concerned for your thoughts.' He halted her protestation with a sharp headshake. 'They are very dark. You are on holiday, you told me. More relaxation is most definitely needed! Think for a moment, please, and you will see I am correct. If the lieutenant did not know who wished to kill him, he could not know they were on this boat.'

'Clifford?' she said with a coaxing hand.

Her butler relayed having seen the lieutenant's cabin in complete disarray. She cocked her head. 'Chief Sharaf, you saw his cabin yourself.'

He sighed. 'Yes, I did. And I think you are asking if it seems a man of his neat and clean habits would make such a mess to find something. My answer is no, I do not. However, it changes nothing.' He frowned at Clifford. 'I think only that the shock of seeing a man dead like that has upset Lady Swift so much as to have wild imaginings.'

'Would that I could agree, Chief Sharaf,' Clifford said. 'And I might, were it not far from the first time her ladyship has seen such.'

For a moment, Sharaf seemed floored. Then he shook his head slowly. 'There is no evidence that Lieutenant Baxter's death is murder. Only two strange remarks. And some strange behaviour. It is all... what is the word in English? Oh, yes, flimsy!'

She nodded. 'You're absolutely right. It is.'

He held his hands up as if he was going mad.

'But I have concrete evidence,' she said firmly. 'Which I will show you in confidence.'

She slid the letter she and Clifford had found in the plaster statue of St George across the table to him. His intelligent eyes moved slowly along each line. But as he passed it back, her insides twisted at his dismissive tone.

'An elaborate hoax. In my experience of these matters, which is admittedly not extensive, the suicide note is still far more likely to be genuine. Not this other way around. I am sorry.'

'Perhaps you are right, Chief Sharaf,' Clifford said smoothly. 'However, dare you take that risk? Particularly in these politically charged times between our two countries? Surely it would not look good if your first act as the new Chief of Police of Bawaaba was letting the murder of an Englishman go uninvestigated?'

Sharaf looked between them. He sat back in his seat and clasped his hands in his lap.

She crossed her fingers under the table. He stayed silent for a moment, then turned to her.

'Lady Swift. Why do you believe Lieutenant Baxter chose to ask *you* for help?'

'I'll answer that with a question to you. What did you hear Ludo de Groot tell the lieutenant about me when you were eavesdropping?'

He smiled thinly. 'Nothing that surprised me. Having spent but one day on this boat with you, I had already realised you are not the usual English lady.'

She pretended to whisper behind her hand. 'Don't tell Clifford. Poor fellow still believes I might be one day.'

Sharaf laughed. 'How long a life do you hope to have, Mr Clifford?' Quickly sobering, he fell back into thought.

She waited with all the patience she could muster.

'I will tell you something,' he said finally. 'But only in strict confidence. It cannot be repeated beyond this table. Agreed?'

'Agreed,' she chorused with Clifford, as they both leaned in closer.

'I have orders to hold the SS *Cleopatra* for a few days when we dock in Bawaaba.' He held up a finger. 'Let me make this absolutely clear though. This is *not* related to Lieutenant Baxter's death. I cannot say more than that.'

'And we won't ask,' she said.

He nodded. 'Good. So, to be blunt, to cover myself in the extremely unlikely event that there is something more to Lieutenant Baxter's death than suicide, I will do certain things. For a start, I will arrange for the passengers to stay in Bawaaba. There is only one hotel. The El Asafa. The town is surrounded by miles of desert, so none of them can leave. And none will try, when they learn the only road out is but a track and the sands are home to dangerous bandits. If you travel three days further from here up the Nile, you can disembark and from there travel by vehicle to Aswan, another day's drive away. There are no bandits on the road there.'

'So to travel further, anyone must take a boat. So, couldn't one of the passengers leave that way?' she said.

'Of course, Lady Swift. However, there is only one jetty, which I will have guarded by an armed policeman at all times.'

'Just the passengers to be held over at the El Asafa Hotel, Chief Sharaf?' Clifford said.

'No. Captain Anders also. And First Mate Jabir.'

Eleanor frowned. 'But, when the three of us heard the shot, Jabir was in the wheelhouse with deckhands Farah and Ali. So he cannot be suspected of having any hand in... anything,' she finished diplomatically.

Sharaf nodded again. 'True. But this is not the reason he must stay at the El Asafa. That is for my own reasons. The deckhands I will let stay on the boat to keep the pumps going.'

'You mean the bilge pumps?' Eleanor said.

'To keep the water from growing too high in the bottom of the boat, yes. Too many boats like this have sunk in the Nile without constant watch of the pumps.'

'Marvellous,' Clifford muttered, catching her eye.

'And,' Sharaf continued, 'I will make sure all the cabins are locked and the keys safe at the police station. Again, for my own purposes. But also so the deckhands cannot interfere with any evidence of wrongdoing in the case of Lieutenant Baxter that might be present.'

That rekindled her curiosity over why he wanted to impound the boat, but she bit her tongue.

'Thank you. And might you, just to be sure, check the fingerprints on the gun found beside his body? And also, perhaps, have the handwriting of his suicide note examined, to verify it was his?'

He looked at her with a hint of admiration. 'These I can do. The fingerprints I must send to Cairo. But for the handwriting, I will need something more that he wrote.'

'The gentleman's passport, Chief Sharaf?'

'A fine suggestion, Mr Clifford. Both checks will take several days, however.'

She raised her hands. 'That's not a problem. You'll have all the possible suspects in the El Asafa Hotel for as long as—'

'For as long as I need the SS *Cleopatra* to be held. Not the people.' Sharaf tapped the table. 'When my business with the boat is complete, I will let everyone continue on their way. And no, you cannot persuade me otherwise. But I have more news you do not wish to hear.'

She groaned inwardly, but slapped on a neutral expression.

'I cannot be seen investigating the lieutenant's death without any evidence that it was murder. Which I still categorically believe is not the case.'

'But this letter!'

'Is not evidence enough. I will not, repeat *not*, have my first act as head of police in my new station end up being my last!'

'We understand, Chief Sharaf,' Clifford said smoothly again. 'Incidentally, the information you overheard Mr de Groot telling Lieutenant Baxter. Was that about her ladyship's travel adventures only?'

'Yes. But "only"? There cannot be anything more that is so unusual about the lady?' Sharaf stared at her. 'Can there?'

Clifford shrugged. 'Unless you call helping the police in England, and abroad, solve more than a handful of murders in the last few years "unusual"?'

'You?' He pointed at her in disbelief.

She nodded. 'Regrettably, yes. But Clifford deserves equal credit.'

Sharaf shook his head slowly. 'I did not realise how right I was when I said you are not a typical lady of your country.' He switched his gaze. 'Nor you a typical butler, Mr Clifford.'

She laid her hands on the table. 'So, as you have stated you cannot openly investigate this matter, Chief Sharaf, we will also stay in the El Asafa rather than our rented townhouse. Then we can discreetly interview witnesses and suspects without arousing suspicion.'

He nodded. 'Yes. But we will need to discuss how this will work in more detail.'

She smiled easily. 'Of course. Please come to lunch at our townhouse and I will be all ears. Clifford will give you the address.' She rose. 'In the meantime, thank you. I've held you up enough. Particularly as I'm sure you wish you'd never set eyes on me now.'

As she left with Clifford in tow, she caught Sharaf's vehement nodding.

13

Eleanor felt her face instantly burning as she left the protection of the covered deck and leaned over the rail as the SS *Cleopatra* drew up alongside Bawaaba's jetty.

'Gracious, Clifford! The heat has really picked up today.'

'Indeed it has, my lady.' He passed across her parasol. Then, a moment later, turned to one of the other passengers.

'How fortunate, Mr Merrick, that you will now have the chance in Bawaaba to purchase a sun protector appropriate for a gentleman.'

The Welshman coloured and shuffled backwards out of the shade of Eleanor's parasol. Standing nearby among the suitcases and bags cluttering the front deck, Trott sniggered.

'Fortunate!' Merrick huffed. 'There is nothing fortunate, Mr Clifford, about having what was too long a journey to Aswan in the first place now delayed further by bureaucratic interference!'

'Mr Merrick!' Sharaf's voice came from behind him. Stepping out of the dining room, Sharaf fixed him with a steely look, his thick moustache set in a firm line. 'The unavoidable delay is caused by the suicide of Lieutenant Baxter, as I explained most clearly in my briefing.'

'A strange word, this,' Herr Piltz's barbed tone cut in. 'Because I found nothing "brief" about it!'

Eleanor quietly let out a long breath. The lack of regard among the other passengers for Baxter's death was troubling her. Even more so because it seemed almost certain he had died by one of their hands.

She lurched forward as the boat came to an abrupt stop. Up in the wheelhouse, Anders barked commands down to the deck-hands. Farah leaped lithely onto the jetty, deftly throwing the front rope over a thick wooden mooring post. Ali slid the gangway over the side with a grunt, gratefully nodding to Clifford as he stepped over to offer a hand.

From the elevated position on deck, she could see that beyond the narrow patchwork of crops dotting the banks of the river, a compacted dirt road led up to Bawaaba. From its central domed mosque, the small town sprawled out across the immediate landscape, its buildings predominantly honey-brown stone, reminding her of butterscotch. In the distance stretched nothing but an endless vista of sand.

Her gaze fell on the motorised charabanc waiting on the riverbank, beside a dejected-looking horse and trap. A policeman stood next to it with a rifle swinging from his shoulder.

'No escape, it seems,' Ludo muttered as he swung a large canvas duffel bag onto his back.

She frowned. 'The officer is here to guard the boat, I would imagine. Whatever would any of us want to escape for?'

'Not for. *From,*' Frederika cut in, elbowing Ludo hard enough for him to grimace. 'From the tedium of time-wasting, Lady Swift. You don't seem like one to enjoy an enforced break in your plans, either?'

She opened her mouth, but quickly closed it. She didn't want any potential murderer to know she'd originally intended to stay in Bawaaba and had a townhouse there. Next thing, they'd be turning up on the doorstep!

She smiled. 'How right you are. Which is why I shall endeavour to make the best of the situation.'

Sharaf beckoned the armed officer aboard and, after a brief talk with Farah and Ali, he turned back to the restless passengers, captain and first mate.

'The bus will take you to the El Asafa Hotel. Please remember that no one may re-board the SS *Cleopatra* until I say so. And any attempt to leave Bawaaba by river, or overland, would be very foolish. Thank you all for your cooperation.' He stood by the gangplank as those ordered to leave surged off the boat and onto the bus.

'Look forward to catching up with you later!' Eleanor called, waving from the horse and trap as the bus rumbled off.

Clifford's eyes twinkled. 'Fibber.'

She cocked her head. 'As were whatever surreptitious mutterings you made to each of them on the pretext of helping with their luggage. What on earth were you saying?'

'Merely that those first on the bus could choose where to sit and therefore be first off. And thus at the head of the queue at the check-in desk for the best rooms in this town's one and only hotel.'

'In the hope none of them would therefore want to tag along with us and hamper our plans for this afternoon?'

He tutted with mock affront. 'Hardly, my lady. It was in the hope the quarrelsome lot might rush down the gangplank and straight into the Nile.'

She shook her head, laughing. 'Clifford, you are a terrible man! Keep it up, I love it.'

He bowed from the shoulders. 'If the lady insists. Now.

Shall we proceed to your townhouse and band of aproned elves?'

She grimaced. 'Y-e-s.'

He nodded comfortingly. 'Do not fret, my lady. I will assist in breaking the news as gently as possible.'

'Thank you, Clifford. Now, let's enjoy the delights of Bawaaba as we go.'

She was immediately captivated by the hotchpotch feel of the closely packed sandstone buildings. Everything they were passing seemed to have been designed and built in equal part from necessity and imagination, using whatever minimal wood, brick and glass had been available at the time, alongside the plethora of sandstone. The road curved gently, offering tantalising glimpses of the central mosque's dome. Her eyes darted hither and thither, equally fascinated by the eagerly calling street sellers gesturing over their myriad wares, and the bustling townsfolk swathed in ankle-length robes, headscarves and fezzes, hurrying by.

A short while later, the horse and trap pulled up outside an ornate walled garden filled with lush greenery and dominated by a magnificent palm bursting with dates. A path from the gate led to a three-storeyed, yellowy-cream house so architecturally detailed it would have been called a villa in many other parts of the world.

'It's perfectly lovely,' she said excitedly, wishing her original plan to do nothing but relax there with her staff was still an option. 'It's like a study in exotic arches and exquisite columns. And just look at that shady terrace. And the intricate tiling around the arched windows. There's even a half-round tower.'

The driver paid, they climbed the blue and white tiled steps to the front door which flew open.

'Welcome, my lady, Mr Clifford!'

Her housekeeper, Mrs Butters, stepped aside to let them into the elegantly tiled hallway, then hurried to join the remaining three female staff flustering into a line. She curtseyed along with the others, her grey curls bobbing, her smile as soft as her motherly nature. Next to her was Eleanor's taller, pear-hipped cook, Mrs Trotman, equally forthright in manner as she was cheeky in humour. Then there was Lizzie, the older of the two maids, and as sweet-faced as she was natured, her strong Scottish burr never failing to delight Eleanor. And at the end of the line was her youngest maid, the willowy Polly, whose wide-eyed wonder at life itself was as endearing as her ever unsuccessful efforts to be less clumsy.

'Hello, ladies. What a treat we're together again!' Eleanor said genuinely. She pretended to whisper behind her hand. 'Clifford has been positively fizzing the starch from his collar with excitement. But he thinks I haven't noticed.'

He rolled his eyes good-naturedly at the women's collective giggling, led as ever by Mrs Trotman. 'Ahem! I trust your journey here went smoothly, ladies?'

Order restored, Mrs Butters nodded. 'That it did, Mr Clifford. The gentleman guide you arranged for us couldn't do enough.'

'He could have done one more thing for me!' Eleanor caught Mrs Trotman murmur as she gently bumped hips with Mrs Butters, who failed to hide a wince.

'Gracious, whatever happened to you, Mrs Butters?' Eleanor said in concern. 'Not overexerted yourself trying to make everything perfect before I arrived, I hope?'

'Oh, 'tis nothing.' Mrs Butters flapped her apron. 'Just a little reminder of when to know better.'

It was clear the other ladies were trying to keep a straight face. Even Clifford's lips were quirking. He inclined his head. 'Which of you would care to explain?'

Mrs Trotman glanced at the two maids with a conspiratorial

grin. 'Well, Mr Clifford. You told us we should appreciate everything Egyptian-like, since her ladyship was so kind as to bring us aprons along.'

'Indeed. By which I meant Egyptian culture, architecture and—'

'And dancing, of course,' Mrs Trotman said innocently.

'But nobody saw us down in the little café square where the musicians were playing,' Mrs Butters added hastily.

Lizzie nodded vigorously. 'Honest they didn't, Mr Clifford. 'Cos Mrs Butters insisted we only dance in the wee tower at the back of the house here which looks down on the square.'

'So as to practise our whirlin' and wigglin',' Polly added brightly, unwittingly undoing the others' efforts to play down what they'd been up to.

Eleanor couldn't contain her laughter any longer. 'Egyptian dancing, was it that you were trying, ladies? The kind that's all rolling the tummy and snaking the hips, perhaps, Mrs Trotman?'

Her cook grinned. 'That's the one, m'lady.' She pointed at her friend. 'Though Butters near as dislocated hers going at it like a spinning top.'

That finished the ladies and Eleanor off. Eyes closed, Clifford pinched the bridge of his nose.

The sound of exuberant woofing and meowing made her glance down the hall.

Her portly bulldog bounded up but on trying to stop, skidded past her on the shiny tiles. He was followed by her tomcat, who spun in a circle. As they scrabbled back to her, she dropped to her knees. She failed to dodge the soggy leather slipper Gladstone thrust in her face, and equally the paws an eager Tomkins batted at her red curls. She pulled them both into a sorely missed hug.

'What ho, you terrible two! I can't wait to hear what

mischief you've been up to as well. And for a tour of our wonderful holiday home.'

'Although,' Clifford said gently, 'perhaps there might be another, more pressing matter before either, my lady?'

She looked up and winced. 'Oh, dear. I'd almost forgotten.'

Oh, well, Ellie. Time to bite the bullet.

14

Eleanor looked around the ring of expectant faces.

'Umm. Ladies, we have an... unexpected visitor for lunch.'

'Ooh, entertaining so soon? What a treat, m'lady.'

Eleanor smiled weakly. 'Ah, yes, Mrs Trotman. But with apologies for the short notice.'

Her cook shrugged. ''Tis never a bother. I've made heaps, just in case. Same as always.'

'Thank you. The thing is, it's all because, well...' Eleanor floundered for suitable words. Her housekeeper stepped forward with that caring look that made everything better whenever life had spun off the rails.

'Whatever 'tis, m'lady, it's likely to be easier with a cup of tea and a slice of Trotters' new cake, perhaps?'

Clifford nodded. 'For everyone, Mrs Butters, thank you.'

'Certainly, Mr Clifford. I'll serve it in the "inside-out", as the young 'uns have named it, if that suits? It's straight on through that door and out the next.'

Eleanor followed Clifford down the hallway, marvelling at the decorative giant urns and golden-framed paintings of what she took to be Egyptian gods and goddesses, given their exquisite head-dresses. At the end, they passed through an exquisitely appointed room hung with silk wall coverings. Stepping through an arched door, they arrived on a terrace dotted with exotic pot plants and screened on three sides with intricate lattice panels in dark wood. In the garden, a multitude of palms rustled in the morning breeze.

'Evidently, this is the "inside-out", my lady.' Clifford pulled a sumptuous purple cushioned seat out from the table for her, then a long carved wooden bench over for the ladies.

'Something for you too, please?' she said. 'Though given you'll only perch, I'm sure you'd best pull up a bird cage.'

Before he could reply, she heard the ladies approaching.

'Ready, my lady?'

She took a long breath. 'Not at all, Clifford. So, let's get it over with.'

A moment later, the rest of her staff appeared, all bearing trays and struggling not to trip over the bulldog and tomcat eagerly winding in and out of their legs.

'Masters Gladstone and Tomkins,' Clifford said firmly. 'Best behaviour, please! No doubt you are catered for amongst the offerings the ladies have brought?'

'Ach aye, sir.' Lizzie held out a tray. 'The two of them can nae get enough of these little silvery fried fish treats. They're meant for people, mind.'

'How delightful,' Clifford said, looking as if he thought it anything but.

He inclined his head, and the ladies slid onto the bench except Mrs Butters, who served everyone a cup of tea and a slice of honey and almond date cake first. Eleanor took hers, thinking it looked too heavenly to sour with what she needed to say. Her brow furrowed as she tried to work out an easy way to put it.

Clifford came to her rescue. 'Ladies, it has become necessary for her ladyship to change her plans. Thus, the two of us will be staying, for the most part, at the hotel here in town.'

'But popping back here regularly. And it's for a few days only,' she added quickly at their obvious disappointment.

'Hopefully,' Clifford muttered. 'Ladies, something regrettable occurred during her ladyship's cruise here. Hence the visitor for lunch today will be the Chief of Police of Bawaaba.'

'Ooh! A uniformed gentleman, Butters,' Mrs Trotman murmured cheekily. 'Haven't had one of those since we was back home.'

Despite the gravity of the conversation, Ellie couldn't help smiling. Whenever her fiancé came around to Henley Hall, her female staff swooned over him. Particularly her irrepressible cook. Not that she could blame her. She tutted to herself. She really should try and finish her letter to Hugh. Leaving out any mention of the regrettable business they had found themselves in again, of course!

Mrs Butters poked Mrs Trotman in the arm. 'Not now, Trotters,' she hissed. She turned back to Eleanor, clucking like a mother hen. 'Oh, m'lady, say the occurrence wasn't a too unhappy one?'

Eleanor shrugged sadly. 'I wish I could. But one of the passengers passed away on our boat.'

Mrs Trotman looked abashed. 'Poor soul to go amongst strangers. And, beg pardon for askin', but the police is coming because, m'lady?'

Eleanor hesitated.

'In strictest confidence, ladies,' Clifford said solemnly. 'There is a question mark over how the gentleman passed away.'

The rest of her staff gasped in unison. Her cook found her tongue first.

'Meaning, someone might have up and done for him?'

'That cannot be entirely ruled out, Mrs Trotman,' Clifford said gently.

Eleanor spotted her two maids linking arms as Mrs Butters rose and came around to her side. 'Will you be alright, my lady?'

She nodded. 'Yes, I'm sure. I'm only sorry to have to mention it. After all, this is your holiday too.'

Her housekeeper patted her arm. 'Then when as the matter is all sorted, m'lady, please come straight home here for a goodly dose of spoiling by us all.'

'I can't wait, thank you. Nor for hip-wiggling dance lessons!'

'Not to fret,' Mrs Trotman said, looking as relieved as the others. 'Butters'll whip up a blindfold so as Mr Clifford can play for us without blushing on one of those peculiar guitars folks was plucking at faster'n chickens on roasting day last night.'

'Lucky me,' he said playfully, clearly joining in to ease Eleanor's worry she had ruined the ladies' holiday. 'Now, let us change topic. Had you planned anything... er, decorous for tomorrow? Polly?'

The young maid nodded eagerly. 'Yes, Mr Clifford. 'Tis the day for the special market, we heard.'

Eleanor clapped her hands. 'Then, how about we all go? I'm sure we can be free for that. If my tagging along won't cramp your style, of course?'

Mrs Butters tutted. 'You don't need no invitation, m'lady.'

Mrs Trotman rose. 'Speaking of invitations, if there's one more to lunch, there's work to do. Excuse me, my lady.' She turned to the maids. 'Hurry scurry, girls!'

As all the ladies left, Eleanor sighed.

'That didn't go too awfully, did it, Clifford?'

He shook his head. 'On the contrary, my lady. They are concerned only for you, rest assured. As your butler would also admit to, were it his place to say so.'

She smiled. 'In that case, please tell him I'm immensely grateful he cares.'

A clanging downstairs made her jump. 'That isn't the door-bell and Sharaf already, is it?'

He pulled out his pocket watch. 'I believe it is, my lady.'

She eased out from under her bulldog's heavy head. 'Then let me greet him, please. I know you should, but I want to start things off a little less formally.' She groaned at her butler's hesitation. 'Look. If he's to take me seriously, it's no good him being escorted in to find me languishing like a vaporous princess.' Something in his silence gave her goosebumps. 'Clifford, what is it?'

He sighed. 'My lady, I have a... concern.'

15

Eleanor anxiously scanned her butler's face. 'Concern? About what? Investigating Baxter's death?' She tutted gently. 'We've done this sort of thing before, you know? And we've always covered each other's backs.' She pointed between them. 'And, unless we're just mirages from this relentless heat, we're both still here in one piece.'

He nodded slowly. 'I concur. However, I have a feeling this time. A bad one, my lady. The worst of it is, I cannot begin to articulate what is at the root—'

'Beg pardon for interrupting, m'lady,' her housekeeper said, hurrying in. 'Only it seemed far too hot to leave your gentleman visitor waiting on the step.'

'Indeed, Mrs Butters, thank you. Ah! Good afternoon, Chief Sharaf,' Clifford said smoothly, his ever-impassive expression back on his face. 'Allow me to relieve you of your hat. And, ahem, her ladyship's wilful bulldog and tomcat!'

Eleanor felt a prickle of apprehension as she settled into the carver chair Clifford held out for her in the dining room. Sharaf's expression was genial enough as he sat opposite, but there was a disconcerting steely look in his intelligent black eyes.

She forced herself to relax and admire the room. The table was dressed in ivory and gold linen with glistening glassware and a centrepiece of cream and vanilla jasmine sprays set among silky soft ruby-tipped grasses. Outside, the magnificent palms cast captivating patterns over the room's ochre walls as they rustled in the light breeze.

'What delectableness has Mrs Trotman conjured up for us, then?' she said to Clifford.

'Evidently, the luncheon menu is a creative blend of English and Egyptian cuisine from Mrs Trotman's own inimitable culinary expertise.' He glided over with a silver tray bearing two cocktails. 'Including this aniseed and mint aperitif.'

'I would watch out, Chief Sharaf,' she said as she took one. 'My cook's home-brewed concoctions are invariably lethal!'

Clifford offered the policeman the other glass. 'I can assure there is no alcohol included in any of the luncheon fare. As all dietary preferences have been strictly respected.'

'Most kind.' Sharaf smiled and took the glass. 'I had not appreciated your cook was here with you, Lady Swift?'

'Yes. All my ladies are, in fact. As well as the terrible two, Gladstone and Tomkins. I brought us all out here for a well-deserved holiday.'

'Interesting,' Sharaf muttered.

After several failed attempts at small talk, she finished the last sip of her refreshing aperitif and sat back. She had to steer the conversation around to Baxter's death somehow.

'What do you think of your new police station?' she blurted out, catching her butler's almost imperceptible wince as he set down a bowl of delicious-smelling soup in front of her.

Sharaf shrugged. 'It is fine enough for my time there. However long that is.'

'Oh! Are you regularly seconded to different posts, then?'

'I go wherever I am sent. My town of birth is not large. Nor important. And never receives any tourists or foreign businessmen.' He sighed quietly. 'Which is why I am mostly sent to other small, unimportant towns.'

'Like Bawaaba?' She savoured a spoonful. 'Sublime starter, Clifford. Chicken with bay leaves and...?'

'Saffron, cumin, and a soupçon of hibiscus, my lady.'

Sharaf smiled. 'It is a delicious combination. I too was wondering. And, yes, Lady Swift. Small towns like Bawaaba. It means "gateway" in Egyptian. It is not its original name. It was renamed recently when the touristic desire to see and experience the ancient wonders of my country first began to grow. The local authorities thought they could capitalise on an old underground part of the town located in the "empty quarter", as they call it. Apparently, it is a little like the Rome or Paris catacombs, but much less extensive and interesting! Indeed, some people here refer to it as the Bawaaba Catacombs, but I was told no tourist ever came.'

Over their second course of dill-infused perch terrine on toasted sesame bread fingers, Eleanor decided enough pleasantries had been exchanged.

'Chief Sharaf, about Lieutenant Baxter's death?' His gaze gave nothing away. 'It's clear the murderer must have been someone on board the SS *Cleopatra* since we left Cairo.'

He put down his fork. 'Your reason, Lady Swift?'

'Well, it had to be as no other passengers had boarded. Unless someone climbed aboard, killed the poor fellow, and then disappeared without anyone seeing them. Which strikes me as unlikely, given that the three of us were on the front deck, and Captain Anders was on the rear.'

Sharaf nodded. 'I agree. To board a moving boat in the night would be a most difficult task. And a foolish one, as the crocodiles are most active between dusk and dawn. If someone had succeeded, they would still have needed to know which cabin was the lieutenant's.'

Eleanor didn't miss his heavy emphasis on "if" among his otherwise seemingly hopeful comments. 'So we agree we should focus on those whom we know were on the boat when we heard the shot?'

'As a precautionary measure against the unlikely possibility of it being murder, yes.'

She nodded resignedly. 'Thank you for making your opinion so abundantly clear.'

'Lady Swift, I am a policeman. Facts form my opinions.'

She laughed. 'Chief Sharaf, you have no idea how many times I have been told that!'

Mostly by your own fiancé, Ellie.

'I am beginning to imagine,' he said with a half-smile. 'So, to continue. We three are above suspicion as we were together at the time of the gunshot.'

'Yes. And First Mate Jabir. Plus Farah and Ali. I saw them up in the wheelhouse moments before. None of them would have had time to sprint to Baxter's cabin and arrange a fake suicide.'

Sharaf raised his glass to her. 'Thank you for making your opinion of how the lieutenant died so abundantly clear, Lady Swift. I prefer straight talking.'

'Can we talk freely, then?' she said with relief. 'I'm hopeless at pretending anything.'

Clifford nodded emphatically at Sharaf. 'You may trust her ladyship on that score.'

Sharaf chuckled over her mock huff. 'Yes. Let us talk freely. And I freely repeat that I do not believe Lieutenant Baxter was murdered. You need to present me with evidence, *firm* evidence, before I will change my mind.'

A moment later, while serving the main course, Clifford

slipped her investigation notebook onto the table next to her, then gestured at their meals.

'Mrs Trotman informs me the squab wellington has been cooked with a turmeric and cardamom crust in lieu of the more traditional English mustard.'

She looked at him innocently. 'Squab? As in squabble? The disgraceful art which we titled ladies never engage in?'

'Squab, as in pigeon,' he said, eyes bright with amusement.

Sharaf nodded. 'Pigeon is popular here in Egypt. But never before have I seen it in a kingdom of pastry. And one so golden, like the desert itself. Neither have I tried it with rich mushrooms as were once eaten only by our kings and queens. Man gave them to Osiris in ancient Egyptian religion, it is said.'

'As a gift of immortality, if memory serves,' Clifford added.

'What a shame poor Baxter wasn't granted some the night he was murdered,' Eleanor said sadly.

Sharaf seemed about to say something, then closed his mouth.

'On to our suspects, then.' She hurriedly opened her notebook at the list she and Clifford had prepared earlier, as if it was the most natural thing to do over lunch with a barely acquainted guest.

BAXTER'S DEATH

Crew of SS *Cleopatra* **Alibi**
Captain Anders **?**
First Mate Jabir **Yes**
Deckhand Ali **Yes**
Deckhand Farah **Yes**

<u>Passengers</u>
Chief Sharaf **Yes**
Ernst Piltz (following Baxter) **?**

Frederika de Groot **?**
Ludo de Groot **?**
Felix Trott **?**
Wesley Merrick **?**

She cleared her throat. 'I'll only go through the ones we have something on. Herr Piltz first.'

Clifford spooned more of the tangy prickly pear and grape coulis onto her plate.

'Now then,' she continued. 'Piltz's cabin is number eight. Almost directly opposite Baxter's, which was number four. And Piltz was the first one to bluster out into the corridor when the three of us arrived. Which can't have taken us more than a minute or so from the time of the shot.'

Sharaf nodded but failed to pull out his own notebook. 'Not enough time to have killed the lieutenant and placed the gun in his hand. Particularly as, before returning to his own cabin, he would have had another task. To turn the key in the lock on the inside of the door from outside, which would be very slow to do.'

He looked up at Clifford's quiet cough. 'Ahem, if you will forgive the observation, Chief Sharaf, it takes a matter of seconds if one uses particularly long, or specially adapted, needle-nosed pliers.'

Sharaf's eyes narrowed. 'I think it would take longer. Even for an... expert hand?'

Eleanor forced a laugh. 'Clifford's really not a housebreaker on the quiet, you know.'

'Perhaps only when he wishes to enter the padlocked cabins of dead men?' Sharaf said pointedly. 'Or am I mistaken about how you came to find the letter you showed me hidden in the statue?'

An awkward silence filled the room.

'Have I mentioned I caught Piltz following Baxter earlier

that evening?' Eleanor said quickly. 'It was just before I ran into you.' Sharaf shook his head. Hurrying on again, she tapped the page. 'As we discussed, timing seems very tight, but I say we leave him on the list until we can investigate further?'

'I agree,' Sharaf said. 'Who do you wish to discuss next?'

'The de Groots. It's hard to imagine one could have murdered Baxter without the other knowing. However, I did catch Baxter and Ludo arguing the night of his murder.' She paused to savour another mouthful of the succulently sweet pigeon which paired sublimely with the sharpness of the coulis. 'As to Trott. He emerged in a state of undress from his cabin, so must have been inside. But, Merrick. He was in the lounge when the three of us ran in after the shot. Could he have sprinted there from Baxter's cabin? Doubtful, even though he seemed extremely flustered.'

'I think he is a man of exhausted nerves,' Sharaf said.

'Yes. And I do have something on him, too!' She scrabbled for her jacket pockets, then frowned.

'Your jacket is hanging in the wardrobe, my lady. Are you looking for this?' Clifford placed the broken pen clip she'd picked up on her notebook.

'Has Gladstone been going through my pockets again, the devious scallywag?' she said, fleetingly piqued her butler was one step ahead of her again. Placing the pen clip on the table, she sat back. 'I found that in Baxter's cabin. Under the very desk where the suicide note had been planted, sorry, placed so as not to be missed.'

Sharaf pulled a pair of thick-rimmed spectacles from his jacket pocket and looked the clip over. 'You think this is like the ones Mr Merrick wears in his jacket pocket, I suppose?'

'I do. And it's the first thing I shall check when I see him at the El Asafa Hotel this afternoon.' She cleared her throat. 'So, we've drawn nothing conclusive for Merrick except possibly the pen clip, but agree he should be on the list?'

He nodded. 'Agreed. Which leaves only Captain Anders.'

'It does. We've already noted he came into the cabin corridor from the back deck.'

'And arrived *after* us,' Sharaf said, sounding interested in what she was saying for the first time.

'True. And the distance from the rear deck compared to the front deck where we came from is considerably less.'

Clifford set down a long platter of divine-looking cheeses, surrounded by dates and figs. She dived in. The policeman waited before taking some himself.

'Forgive me saying so, but I believed English tourists found the heat in Egypt blunted their appetite?'

Clifford nodded. 'Usually, Chief Sharaf. However, in her ladyship's case, dining on the surface of the sun might be the only possible cause of such.'

Sharaf chuckled as he dropped his napkin and sat back. 'So, Lady Swift, we have discovered nothing except all your suspects possibly had the opportunity.'

She winced. 'True. But next we need to establish if any of them had a motive. For instance, to ensure Baxter never got to put right this "great injustice" he mentions in his letter.'

Sharaf pulled the folded letter from his pocket and held it up. 'The words "great injustice" are indeed written here. But by who, I cannot say. And for what purpose, the same. It may still just be the ramblings of a disturbed mind, as I said. But let us believe, for the purpose of your murder theory, it is not.' He leaned forward. 'I made an agreement with you. For my reasons. So, I will tell you what I have done. And am doing. As I promised, I have sent the fingerprints found on the gun to Cairo to be matched with others found in the cabin that can only be the lieutenant's. And also I have sent the suicide note, the letter you discovered, and another sample of his handwriting to be matched.' At her gasp, he waved the letter he still held. 'This is a copy I made myself and the original letter was sent sealed, so it is perfectly secure. Now, while I am waiting for the results of all these tests, my men have been searching the SS *Cleopatra*. Again, for my own reasons. However, anything they find relevant to your interest in this matter, I will share with you.'

She nodded eagerly. 'Thank you. And it was an excellent idea to send off the letter to confirm it is genuine as well. On our part, Clifford and I will do what we do best at the hotel with each of the people on this suspect list. Discreetly, of course,' she added hurriedly. 'While trying to work out what the "proof" is that Baxter mentioned in his letter.'

'By Friday,' Sharaf said firmly.

She grimaced. 'But that's only two days.'

He shrugged. 'I did not promise any more. By Friday, if my reasons for holding the SS *Cleopatra* are resolved satisfactorily, she will sail. That is all I will say.'

Let's hope they aren't then, Ellie.

He smiled thinly. 'Unless, that is, you have in the meantime uncovered evidence that convinces me the lieutenant's death was, in fact, murder. Otherwise, the moment the SS *Cleopatra* leaves Bawaaba, his death will be officially recorded as suicide and any investigation will be closed.'

Along with any chance of catching Baxter's killer, Ellie!

He fixed her with a steely gaze. 'Do we understand each other, Lady Swift?'

She nodded resignedly. 'Yes, Chief Sharaf. We do.'

16

Eleanor paused on entering the lobby of the El Asafa Hotel as a tantalising earthy scent of spiced musk overlain with jasmine tickled her nose. The paprika-red walls of the hotel were each hung with a large geometrically patterned carpet in varying combinations of dusky pink, midnight blue and sandy yellow, while the polished, dark-wood floor was bare except for one central rug of similar design. Three high arches led off the lobby, each offering glimpses of latticed panels, coloured glass lanterns and comfortable-looking lounge chairs.

She and Clifford had come straight from their talk with Sharaf to book in. Once they'd done that, she was determined to waste no time and start interviewing her fellow passengers immediately. *Discreetly* interview, she reminded herself grudgingly as she looked around. Discreet wasn't her happy place.

A petite, copper-faced man held his arms wide behind the reception desk.

'*Marhaba*!' he declared with a broad smile. Stepping out, revealing his ankle-length white robe, he gestured around him. 'Meaning welcome to my hotel. I am the owner and manager. It is rare for me to have the pleasure of tourists as my guests.'

Although one of them is almost certainly a murderer, Ellie.

She smiled broadly to cover up her thoughts. 'Thank you for such a wonderful greeting. We haven't booked ahead though, I'm afraid.'

'No problem.' He beamed back as he pulled a basket out from under the desk and selected two keys on fobs. 'Chief Sharaf tell me six rooms required. Two are waiting for you. On the third floor with the special view of the sun as she brings the first golden light of the morning.'

'How perfect for such an inveterate early riser, my lady,' Clifford teased as he signed the register.

The manager raised a finger. 'Ah! The lady would like the five o'clock breakfast, I think, yes?'

She tried to hide her horror. 'Oh, well, perhaps I could confirm a little later?'

He nodded. 'Whatever' – he examined the register – 'Lady Swift wishes. Which I think now, is maybe to rest in the cool air of your room?' He clapped his hands, and a porter appeared and took their cases.

She was about to follow him when, through one of the arches, she noticed a pair of stout walking boots and loose-fitting khaki trousers poking out from behind a chair.

This is your chance, Ellie. Let's see if you can find out what his argument with Baxter was about.

'I believe her ladyship will take coffee in the lounge first,' she heard her butler say. 'A pot for three, please.'

Clifford's spotted him too, Ellie.

Once through the arch, she made a convincing show of being surprised. 'Oh, hello, Ludo. You feeling marooned too?' She glanced around quickly but, as she thought, Frederika was nowhere to be seen. It would be easier to get Ludo to talk without his domineering partner around.

Ludo unfolded himself from his chair and ran a hand

through his shock of straw-blond hair. 'Umm, marooned, did you say, Lady Swift?'

'Yes. Like a fully rigged galleon straining at her mooring ropes. Or the SS *Cleopatra*, of course.' She dropped into the chair opposite him as if all the wind had gone from her sails.

Her butler nodded. 'Quite so, Mr de Groot. In ordinary circumstances, containing her ladyship might only be achieved with the aid of a locked trunk in a cellar patrolled by a hungry tiger!'

Eleanor laughed. 'Which he's often wished he could arrange, trust me.'

As Clifford took the coffee pot from the hovering waiter and set out the cups, she leaned forward.

'Mind you, it does feel better all of us being in this frustrating pickle together, doesn't it?'

Ludo nodded hesitantly. 'I guess it does. And I should not complain. The dig I am heading to is not going anywhere. That is one advantage of archaeology.'

Eleanor noted he said 'I', not 'we', but it was none of her business whether Ludo regarded his wife as an equal partner or not.

But then again, they are both on your suspect list, Ellie, so maybe it does? And he sounds far too casual about arriving late at the dig Frederika said was so important to their careers. Could that have anything to do with a motive for Baxter's murder?

She accepted her cup of coffee from Clifford, delighted it was accompanied by two squares of what looked like rice pudding topped with grated nuts. 'By the way, Ludo, I hope I didn't sound as if I was complaining? It's only right that everything is done properly for poor Lieutenant Baxter, after all.'

He shrugged, but not callously, she thought. 'It is sad, of course. But the rest of the journey will be quieter without him. A few less arguments, at least.'

This was her chance. 'Bless him, he did seem to ruffle everyone's feathers. Even such an even-tempered man like you.'

Ludo's smile stiffened. 'Me? I did not argue with him.'

'No? My mistake then.'

She busied herself with her coffee.

'Why would you think I had?' he said a moment later.

'Oh, nothing in particular. Although, yesterday evening when I bumped into you and Baxter up on the second deck, you both did look as if you'd been arguing.'

He shook his head. 'No. We... we were just having a lively, but friendly discussion of the cricket scores. As you guessed at the time.'

Clifford placed a filled cup in front of him. 'Incidentally, Mr de Groot, how are both sides faring? My copy of the *Egyptian Gazette* omitted to report the score. Perhaps because the tournament does not start for a few days yet?'

Ludo sighed. 'You are unsettlingly sharp-witted enough on your own, Lady Swift. Joining forces with your butler is unfair. You obviously overheard us.' He held his hands up contritely. 'I am sorry that Lieutenant Baxter and I were talking about you. But he said he was curious. And there seemed no harm in his question.'

She smiled reassuringly. 'I'm sure there wasn't. But I admit to being intrigued that you could answer. I've a terrible memory for some things, but I would remember if we'd met before?'

'We have not. But Frederika read... I mean, we read about your adventures when we were at a dig in Turkey. It was in the local newspaper the day after you passed through the area. Or that week, I think, anyway. It said you were cycling around the world on your own. That surprised Lieutenant Baxter, alright! You should have seen his face. He was dumbfounded. It is a remarkable story. Especially for a lady.'

Clifford raised a brow. 'And that was all you told Lieutenant Baxter about her ladyship?'

He shrugged. 'It was. There was nothing else I could tell, as there was nothing else I knew. After all, as Lady Swift rightly said, we have never met before.'

Her shoulders relaxed. It seemed the de Groots knew only about her adventures travelling solo, not solving murders. However, if he was telling the truth and he hadn't been arguing with Baxter, then her one tenuous motive for him killing Baxter had just vanished. Maybe he would trip himself up over his alibi?

She nodded for Clifford to refill her coffee, noting Ludo hadn't touched his.

'You know, I'm still not sure I'm quite over the shock. It was all so sudden. There Lieutenant Baxter was talking with you and me, and only a few hours or so after that, he was dead, poor fellow.' She leaned forward again. 'It would be comforting to learn he exchanged a few pleasant words with someone just before he died. Did you maybe see him once more later on? Nearer the time of that awful shot?'

He shook his head. 'No. He must have been in his cabin for quite a while before he... did what he did and ended it all.'

'How do you know that?' she said lightly.

'I don't exactly. But I couldn't sleep, so I went to the lounge to have a cigarette. Frederika doesn't allow me to smoke in the cabin. It was twenty minutes before midnight, and I did not see Baxter there. Or passing outside, so I assumed he was in his cabin.'

Clifford cleared his throat. 'Did you meet anyone while you were in the lounge who might have spoken to Lieutenant Baxter?'

Ludo frowned. 'Well, I saw Trott. You could ask him. He passed in the corridor about five minutes after I got there. And ten minutes later, he passed back again. But on the outside deck.'

'So, at about five to midnight?'

'It must have been, because I finished my cigarette at five past. Then I returned to bed. That was just before the gunshot.'

'You've remembered that time very clearly?'

He nodded. 'I remember glancing at my watch and thinking I would be in trouble when I got back to the cabin for being away so long.'

'You mean with Frederika?'

'What about her?' a forthright female voice cut in.

Blast, Ellie. Now Ludo will probably clam up. Still, maybe you can check Frederika's alibi instead?

Ludo jumped as if he'd been stung. 'Nothing, dear. Lady Swift and Mr Clifford just invited me to join them for coffee.'

Eleanor smiled genially. 'Which he hasn't had a chance to start in on. There's heaps more. Do grab a seat.'

Frederika glanced coldly between the three of them. 'No, thank you.'

'We were talking about poor Lieutenant Baxter,' Eleanor said. 'I was hoping someone exchanged some nice words with him just before he died, you see? Maybe you did?'

Frederika shook her head firmly. 'No. I went to bed early. Ludo, however, went to the lounge for a cigarette at twenty minutes to midnight. He returned a little after midnight. And I was about to go back to sleep when I heard the gunshot ten minutes after that.'

Eleanor shrugged apologetically. 'Sorry. Perhaps we should talk about something less sombre? You know, Frederika, I haven't stopped thinking about how unusual it was. Ludo proposing to you in a hole in the ground in Greece. How long ago was it now, Ludo?'

She spotted Frederika surreptitiously kick him.

'Three years. I mean—'

'Four and a half, in fact.' Frederika grabbed him by the arm. 'Ludo, we need to go. Now.'

'We do? Oh, I see,' he said blankly. He waved goodbye as he was dragged away.

'Interesting,' Eleanor muttered. 'Let's retire to my room so I can hold forth on the de Groots' strange inability to agree with each other on anything except their potential alibi.'

'A most tempting invitation, my lady,' he said sniffily. 'However, salvation arrives, I believe. In the form of—'

Before he could finish, Trott slid into the seat Ludo had left.

Even better, Ellie. You can check his alibi against what Ludo has just told you.

Trott sniffed the coffee. 'Aha! How did you know I like mine strong and without milk?'

She laughed. 'Lucky guess. Although you'll want a fresh cup. That was Ludo's.'

'Here, Mr Trott.' Clifford poured a stream of the rich dark coffee into what would have been his own cup if he'd actually drunk anything.

'Ah, top job.' Trott took a long slurp. Crossing one ankle over his opposite knee, he leaned back in his seat. 'This is the life alright, I'd say.'

She smiled easily. 'I thought you'd be champing at the bit to get on with your research?'

He took another slurp of coffee. 'Oh, I am. Scaly beasts, especially crocodiles, are really the only thing that excites me. I can't pretend otherwise. But since that policeman Sharaf seems to lack a sense of humour, I'm being a good boy and mostly doing what I should, for once.' He slid his empty cup across to Clifford. 'In between, that is, making the most of an enforced stay at the Egyptian government's expense.'

'And her ladyship's. Since sundry refreshments are not covered.' Clifford poured him a half cup.

'Alright.' Trott took the offering. 'Just trying to make the best of the situation, my friend. Old Baxter—'

'Is dead,' Eleanor said firmly.

Trott shrugged. 'I have to confess I think going that way is a mistake. I'd hurl myself into the Nile and let a croc take me. Just as sure as a gun.'

She shuddered, then remembered Sharaf's remark. 'Tell me. Do they hunt mostly at dawn or dusk?'

'Dusk, not dawn. No, indeed. Don't try coaxing a croc out of bed before he's ready. Definitely bite your head off, he would!'

Clifford glanced mischievously at her. 'Sound familiar?'

She hid a smile. 'So, Mr Trott, were you crocodile spotting when that awful shot went off?'

He frowned. 'What? Why would I be out of...? What an odd idea, Lady Swift. I was in bed like everyone else. Had been for ages. Got woken up before the shot, then heard it and the subsequent ballyhoo in the corridor, actually.'

Her ears pricked up. 'You were woken up before the shot? By what, I wonder?'

'Not what, *who*. Someone not very considerate. Heard the cabin door next to mine bang open at ten to midnight. And footsteps go across the corridor to the cabin opposite. Then more footsteps and another door further along open and close. Rotten lack of decency. I'd just got back to sleep when the shot went off. Thought I was dreaming, actually. Until someone hammered on my door and frightened the daylights out of me, that is!'

'You say you were asleep, but when you came to the door, I seem to remember you were still doing up your pyjamas?'

Trott tutted in mock disapproval. 'Really, Lady Swift! I thought titled ladies weren't supposed to ask a chap about his bedtime habits?' He eased out of his chair. 'But since you're curious. I had no clothes on because I sleep in the raw.' He ambled away, calling back to a horrified-looking Clifford. 'Thanks for the coffee and a half, my friend.'

17

In her hotel room, Eleanor dropped onto all fours as she wrestled with the latches of her suitcase. 'Dash it! Why is it too stubborn to yield to reasonable persuasion?'

From outside her half-open door, Clifford's amused voice answered, 'It is a troubling trait in a titled lady, I agree.'

'Very droll,' she huffed. 'But hardly helpful.'

'Perhaps you might find your luggage less stubborn with this?'

He held out a small silver key. Before she could insert it, her investigation notebook slid into her eyeline, followed by Clifford's fountain pen.

'Ah, of course, that's where it was. Thank you.' She perched on her case, flipping through to the suspect list she'd written out during lunch with Sharaf. She ignored her butler's sniff in the direction of the cane chair by the window.

'Now, let's see what progress we've made. Starting with Frederika. She backed up what Ludo said about the times either side of the gunshot, yes?'

'To the precise minute.'

'Exactly! But conversely, she then contradicted him about

how long ago he'd proposed to her. So, was that a simple error on Ludo's part, or...?'

'Or have the de Groots expanded more effort rehearsing their alibis for the time of Lieutenant Baxter's death than their personal details as a married couple?'

'And why should they need to?' She added a note. 'Also, was Ludo telling the truth about not arguing with Baxter?' She thought for a moment and then shook her head. 'Let's ponder that later when we've got more to go on. So, Trott.'

He nodded. 'Who did not contradict himself, but did make an amateur error for a supposed expert. I happened to read up on the Nile and its inhabitants before leaving England and it seems the crocodiles therein are most active at dusk *and* dawn.'

'Bit sloppy for an expert?'

'Although whose word other than his own do we have that he is one?'

'Excellent point. We'll have to follow that one up as well. But, perhaps more pertinently, he gave an entirely contrary story to Ludo's about where he was either side of that terrible gunshot.'

He nodded. 'Mr Trott said he heard the door of the cabin next to his open.'

'Trott was in number six, the last starboard cabin, so that must have been number seven. Merrick's.'

'He then heard footsteps cross the corridor.'

'And opposite number seven is number four, home to one Lieutenant Baxter... now deceased!'

She rocked back and forth on her suitcase, deep in thought. 'So whose version of where Trott was between twenty minutes to and five past midnight is true? Ludo's? Who said Trott passed him twice within that time span. Or Trott's? Who swore the whole time he was in bed in—'

'Ahem! His cabin.'

'Exactly. In his cabin in nothing but his birthday suit.' She hid a smile as Clifford cleared his throat pointedly. 'But if Ludo is lying and Trott is the one telling the truth, did he really hear Merrick entering Baxter's...'

They shared a look of realisation.

'The broken pen clip I found at the scene of his death!'

Clifford stroked his chin. 'So Mr Merrick would have been in Lieutenant Baxter's cabin around twenty to twenty-five minutes before we heard the shot. Long enough to coerce a man into writing a false suicide note, kill him and then arrange for it to look like suicide?'

She leaped up, knocking her case over backwards. 'Let's go ferret out Merrick, and find out!'

They tried everywhere else they could think of with no success, finally buttonholing the manager in the lobby.

'Has Mr Merrick left the hotel?'

'I am most certain not, Lady Swift. His key is not behind the desk. Maybe the gentleman is in the games room?'

'I didn't realise you had one. If you do run across him, please tell him I am looking for him.'

They left the lobby and crossed the courtyard. But inside the games room, there was no sign of their prey. There was, however, a consolation prize.

'Ah! Good afternoon, Herr Piltz.'

The German turned slowly and nodded. His pale-blue eyes narrowed as he continued puffing on his cigar. She waved around the room, indicating the three tables on which sat various board games, packets of cards and dice. 'Which do you fancy trying your hand at first?'

'None, thank you,' Piltz said coldly.

'As you wish. You'd only have denied Clifford the delight of trumping me anyway.'

She slid onto the bench seat nearest him, blocking his escape route. In her mind, she'd promoted the German to second place in her list of suspects after Merrick. She had to try and find out why Piltz had been following Baxter the evening of his death. But asking such a cool customer as Piltz directly was unlikely to elicit the truth.

She tutted. 'A pity. There's enough of us stuck here at Chief Sharaf's insistence to have made up proper teams. It's going to feel even longer an incarceration if we all just mooch about being bored, wouldn't you say?'

Piltz snorted. 'Bored, Lady Swift? A condition affecting only those not in charge of their thoughts. Not wishing to be rude, of course,' he said in a tone that hinted he wasn't particularly concerned if he had been.

She turned to Clifford. 'There you go! I was absolutely wrong about Herr Piltz. That's one wager to you.'

He nodded. 'One up, but still three down overall.'

She bit back a smile. *Only Clifford would make up false scores, Ellie, for an imaginary betting competition you've just conjured up.*

He joined her on the opposite side of the table and set out a row of seven palm-sized figurines from a box, each with the head of a dog or bird. The top of the box was inset with three lines of ten alternating ivory and crimson tile squares.

Piltz seemed to lose a battle with himself. 'I don't understand what you could have found to wager about me?' he growled.

She shrugged. 'I bet Clifford that you were easily bored. You see, I couldn't think of any other reason you would have been following Lieutenant Baxter around the SS *Cleopatra*.'

Piltz froze for a moment. Then slowly removed the cigar from his mouth. 'You are quite mistaken, Lady Swift. It must have been one of the other guests.'

'I clearly saw you the evening of his death follow him down the rear crew stairs to the lower deck.'

'You mean the fr—' Piltz stared at her furiously, then looked away.

Got him, Ellie. It was the front crew steps.

Piltz ground his cigar into the ashtray. 'I think, Lady Swift, you are the one who is easily bored. Bored with life!'

She bristled. 'Is that a threat, Herr Piltz?'

Clifford's quietly strangled cough brought her to her senses. 'Ahem! Your turn, my lady.'

He's right, Ellie. What happened to discreet?

She dutifully re-threw the dice, then held up her hands. 'I'm sorry, Herr Piltz. It... it must have been someone else.' She moved another dog along the board. 'Tell me, how long were you in your cabin before you heard that terrible shot? Clifford bet me—'

'Enough!' He flapped his hands for her to let him pass.

The courtyard door was flung open.

'Ah! There you are, Lady Swift,' Merrick panted, pointing at her.

She waved at him. 'Ran me to ground at last, eh?'

'What?' he said, abashed. 'I haven't been chasing you!'

With a grunt, Piltz pushed past the Welshman and stomped out.

Merrick sank down onto the bench beside Clifford. 'I have never once engaged in such a disreputable thing as chasing after a lady. The very idea! I was only looking for you because the manager made a complete song and dance about how desperately you needed to see me.'

She nodded. 'I did casually ask our clearly over-helpful hotel owner if he had seen you.'

Merrick looked uncomfortable. 'To make up a threesome at whatever you're playing?'

'Later, perhaps. We could all do with some diversions from being forced to hole up here. But I wanted to ask you a couple of things first. How are you holding up after that terrible business with Lieutenant Baxter?'

'Perfectly alright, thank you,' he said stiffly. 'Though why wouldn't I be? No disrespect to the fellow and all that, but he was just another passenger.'

'But you were so agitated when Clifford and I burst into the lounge after that awful gunshot went off.'

'That was only on account of the noise.'

'Inner ear problem, was it?'

'Yes. No! Well, if you must pry, I was worried one of the crew was shooting... at a crocodile that had got on board.'

'Gracious, that would have been an unsettling occurrence if one had.'

'Albeit an extremely unlikely one,' Clifford said smoothly.

Merrick's fingers fidgeted with his pens. 'That's as maybe. But phobias play tricks, don't they? They're as mean as... the thing that causes them.'

He was looking so flushed, Eleanor hurried onto a different tack. 'It was a shame your peaceful time in the lounge was interrupted, Mr Merrick. I hope you'd managed to relax in there for a significant time before that?'

'That was the worst of it. I left my cabin to get a glass of brandy but only got to sit down for fifteen minutes before that great bang of a shot went off.'

'I can see it would have rattled you. And whoever else was in there with you.'

He shook his head vigorously. 'There was no one. It was empty when I arrived so I never got my brandy. And not a soul came in all the while I was there.' He ran his hand over his face. 'Though a soul went out alright. Lieutenant Baxter's. Oh, this heat is too much, you know! I have to get something cool to drink.' He leaped up.

She half rose too. 'Wait! You didn't hear my second reason for wanting to see you. It was to return this.' She reached into her dress pocket. She placed the broken pen clip on the table in front of him.

'That?' he said dismissively, but his wide-eyed gaze didn't

leave it. 'Kind thought, Lady Swift. You've noticed I carry a few pens myself, then? But that isn't from any of mine.'

'Do you know, I'd swear it was,' she said casually.

'No. No.' He fumbled in his pocket for his pens and spread them in his hand, running his other fingers over them so they spun.

Her eagle-eyed butler pressed a fingertip to one, halting its revolution. 'This one is not the original clip, Mr Merrick. How difficult it must be to find a replacement in Egypt for a fountain pen of such long-standing British heritage as a Gillott's. Almost impossible, perhaps!'

'"Almost impossible, perhaps!"' Merrick said, imitating Clifford's voice perfectly. His face reddened. 'It's not, I tell you! A replacement, I mean. You're seeing things. Now, excuse me!'

His footsteps faded across the courtyard.

She tutted. 'Aren't we doing well at making new friends, Clifford? Almost as well as getting answers!' She shook her head. 'If Merrick really did arrive in the lounge fifteen minutes before the shot, he should have found Ludo already there, ten minutes ahead of him. Unless Merrick's lying, that is?'

'Or Mr de Groot?'

With Clifford's prompting, she quickly jotted down what they had been told:

Baxter's Murder – alibis and timings

11.40
Ludo de Groot – in lounge (according to Ludo and Frederika)
11.45.
Felix Trott – passed in corridor (according to Ludo)
11.50
Wesley Merrick – in cabin (according to Merrick BUT left his cabin and went to Baxter's according to Trott)

11.55.
Felix Trott – passed back towards cabins (according to Ludo)
12.00
Wesley Merrick – in lounge until gunshot (according to Merrick)
12.05.
Ludo de Groot – returned to cabin (according to Ludo and Frederika BUT not seen by Merrick in lounge)
12.10
–
12.15 (gunshot in Baxter's cabin)
First Mate Jabir – in wheelhouse (seen by me, Clifford and Sharaf)
Deckhand Ali – in wheelhouse (seen by me, Clifford and Sharaf)
Deckhand Farah – in wheelhouse (seen by me, Clifford and Sharaf)
Captain Anders – on rear deck (according to Anders)
Chief Sharaf – on front deck (seen by me and Clifford)
Frederika de Groot – in bed (according to Frederika and Ludo)
Ludo de Groot – in bed (according to Ludo and Frederika)
Ernst Piltz – in bed (according to Piltz)
Felix Trott – in bed (according to Trott)
Wesley Merrick – in lounge (seen by me, Clifford and Sharaf)

She sighed in frustration. 'Well, one of them is definitely lying. But which one? And why?'

18

'Stolen?'

'Regrettably, yes, my lady.'

Eleanor shook her head. They were standing outside her rented townhouse, the early evening sun beating down on her disbelieving features.

'Do you have any idea who'd do such a thing?'

'Indeed. A most unmannered reprobate who will doubtless never see the error of his ways now.'

She frowned. 'Why now? My hat is hardly much of a prize for a professional thief!'

'Because this thief has been shamelessly overindulged from the day he first arrived. Like his ginger menace of an accomplice.'

She gaped, then laughed. 'The terrible two?'

'None other. Apparently, Lizzie caught Master Gladstone dragging your regally posed tomcat through the herb border in your upturned silk sun hat.'

'Didn't she stop them?'

'She tried, but, regrettably, it was too late. The entire entourage ended up in the ornate lily pond.'

She burst into laughter at the image, which made Clifford lose his composure too.

'They're total monsters,' she chuckled, draping her scarf artfully over her head as a make-do hat.

'Most assuredly, my lady. Shall we continue?'

She nodded. They had spent a few pleasurable hours relaxing at the townhouse but wanted to interview Anders next, so were returning to the El Asafa where they hoped to find him. The fact that Sharaf was detaining the SS *Cleopatra* for his own, separate purposes made her suspicious. Was Baxter's murder on board that same boat just a coincidence? Or was it connected? And was Anders, as captain, somehow mixed up in it?

They walked on down the street past blacksmiths, woodturners, coppersmiths and weavers, all plying their trade outside despite the fierce sun. The cacophonous clanging, hissing of steam and rhythmic creak of manual looms and treadle boards accompanied them as they worked.

She steered Clifford right at the second corner, having spotted it led to a small square flanked on three sides by ancient domed buildings with porticoed entrances. What had also caught her eye was that it was home to an outdoor café.

She held up her hand as he opened his mouth. 'I know we are on a mission, but we can spare a minute or two. And I also know that tea and coffeehouses are firmly the province of men here. But I just want to enjoy the sight, and sound, of the hookah pipes being smoked at every tab—' She nudged his arm. 'Look! Those mahogany curls fluttering against that jaunty red neckerchief could only belong to one man!'

Clifford glanced over. 'You are correct, my lady. Captain Anders himself. A true pirate of the Nile.'

She imitated his disapproving sniff. 'Tsk, Clifford, that's hardly an objective start to sounding out our most suspicious of suspects.'

He eyed her sideways. 'You too, my lady?'

'Yes. But may I ask you first why Anders has achieved such an accolade as being a pirate in your estimation?'

'Because, my lady, Chief Sharaf obviously has information that the man is engaged in something illegal. Hence holding the SS *Cleopatra*. Which does not mean, of course, Captain Anders has anything to do with Lieutenant Baxter's death. But it does make me curious to know what exactly is the captain's game. And you?'

'That and because I'm still not sure he was even on the SS *Cleopatra* for the start of our journey from Cairo! And he took an awful long time to come from the rear deck after that shot rang out.' She groaned. 'It's no good, Clifford. You'll have to go and grill him intently while he puffs on his hookah pipe. Try and learn something more about the crew as well. I'll loiter in the shadows and listen.'

'Or perhaps a modicum of patience might be unearthed, my lady? Since it appears his coals are almost burnt to ash, given the paltry plumes of smoke he is exhaling.'

'So, he might leave soon, his pipe exhausted? Fair enough, I'll unearth what patience I can.'

Waiting for Anders, however, soon made her prickly. Or maybe she was finally feeling the effects of the fierce heat as she only had an improvised hat made from her scarf.

Finally, Anders rose, shook out his shoulders as if stiff, and threw some coins onto the table. But instead of turning towards them, he headed across the square.

They hurried around the opposite way, making sure not to be seen. Clifford's long stride allowed him to arrive at the other side of the square without losing his dignified comportment. Eleanor didn't fare quite so well, arriving red-faced and sweatier than a respectable lady should ever be.

'Another fine example of arcuate construction, my lady.'

Clifford pointed at the domed building in front of them. The one Anders was leaning on the porticoed entrance of as he took a surreptitious swig from a hip flask.

'Simply fascinating!' She feigned surprise as she stepped inside. 'Ah! Captain Anders. An architecture lover, too, are you?'

He ran the back of his hand over his mouth before offering a guarded smile. 'Only for the lines of a boat, Lady Swift.'

'Well, you must be fretting over having to leave your own boat, I'm sure?'

He nodded with a scowl. 'Ordered to leave, you mean! And given she's been my whole life for fifteen years, Sharaf might as well have cut my legs off. I'd feel just as stranded.'

'I can understand that,' she said genuinely. 'Having grown up on a sailboat.'

He looked bemused. 'Is there anything about you that fits the mould of a titled English lady?'

She laughed. 'Suffice to say Clifford here is working feverishly on that.' She pointed at him. 'That's why he looks so harried and haggard.'

Anders scowled. 'And why he's been so persistent in demanding my crew run my ship purely to your liking, Lady Swift!'

She shrugged. 'Well, Captain, someone had to in your absence at the beginning of the cruise.'

A look of surprise passed over his face, telling her she'd hit a bullseye. She hesitated.

Remember Piltz, Ellie. You can't push Anders too far. He'll get suspicious.

Clifford stepped in. 'Returning to your crew, Captain Anders. Have the three of them been with you long?'

Anders rubbed his chin. 'First Mate Jabir has been with me for seven years. And almost that for Deckhand Ali. Farah, I took him on about four months ago after my original deck-hand... changed his mind about wanting to follow orders.'

She mentally filed all that away. Especially Jabir's long service with Anders. Why, after all that time, would he kill one of the passengers?

'Well, all your crew have been wonderful. Especially given the unexpected events that have dogged the SS *Cleopatra* since leaving Cairo.'

Anders looked at her sharply. 'I know of only one. Lieutenant Baxter's suicide.'

'Oh, yes. Poor man. Had he been a passenger previously?'

He shook his head. 'I'd never clapped eyes on the fellow until he boarded at Cairo.'

'Goodness, though!' she said emphatically. 'It was such a shock when we heard that shot. I remember Clifford, Chief Sharaf, and I were on the front deck and reached the cabins just before you arrived from the rear deck.' She frowned.

He shrugged. 'So?'

'So, as you arrived in the cabin corridor after us, you must have been doing something frightfully important not to drop it immediately on hearing the shot?'

He opened his mouth, then snapped it shut. His eyes roved over her face, then turned to Clifford. 'I was making sure that everything was up to the exacting standards of some of my more demanding passengers!'

'Most dutiful, Captain Anders,' Clifford said smoothly. 'But how exactly did that delay you? Did you not fear a tragic incident may have occurred? One that necessitated your immediate attention?'

Anders leaned forward threateningly. 'I told you where I was when I heard that shot. What do you want? A signed testimonial to that effect!'

'Not at all, Captain Anders,' Clifford said smoothly. 'But I imagine Chief Sharaf might.'

Anders' face darkened. 'That over-righteous buffoon!'

Eleanor shrugged. 'Buffoon or not. I almost fell off my chair when he announced he was a policeman. But I realise now you must have known already?'

Anders looked away. 'No, as it happens. I didn't know a thing until a few minutes before he told everyone publicly!'

She kept her expression neutral, even though she no more believed him now than when he'd told them why he'd taken so long to come from the rear deck.

Before she could lead into another question, Anders spoke. 'You know, you didn't strike me as an architecture lover yourself, Lady Swift?'

She shrugged. 'I'm not. It always feels like a sack of mumbo-jumbo to me. A doodah arched this, and flange-fluted that. But it's Clifford's special thing. And, to be fair, I'll bore the starch out of his collar tomorrow with endless shopping. We're trying to keep each other sane during this incarceration of Chief Sharaf's, you see.'

Anders snorted. 'Messing about with a man's livelihood should be against the law! It's outrageous!'

She nodded sympathetically. 'I do understand why you're so upset about the SS *Cleopatra* being... oh what's the word, Clifford?'

'Impounded, my lady?'

Anders shrugged. 'Please excuse me, Lady Swift. I must be elsewhere.' Turning back to her butler, he smiled thinly. 'A word of advice, Mr Clifford. It is rather neglectful of a lady's aid to let her out in this heat without a hat, isn't it? She is likely to get burned. Badly. A fate you may well also suffer. Hat or no hat!' He bowed courteously to her and sauntered away.

She watched him go. 'Well, Clifford, our Captain Anders is definitely not telling the truth. Either about why he took so long to respond the night of the shot. Or about being on the rear deck at all! The question is, either way, was it related to Baxter's murder?' She shook her head. 'At the moment, the jury's out on that one.'

Clifford nodded. 'I agree, my lady. Perhaps, then, it would be more profitable to turn our attention to another equally pressing matter...'

19

Eleanor frowned. 'What matter? We've already spoken to all the suspects we've got at the moment. Who's left?'

'Not who, my lady, *what*. The matter of your mission from Lieutenant Baxter. If that is what the gentleman intended in his letter.'

Her eyes widened. 'Ah! And, yes, it is. I'm sure of it. Even if I'm not sure at all of what I'm supposed to do. Right. We need somewhere quiet. The El Asafa. Your room or mine?'

He paused outside a shop and looked at her questioningly. 'Bamboo or papyrus?'

Her brow furrowed in puzzlement. 'What am I choosing? Between the wallpaper in our rooms? Because, honestly, I haven't even registered what mine is like.'

He held up two rather attractive-looking hats. 'Bamboo or papyrus?'

In what seemed like a blink, she was sitting on a quiet, centuries-worn bench in a triangular patch of shade. The shade was created by a stone obelisk about eighteen feet high and carved with a formidable figure with a peculiar, long, downward-curving snout. Grateful her papyrus brim was keeping the sun's glare from her eyes, she looked up at Clifford, who had respectfully declined to sit.

'As you're always infuriatingly prepared and I'm not, have you...?'

His lips quirked at her teasing compliment as he slid two slim pads of paper from his inside pocket. 'I think you'll find this one suits your artistic style best, my lady. Being robust enough for even the over-exuberant strokes of an impatient hand.'

'What mischievous ruse is this, you terror? Papyrus paper? Oh, I see,' she ended in an appreciative whisper, having discovered the copy of Baxter's letter tucked under the first page. Her shoulders fell. 'If I'm honest, it feels a horribly daunting responsibility.'

Clifford paused in his sketching of the obelisk and scanned her face. 'Even together?'

She shook her head with a smile. 'Certainly, less of one. Thank you.'

For a moment, she wished her fiancé was there. But only for a moment. She'd involved him in enough matters like this already. And being a senior police detective, one thing he really didn't need was more murders to deal with! She sighed, wishing they could be together for just one day with nothing more to do than delight in each other's company.

Shaking herself, she read Baxter's letter twice, then accepted the pen Clifford passed her. 'Perfect, I'll underline the pertinent points. Here goes. Baxter stated if we are reading this, he is "dead by the hand of another". Killed before he could leave the SS *Cleopatra* early. His conscience had been troubling him since "that terrible day". A miracle loomed, but then never happened. His conscience was mortified. He knew he had to "put right this great injustice", which he felt partly responsible for. He begs me to finish what he started. And, as he is not able to attend himself, present an alternative "proof" by the sixteenth of this month.'

She let out a long breath. 'What injustice? What proof? Present it to who? Where? And more to the point, why, Clifford, isn't he asking that I bring his killer to justice?'

He held his hands out. 'One puzzle at a time, perhaps, my lady? Let us start with this puzzling "proof" the gentleman talks about. Without which, it seems, the mission is doomed.'

'But hang on,' she hissed. 'If Baxter was killed, then it was likely for this "proof". And if we find it...'

Clifford's tone turned grave. 'Disgracefully, yes. I will have let my mistress march into danger once again.'

'Only if we work out what and where this "proof" is.'

His expression told her that offered him little consolation.

She pushed on. *After all, Ellie, we've only got until Wednesday the sixteenth!*

'Please think, Clifford. What could possibly put right this "great injustice"?

He thought for a moment. 'Off the top of my head, a photograph? A personal item which proves the lieutenant's part in it and therefore... absolves someone else, perhaps?'

'Mmm.' She rubbed her face with her hands. 'You've made me think, though. You're right. It's most likely the "great injustice" is going to be inflicted on a third party. Otherwise, why would he be travelling on the SS *Cleopatra* to deliver his "proof?" Also, he refers twice to his conscience. Which makes me also think the wrong has been done to another person, or persons. At least to his mind.'

'I concur, my lady. And the killer seems to have shot Lieutenant Baxter to stop him reaching his destination. Where, one assumes, he was to present this "proof". Now, in the letter he stated he was the original proof.'

She grimaced. 'Gracious, it's too macabre to think we might need to drag his body along with us on the sixteenth! Especially in this heat!' She drummed her fingers on her forehead. 'Clifford! Captain Anders!'

He glanced around. 'Where, my lady?'

She shook her head. 'No! I mean his testy reply to you when you hinted that he was lying about being on the rear deck when we all heard that shot. He sarcastically offered you a *signed testimonial*.'

He thought for a moment. 'Of course! Lieutenant Baxter was very probably on his way to unburden his conscience by telling his, one assumes, eyewitness account, of what really happened. Otherwise, why the guilt?'

'Exactly! And having found his cabin ransacked, he realised he might not make it.'

'Which he did not, due to being murdered!'

'Tragically, yes. Then, in his place, a signed testimonial would be the next best thing.'

She nodded to herself. 'Let's assume for the moment then that's what he's talking about by "proof".' She sighed. 'Unfortunately, as he never got to finish the letter, we have no idea where this testimonial, if it is one, might be hidden.'

Clifford thought for a moment. 'Although, as his manner only changed when he was on board the SS *Cleopatra*, it would suggest he hid it somewhere on the boat itself.'

'He could have hidden it in the tomb we visited?'

'Possibly. But he was aware that there wasn't much time. Therefore, to expect you to return to the tomb, find it, and then arrive with it by the required date seems foolhardy.'

She nodded again. 'Agreed. We're definitely getting somewhere. So, let's recap. We're assuming this proof is some kind of signed testimonial and it is hidden on the SS *Cleopatra*. And it's obvious from the last sentence of the letter he was about to give me more information, including, I assume, where to go. So, are there any clues outside of the letter that might help?'

'Yes,' Clifford said slowly. 'Cryptic ones.'

'Go on!'

'Lieutenant Baxter's letter, my lady, is written in unequivocally plain language. And he spoke very plainly too.'

'Sometimes too plainly!'

'True. Yet he approached you with two very cryptic remarks. And he also inscribed a cryptic clue in his trunk. Could we obliquely glean more from those?'

He paused, pretending to be still sketching the obelisk as a couple passed.

She rocked her head. 'I suppose we might. But where to start? The two cryptic things he said to me – "To bury the secrets of the dead!" and "It is never too late to uncover the secrets of the dead" – don't seem to lead anywhere. Which only leaves the quote in his trunk?'

'"*We aren't no thin red 'eroes, nor we aren't no blackguards too, But single men in barricks, most remarkable like you,*"' Clifford intoned. '"*An' if sometimes our conduct isn't all your fancy paints, Why, single men in barricks don't grow into plaster saints.*"'

She jumped up. 'That's it! You said that was from Kipling's *Barrack Room Ballads*. And it mentions barracks in the lines he chose. So that's a double reference. It's a long shot, I know, but do you think this "great injustice" may have a military connection to do with Baxter's old barracks, wherever they were?'

'Indeed, my lady!' He tapped his forehead. 'Fool, man. How did you miss that?'

She laughed. 'You just needed to bow down to a more chaotic way of thinking.'

'Silly me,' he said with a wink, pointing at the carved figurine on the obelisk. 'Why did I think Seth, the Egyptian God of chaos, would be required when you are present, my lady? Now, at the pre-dinner drinks on the first night, the lieutenant said he had been protecting British interests abroad almost his entire career.'

She nodded eagerly. 'The Suez Canal was one. For about ten years, I think he said. And... and—'

'"Other strategic points in this wretched country."'

'Well remembered. So, my infallible boffin, what are some "other strategic points"?'

'Mmm. The Suez Canal was completed in 1869 and strongly guarded for decades by the British. Then there is the Aswan Dam completed in 1902. That remains fiercely defended to this day. Albeit contentiously given the current unfortunate relationship between Britain and Egypt.'

'So there would have been barracks at both locations?'

'Several, my lady. Certainly along the Suez Canal. But whether all of them are still active given Egypt has become independent, I don't know. Also, Lieutenant Baxter could be referring to any of them. Or, if we're wrong, none of them.' He frowned in thought. 'The SS *Cleopatra* stops at Aswan, but that could be coincidental as all the major towns in Egypt are situated on the Nile, so where else could it go?'

She grimaced. 'True. But Baxter did write that he only intended to leave the boat early, at Bawaaba I assume, to fool the murderer. So it's a possibility he originally intended to travel all the way to Aswan.' She rubbed her face with her hands. 'So, when did this "great injustice" happen, do we think?'

Clifford's brow furrowed. 'I really couldn't say. But, if I had to guess, the tone of the letter suggests it was in the recent past.'

She crossed both sets of fingers. 'Tenuous. But it's all we've got.' She groaned. 'We really need to find that wretched testimonial. Hopefully, it will answer more questions than it poses. The only question in my mind at the moment, however, is...' She stared at Clifford.

He nodded slowly. 'Is whether we are too late and the killer already has the testimonial!'

20

The only truly effective remedy for frustration or anxiety, Eleanor had learned, was spending time with her wonderful staff. And this morning, particularly, their familiar presence felt more soothing than ever. Still, she had taken some persuading from Clifford that an hour would not be time lost in finding Baxter's killer. Or his testimonial. Rather, it would reinvigorate her to come at the case anew.

As Clifford led her and her four ladies into the open-air market, her ears were assaulted by the animated calls of buyers and sellers alike. Her nose tingled with the exotic mix of fragrances, some so tantalising she felt she was tasting them. What struck her most, though, was the colours. And not only the myriad rainbow swathes of cloth stretched across the stalls and walkways above her head to keep out the already savage sun, but also a kaleidoscopic offering of vibrant-hued spices, fruits, vegetables, fabrics, pottery, leatherware and rugs. All displayed in drums, sacks, baskets, pails, and even colourful red and yellow painted wheeled barrows.

Mrs Trotman chuckled as Polly, open-mouthed, ran a tentative hand along the flank of a passing honey-cream camel. Eleanor beamed at her ladies' bright-eyed gazes, overjoyed they were part of such a memorable experience. They'd never looked more excited and filled with wonder as they wove in and out of the dense crowd which was surely made up of the entire population of Bawaaba.

Clifford tutted teasingly. 'Spoiling your staff again, my lady, tsk!'

She smiled as he produced four cloth bags from his jacket with a magician's flourish. With his usual seamless wizardry, he artfully distracted the ladies as they mingled among the captivating displays while she chose a few things for each of them unnoticed. In no time at all, the bags were hanging from his shoulders, filled with exquisite aromatic balms, beautiful glass beads, buttons, shimmering embroidery threads and ribbons. And a pair of traditional Ali Baba slippers and a set of brass finger cymbals each, to encourage their mischievous attempts at belly dancing.

In the centre of seven wicker stools arranged around a wooden barrel, a wrinkle-faced, black-haired woman with lively eyes waved at them to come over.

'No sense waiting until we're too parched!' Eleanor said.

Her staff waited for her to sit, which she did without ceremony, dropping onto the nearest stool. Clifford gave the barest of nods and her ladies flustered onto the others, whispering excitedly. In a blink, she was transported back to her favourite moments, enjoying time with her staff at home in Henley Hall's kitchen. The black-haired woman returned with fragrant tea topped with mint leaves on a brass tray, which she placed inside the barrel rim to form the table top.

''Tis too kind of you to spoil us like this, m'lady.' Mrs Butters ran an admiring finger over the filigree holder of their fluted glass cups.

'Butters is right, m'lady.' Mrs Trotman shared a cheeky

glance with the other women. 'There's nothin' so welcome as wettin' the whistle afore eyein' up more of what's on offer.'

'Ahem!' Clifford said with a chiding look.

Eleanor's cook pulled an unconvincing innocent face. 'I only meant gogglin' over all the exotic treats the likes of us have never rubbed up against afore, Mr Clifford.'

Eleanor tried to stifle her chuckle but lost the fight on catching her housekeeper's shoulders shaking.

'So did I, Mrs Trotman,' Clifford said, turning his head so the ladies couldn't see the twinkle in his eyes.

The six of them looked up as a short, middle-aged man in a dusty, worn buff-brown jacket plonked himself down on the last stool and rubbed his hands. His dark hair lay damply against his sun-weathered forehead, but his bright-blue eyes shone with life.

'Here we are! Sorry, I'm late, folks,' he said in a coarse London accent, tipping his battered straw hat to each of the women in turn.

Clifford's brow flinched. 'Actually, you are not, in fact, "late", sir. As one cannot be late to something one has not been invited to!'

Eleanor shook her head to herself.

I'm sure you could, Ellie!

The man seemed unfazed. 'That's just a rumour, squire. But nothing wrong with a bit of notoriety, they say.' He let out an infectious guffaw and wiggled his eyebrows. 'Am I right or what, ladies?'

Despite wanting to support Clifford in his chivalrous defence of her and her staff, Eleanor couldn't help finding something roguishly charismatic about the new arrival. She hid her amused smile though as her butler's already rigid posture stiffened even further. He eyed the man firmly.

'I meant, sir, it was an unseemly presumption to join our

group without awaiting an invitation. And most particularly without even introducing yourself!'

'Cor, swallowed the whole barrow of plums, didn't he?' the man whispered loudly to Eleanor. He turned back to Clifford. 'Only larkin', guv. Everyone in these parts knows me.' He spread his short arms. 'I'm Arthur. Arthur Barr!'

'Which means nothing to any of us,' Clifford said in a clipped tone.

Barr beckoned his audience nearer with a conspiratorial finger. Even Eleanor leaned forward. 'It's mighty lucky for you all I made it here, then. 'Cos whatever it is you need, I'm your man!'

Eleanor was intrigued. 'Are you offering some sort of service, Mr Barr?'

He held up his hand. 'Arthur, please, lady. No need for formalisin' with me.'

'"Lady" is correct,' Clifford said sternly. "Lady Swift" to you!' His lips pursed as the black-haired woman arrived with a cup of tea for their unexpected companion. Barr launched into what sounded to Eleanor more than passable Arabic. The clearly flattered waitress retired with the tray.

'Where was I?' Arthur said, glancing cockily at Clifford.

'Making a spectacle of yourself, I believe,' he said drily.

Arthur laughed again. 'I'm goin' to like this gig! Now, Lady Swift's question should a' been, what *can't* I do for you? I know this place better'n the back of my hands, eyeballs and bits I shan't mention. Been here donkey's years, I have. Speak the lingo. Got the grasp of how it all works. Know all the right people, see?'

'For any legitimate matter, I find that hard to believe,' Clifford replied with a sniff.

Arthur thrust his hand out with a wink. 'Takes one to know one, sir. I'm honoured to be in like company. Put it there!'

Eleanor stifled a gasp as, for the first time she could recall, someone seemed to have seen through her butler's strait-laced exterior into his rather dubious past.

To his credit, Clifford's impassive expression didn't flinch as he shook Arthur's hand wryly. 'Mr Clifford. Delighted to meet you, I'm sure. And rest assured, Mr Barr, among your no doubt sliding scale of charges, character assessment or assassination will not be required.'

Barr nodded vigorously. 'You got it, Mr Clifford. Price of each job's on application.'

Clifford leaned forward. 'Tell me, Mr Barr. How did a man like you end up in a place like this?'

Barr shrugged, his eyes sliding left as if looking for someone in the crowd. 'Oh, you know. I, ah, I'd got into a bit of a rut back in old Blighty and needed a break. So I left. And one thing led to another and...' He shrugged again. 'Here I am.'

Clifford nodded sagely. 'I see. And which of his Majesty's particular institutions did you take a permanent, if unofficial, "break" from?'

Barr chuckled as his eyes slid back. 'One all, I believe, Mr Clifford.' He cocked his chin cheekily at Mrs Butters. 'Now, missus, swap your dainty skirts for my charmin' trousers, would you?'

Eleanor's housekeeper doubled over giggling, which set all the others off.

Clifford rolled his eyes. 'As in "please change stools so Mr Barr might sit next to me",' he translated.

Once Barr had swapped stools, he and Clifford engaged in a murmured conversation. Eleanor was dying to know what was being said, but above the noise of the market, she couldn't quite catch the words. A minute later Barr stood up, slid a card into Clifford's hand, and doffed his hat to her.

'Good day, Lady Swift. We'll catch up later. And you, ladies,' he added with a cocky grin, causing Mrs Butters to blush again.

'Interesting man, Mr Clifford,' Mrs Trotman said, as Barr was swallowed up in the crowd.

Clifford finished paying for the teas, including Barr's. 'Mmm. He may come in useful for... certain matters. But he is currently less interesting than shopping, undoubtedly. Shall we once more to the fray, therefore, ladies?'

21

Eleanor shook her head. It was only now Arthur Barr had gone, she realised she couldn't sneakily buy her butler a heartfelt thank you gift as she had the ladies. He was too eagle-eyed for that. And, besides, she had forgotten to bring anything in which to hide her gift. The ladies, however, suddenly seemed a little shifty, too.

Clifford glanced between them with a raised brow. 'Do I detect a momentary reprieve in the offing?'

'How about twenty minutes?' Eleanor said. 'For each of us to explore the market alone. And then meet back here?'

Mrs Butters nodded. 'Us aprons will stick close together, Mr Clifford. Easier to watch our handbags, that way.'

'And we'll behave ourselves,' Mrs Trotman said, trying to hide a grin.

'And I'll be very careful not to commit any outrageously unladylike acts,' Eleanor said impishly.

Clifford raised another brow. 'Doubtful on all fronts, if I may say so. However.' He pulled out his pocket watch.

'Oh, be off with you!' Eleanor laughed. 'I know you're itching to buy something special to send to Kofi to let him know you're missing him being away at boarding school. You closet softie,' she added in a whisper.

Kofi was the West African boy from the Gold Coast Clifford had recently adopted after he had helped them solve a murder and rescue Eleanor's fiancé's career. A very independent-minded young gentleman, Kofi had made it clear he wanted to remain in Britain long enough to complete his education before returning home. As Clifford had sorely missed out on any formal education as a child, he'd been more than happy to vouch for the lad and become his guardian.

As the party split up, Eleanor wove her way to the edge of the market and began wondering what she could buy for her butler. Anything too ostentatious would embarrass him, she knew. And his passion for unfathomably complex science, engineering and high-brow Latin classics didn't help her either. Every book in the market was in Arabic, so she had no idea what they were about.

She was snapped out of her musings by the sight of someone she recognised. The solidly built Piltz was sauntering along the opposite side of the road. He had swapped his usual burgundy jacket for an inauspicious grey calico one. The legs of his matching trousers clung to him as if he was perspiring from more than just the intense heat. He kept peering over his shoulder from under the low brim of his fedora as he pretended to examine the goods displayed on the makeshift tables.

Whatever he's up to, Ellie, it looks like no good.

She went to follow, then spun around to scour the crowds. If she was more than twenty minutes, the others would worry if she didn't turn up at the arranged rendezvous. A raucous chorus of giggles reached her ears.

'Mrs Trotman!' She pounced on her startled cook with a whispered apology and hastily explained she'd meet them all at the townhouse later.

Darting back to the street where she'd first seen her quarry, she scoured the surroundings. Her fears that she might have lost him were relieved by his rear view sliding out from a doorway further along a run of shops. She carefully crossed the road and shadowed him.

For a man who apparently was only in Bawaaba under duress because of Chief Sharaf's orders, his knowledge of its backstreets seemed remarkable. After five minutes of her playing cat to his mouse, he casually walked around the side of a two-storeyed sandstone building. The windows were barred with thick metal grilles, the interior hidden by dark blinds pulled down low. A sign in gold and red Arabic lettering adorned the top floor. From the pulsating music and vigorous hand clapping she could hear coming from inside, she guessed it was a club of some sort.

She peered around the side of the building to see Piltz at the glassless metal door talking to someone in a low voice through a narrow sliding panel. A moment later, the panel slid closed, and the door opened. With a quick glance around, Piltz slipped inside, the door slamming behind him.

'Dash it!' she muttered.

Was he there just to indulge in a little saucy diversion? Her intuition told her otherwise. Clifford's repeated lament for prudence forced its way into her thoughts, but she needed to discover what Piltz was doing in there. Whatever it was, if it had something to do with Baxter's murder, she couldn't risk missing the chance to find out.

She ruled out trying to bluff her way in through the door. Too risky, especially here, as a woman. She hastened past the front of the building and down a side street. Around the back, the music seemed louder, the clapping more frenzied, but the coast thankfully clear. She peered up at the wooden latticework running from the street to the underside of the first-floor balcony.

There's your way in, Ellie.

Once she started climbing, however, she would be in full view of anyone coming around either corner. Unable to see an alternative, she scrambled up the latticework, hanging on as best she could as it had been treated with something traitorously slippery. Adrenalin won, and she was soon heaving herself over the balcony rail. Dropping the other side, she crouched as low as she could and shuffled quietly along to the first of the windows. As she reached it, she could see it was partially open, the blind raised slightly. Inside, the heat was probably stifling.

She risked a fleeting peek, immediately crouching down again to process what she'd seen. The second floor wasn't a series of rooms and corridors as she'd expected. Instead, it was a viewing gallery down to a colourfully tiled floor below. Groups of cheering men were watching veiled women in sparkling brassiere tops and low-waisted, almost sheer, skirts, swirling their hips and shaking their gold-chain clad ankles. The ornamental balustrade ringing the four sides of the upper landing was a honeycomb of octagonal stonework through which she could see Piltz emerging up a set of ornate stairs.

There were no other patrons or staff on the landing, only a series of pillars luckily offering somewhere to hide and watch. Thinking she'd never forgive herself for not doing everything she could to bring Baxter's killer to justice, she held her breath and slid over the windowsill. Flattening herself against the nearest pillar, she risked another quick peep. This time, through the honeycombed stone, she spotted Piltz standing in front of a large desk. Behind the desk sat the outline of a heavyset giant of a man, his features obscured by the shadows. He wore a pale suit, tasselled white silk scarf and oversized gold cufflinks which matched the patterned braid around the rim of his fez hat.

With the raucous music and clapping below, the two men's voices were too indistinct to hear. She held her breath and inched on her haunches to the next column.

'It is most displeasing,' she heard the giant say in a heavy

Arabic accent. 'As are you!' The man slammed his bear paw of a fist on the desk so hard Piltz recoiled. The giant rose and leaned closer, growling in Piltz's face. 'A small hold-up, I will tolerate this once. But only this once!'

Suddenly the music swelled, drowning out the rest of his words except one: "shipment".

Remember that, Ellie.

She was so engrossed she missed the arched door on her right opening. She was alerted to it by the sound of voices. Heart thumping she slid back to the window and through it to the balcony. Climbing over the rail, she clambered down the latticework, jumping off the last part to land heavily on the compacted dirt below. Regaining her balance, she shot down an alleyway. Only when she'd put some distance between herself and the club did she slow down.

Hailing a horse and trap as her breath was burning in her chest, she told the driver one of the few phrases she'd learned in Arabic and climbed on.

As they pulled up outside her townhouse, she waved at Clifford, who was striding through the gate.

'Just wait until you hear my news, Clifford!'

'I fear I will have to, my lady,' he said gravely, not offering her his elbow to alight as usual, but stepping up into the carriage himself. He pointed urgently forward to the driver and as they pulled away, passed her a note.

She opened it and gasped. 'It is from Sharaf. Gracious! There's been another murder!'

22

Outside the austere prison-like front of Bawaaba's police station, Eleanor took a deep breath and slid Sharaf's note into her handbag.

Clifford cleared his throat. 'If you're searching for a positive, my lady, at least it seems that Chief Sharaf now considers Lieutenant Baxter's death was *not* suicide.'

She nodded glumly. 'Because he's written "another murder", I know. Which is a step forward. But a second person killed! It's simply too awful to think of.'

As they reached the metal-barred entrance, Sharaf stepped out, his thick moustache mirroring the firm set of his mouth.

'We will go straight to the crime scene,' he commanded without any opening pleasantries.

Eleanor turned towards the hotel in unison with Clifford, then shared a confused glance at Sharaf's headshake.

'We are going to the SS *Cleopatra*, Lady Swift.'

'What? But everyone was taken off...' She bit her tongue at his firm look.

'Questions when we arrive, please.'

As they approached the jetty, the quirky charm Eleanor had

found in their cruise boat before had now vanished. The black painted panelling of the forward section shrouded it in the sobering cloak of a funeral carriage.

The armed guard standing at the top of the gangplank saluted with an apprehensive look as the three of them boarded. His hesitant speech was cut off by a rapid fire of Arabic from Sharaf, which left Eleanor in no doubt that whatever the guard had said hadn't gone down well with his new boss. Sharaf beckoned for him to follow, then gestured for her and Clifford to accompany them.

'This murder should not have happened,' he muttered with a grim expression as they entered the interior of the boat.

'To my mind, that is unquestionably true of all murders,' she said emphatically. 'But I thought only deckhands Ali and Farah had been left on board with the guard?'

'You are correct. And too late, yes, but I now have added another of my few available men.'

'To guard a corpse?' she murmured to herself.

In the corridor, another armed policeman stood smartly to attention.

Sharaf nodded at her questioning look. 'It is to number five we go.'

'The only unoccupied cabin?'

'Unfortunately, that is not the case now.' Sharaf blocked her view as they reached the door.

There was no mistaking that the door had been forced open. The left side of the frame was splintered around the hole where the brass plate had been attached. It was lying on the floor, along with its two bent screws.

She frowned. *Wasn't this unlocked the night of Lieutenant Baxter's murder, Ellie?*

Sharaf interrupted her thoughts. 'Lady Swift, normally I would not agree to you coming here. Or seeing what is in this cabin.'

'Yet her ladyship is only here by your summons,' Clifford said pointedly.

'Not summons, Mr Clifford. Suggestion, perhaps. I sent only word that a second murder had happened.' He held Eleanor's gaze. 'But I hoped you would come.'

Not wanting to give him the chance to change his mind, she pointed over his shoulder. 'Whatever I'm about to see can't be any worse than I've seen before.'

'Regrettably,' Clifford muttered as Sharaf stepped aside.

The sight of the lifeless figure sprawled face up on the bed still made her heart falter at the tragedy of a life taken in a blink. For that was all the time a well-aimed bullet to the chest would have needed to do its deadly work. The vibrant crimson bloodstain seemed all the more brutally stark against the white robe the dead man was dressed in.

'Poor Farah.'

She stepped further in, scanning the room. There was no sign of a struggle. The small wooden writing desk stood against the wall, while the glass lamp sat undisturbed in the centre of the bedside table. Likewise, the blue washbowl remained on its tripod stand and the one cushion on the diminutive bench-style settee. Granted, there were no personal effects to have been hurled about in a fight as this cabin hadn't been booked, but even the bed cover hung neatly down the sides. The only item out of place was the other settee's cushion, which lay on the floor near the body with a circular burn mark. Obviously the killer had used it to try and muffle the sound of the shot.

'It's like the poor fellow was caught entirely unawares,' she said thoughtfully.

Clifford nodded. 'I concur, my lady.'

Realising Sharaf was not only waiting patiently for her thoughts, he was also doing so in front of the confused-looking guard, she turned to him. 'For some reason, I'd imagined it was one of the other passengers who'd been murdered. One who'd snuck back aboard somehow.'

'Which nobody should have been able to do,' Sharaf said sharply to the guard. 'Explain yourself. And in the best English you can for this lady.'

'Yes, Chief.' The guard swallowed hard. 'I run when I hear a muffled sound. Like gunshot. Deckhand Ali also. Together we begin the search in this part of the boat.'

'While the murderer escaped along the opposite side deck and down the gangplank with no one seeing him!' Sharaf gruffed.

Eleanor held up a halting hand. 'Wait a minute. How did the murderer get on the boat unseen in the first place?'

Sharaf turned to the guard. 'Your answer?'

He grimaced. 'It was just a small minute I was away, Chief. To this I swear. But there was the sound of much trouble along the riverside.' His shoulders slumped. 'But it was only some boys making a lot of noise.'

Sharaf's black eyes narrowed. 'Which they were paid to do, no doubt, so you would leave your post!'

'This I think now also,' the guard said sheepishly. At Sharaf's finger snap, he rallied himself. 'As I say, after I hear what sound like a gunshot, I make the search of the cabins with Deckhand Ali. We come to this one last. Number five. But I find I have no key. I ask Ali for the key. He tell me it is lost.'

Sharaf pressed his hands over his nose as he let out a very long breath. 'I ordered you to make certain all these doors were locked before anyone left the boat. And to take the keys from every passenger. And also the ring with the spares from Farah!'

'All this is I do, Chief! I take special care of your orders. But no passenger was staying in this number five cabin. And how can I know the keys are not on the ring? I am told to collect and keep safe. Not to count.'

'So you broke this door down, Sergeant?' Eleanor said, deciding Sharaf could finish berating his man on his own time.

'Yes, madam. With Ali. And inside, we find Farah like this.' He pointed at the bed. 'Dead.'

'Back to your post and send Ali to me,' Sharaf commanded.

'Yes, Chief.'

In a hurry of sandalled footsteps, Ali appeared. He hovered in the doorway, head bowed respectfully. Sharaf clasped his hands behind his back.

'Only three of you were on this boat. One is dead. Tell us what you know.'

Ali looked back blankly. Sharaf stared at him for a moment and then spoke in Arabic. After a frustrating exchange Eleanor couldn't understand, Sharaf gestured for Ali to leave them.

'Anything useful?' she asked hopefully.

'Not a thing. He says he has no idea who might have killed Farah. And he saw nobody. He was on the lower deck, trying to keep the pumps working, but they stopped. Apparently, they are very old pumps.'

Ah, Ellie! That's why the guard heard the shot so easily, even with the cushion.

'I will ask more questions of him later,' Sharaf continued. 'But I do not think he has anything of help to—' He broke off at an angry bellow.

'Where is that idiot?'

'It's Captain Anders,' Clifford whispered.

'He can't know we're here with you,' Eleanor hissed to Sharaf as she ducked behind the door with Clifford. 'Head him off in the corridor. Quick!'

Without protest, Sharaf marched out and stood blocking Anders' way. But not Eleanor's view of him, as she squinted through the hairline gap between the door and the frame.

Anders glared at Sharaf. 'What in blazes have you and your men been doing? I went to your police station for an update on when my boat would be released, only to be told my deckhand is dead!' He squared up to Sharaf. 'I hold you personally responsible.'

'I did not kill Farah,' Sharaf said coolly.

'You as good as did when you ordered me and my first mate off the *Cleopatra*!'

Eleanor had to credit Sharaf for appearing unmoved by the tirade. 'Captain Anders, do you have any idea who might have killed your deckhand?'

'No, I do not. As it is obvious, neither do you!' Anders shouted as he stomped off.

'My orders still stand, Captain!' Sharaf called after him. 'Do not board the *Cleopatra* again without my permission.'

He stepped back into the cabin and shrugged. 'Please proceed.'

She nodded and walked to the furthest corner to see if the different perspective of being the unsuspecting victim, rather than the murderer, suggested something. It didn't, other than to increase her sorrow for Farah as she was now level with his lifeless eyes, and the splutter of blood that covered his lips and chin.

Think, Ellie, think.

Clifford rose from his haunches. 'Not so much as a speck of anything anywhere on the floor.'

Catching her glance, he stepped to the doorway, his head almost imperceptibly nodding with each step as if he was counting. He paused before turning to face her, then raised his hand as if aiming a gun. Her gaze ran from him to Farah's body, envisioning the path of the bullet.

'Killed in cold blood. Literally. He had no way, and no time to defend himself,' she murmured, her eyes following the trace of the bloodstain across his chest. Having offered silent words heavenwards for his peaceful eternity, she stared blankly at him as her butler stepped closer. 'I was just thinking, Clifford, of the moment we first met him. I wondered how he could complete any boat duties and keep his white robe so spotless.'

'Indeed. Although, on observing Mr Farah now, he does actually have a small streak of oil on his robe. As well as, ahem...'

She winced. 'Rather academic, I know, given the... hideous mess across his chest, poor fellow.'

Sharaf looked up from his notebook. 'Lady Swift, do you have any thoughts to share?'

She shook her head but caught Clifford's brow twitch. 'I wish I could say yes, but I haven't at the moment. However, judging by my butler's expression, I'd wager he certainly has.'

Sharaf's eyes roved over Clifford's face. 'That is something I wish you to teach me, Mr Clifford. Sixteen years as a policeman and I can tell nothing that you are thinking. Unlike with Lady Swift.'

Clifford's ever impassive features didn't flinch. 'Precisely, Chief Sharaf. It is only her ladyship's unspoken thoughts which have led to my conjecture.'

'Ever the mind reader,' she said, still mystified.

Sharaf waved them both towards the door. 'Whatever it is, we need to hear it somewhere private. If you will both come with me, please?'

With a final sad glance at Farah's body, she followed him out of the cabin.

At a nondescript arched wooden door in a quiet side street, Sharaf slid off his shoes. Eleanor and Clifford were only half a beat behind in doing the same. Thinking they must be entering a mosque or other religious building, she covered her head with her scarf.

Sharaf nodded appreciatively. 'It is good that we can each

respect the others' beliefs and customs. If only our governments might do the same.'

Her assumption of where he had brought them faltered as she accepted the green slippers the smiling elderly lady inside held out. Beyond the simply tiled entrance hall lay a larger room, its two scrollwork-covered windows letting in light, while the partially lowered, woven grass shades cut out the oppressive afternoon heat. Dominating the right side of the room was a large heavy wood table with one high-backed chair at the far end. Behind it, what looked like a tall slatted birdcage was filled with a great number of books. Two low tables were set on intricately patterned rugs, scattered with cushions, while dotted between them were two round padded ottomans. Four unframed paintings of the desert and a detailed map of Egypt adorned the ochre walls.

Sharaf gestured at the cushioned area. 'Please sit. The hand-washing facility is behind the screen there.' He indicated she had no need of her headscarf now they were inside.

As she emerged, smelling of the spicy scent of clove in the soft soap, a quiet tap sounded at the door. Sharaf opened it, and returned with a large tray filled with a pot of rich-smelling coffee, layered pastry triangles, a basket of flattened round breads and a dish of honeyed nut cakes. Alongside it was a tall carafe of chilled water topped with mint.

With them all seated on floor cushions, Sharaf served while talking.

'As the new chief of police, this is my temporary place of residence. Although' – he shrugged – 'I usually find no reason to choose another for myself.' He set down the coffee pot. 'So, Lady Swift, to business, as I believe you say in English?' His steely gaze met hers. 'And this time, the business is definitely murder.'

23

Relieved that Sharaf still seemed eager for their input, Eleanor accepted her investigations notebook from Clifford. 'Absolutely. But I think we need to start by making sure we are on the same page, don't you?'

Sharaf's brow furrowed in puzzlement. Clifford cleared his throat.

'Her ladyship is speaking figuratively. She is actually asking if you also believe the person who murdered Lieutenant Baxter is the one responsible for the death of Mr Farah?'

Sharaf's gaze shot back to Eleanor. 'I have not said that I now believe Lieutenant Baxter did not commit suicide.'

She pulled his note from her handbag and slid it across the rug to him. 'I think you did. Because experience tells me you're not the kind of policeman who would pull a sly trick of writing "another murder" just to bait me into rushing to meet you?'

His moustache twitched along with his lips. 'Your experience, which I have seen evidence of myself twice already, is greater even than perhaps I have imagined?'

She thumbed the multitude of scrawled pages in her notebook in silent reply.

Sharaf smiled thinly. 'We are on enough of the same page then to help each other. Deal, Lady Swift?'

'Deal,' she said without hesitation.

Rather than him now taking charge as she expected, he shuffled back on his cushion and took a long sip of his mint water. She opted to interpret that as a silent vote of confidence.

'Well, first of all, we need to speak to our existing suspects and find out if any of them have an alibi for the time of Farah's death.'

Sharaf nodded. 'I have already sent a message to my men to start asking each of them while we are busy here. The death of Farah is one my police station can investigate without problem as it is clearly murder.'

She hesitated. 'And... while your men are checking alibis, could they check everyone's passport, and record who has been in Egypt for the last few years, and who hasn't? I don't know yet if it's relevant, but I'd like to know.'

Sharaf made a note. 'It will be done. So, now, I will watch the mastermind of the lady and her butler at work. Which I will admit, I am curious to see.'

Eleanor nodded to Clifford that he had the floor, which was a moot gesture, his discreetly arched brow replied, given he was sitting cross-legged on it.

'What struck me in cabin number five is the contradiction of the door. Something I had forgotten until I noted her ladyship's expression before we stepped inside. Firstly, on the night of Lieutenant Baxter's murder it was unlocked.'

She nodded. 'That's right. I remember clearly now. Captain Anders and First Mate Jabir glanced at each other in surprise when it swung open.'

'Exactly.' He turned to Sharaf. 'And yet, Chief Sharaf, your own sergeant checked the following morning before we all left the SS *Cleopatra* and found it locked.'

Sharaf shrugged. 'Which it still was when he and Ali broke it open. What of this?'

'The keys were never lost at all!' Eleanor murmured.

'Quite so. The killer had the keys all along,' Clifford said.

'Ah! Which he picked from Farah's pocket,' Sharaf said with a hint of jubilation.

Clifford cleared his throat quietly.

Eleanor leaned towards Sharaf. 'That's his respectful way of saying he doesn't agree, by the way.'

The policeman tapped the low table. 'Why do you not agree, Mr Clifford?'

'Because, Chief Sharaf, to lift a set of keys from a large keyring is difficult. To do it when they are in the pocket of the slim-fitting *sirwal*, or under trouser, from beneath Mr Farah's all-encompassing, ankle-length robe would take infinite skills. Of both distraction and sleight of hand. Very few, even veteran pickpockets, possess such.'

'Which you seem very certain of?' Sharaf said suspiciously.

'Suffice to say, we're all on the same side here.' Eleanor gulped down a piece of the onion and beef pastry triangle. This was no time for her butler's dubious skills to be questioned.

Clifford gave her a coded look of gratitude. 'At the risk of shamefully slandering a man who cannot defend himself, I suggest Mr Farah accepted a bribe to hand over both keys to cabin five to the killer. Likely not realising for what they were wanted.'

Eleanor nodded. 'Brilliant! And then Farah went to Captain Anders and "confessed" to losing them to cover himself.' At Sharaf's questioning look, she explained, 'On our first evening aboard, I caught Anders berating Farah for his carelessness.'

Sharaf looked perplexed. 'But why would the killer want the keys to the empty cabin five? Why not the one to Lieutenant Baxter's cabin if he had planned to kill him?'

The three of them lapsed into thoughtful silence.

Eleanor paused in breaking off a piece of clay oven baked bread. 'I think I have it. The killer paid Farah to give him both keys as a precaution. In case the suicide aroused suspicion. You see, the killer unlocked the door of the empty cabin just before he shot Lieutenant Baxter, so there was no chance of it being forced open if the boat was searched.'

Sharaf looked unconvinced. 'This person is now sounding more like a madman than the ruthless killer Mr Clifford had me picture?'

Clifford shook his head soberly. 'On the contrary, if you will forgive the correction. I believe her ladyship has worked out what I did not.'

She nodded. 'The killer needed to made sure the door to cabin five would remain intact because they'd planned from the outset on needing that cabin later. To kill their blithely unaware accomplice… Farah,' she ended sombrely.

Sharaf's furrowed brow told her even he was moved by the cruel duplicity of such a plan. 'But why did the killer not murder Farah the same night as Lieutenant Baxter?'

'Largely because of you,' Eleanor said slowly, the tragic irony of both deaths coming into sharper focus. 'And your unexpected revelation that you are—'

'The new chief of police here?' he finished for her.

'Yes. I believe the killer must have been unnerved, at least.'

'In all my years as a policeman, Lady Swift, no one has ever shown delight on learning what I do. Not even perfectly innocent people. Which is why I keep it under my hat,' Sharaf said without humour.

Her thoughts flew to her fiancé, who had ruefully uttered the same sentiment many times. 'That sounds very familiar.'

At Sharaf's puzzled look, she saw no reason to hide that side of her life from him and tapped her engagement ring. 'Hugh, my betrothed, is also a policeman.'

Her host's eyes widened. 'Forgive me to say, but a titled English lady and a policeman! That you should meet is unusual enough, I think? But to be married, very much so.'

'Getting back to poor Farah,' she said, blushing. 'There's another obvious reason the killer might have had for waiting to kill him.'

Clifford bowed his head appreciatively. 'Bravo, my lady.'

Sharaf was staring between them like the only player left on the bench unpicked for the team.

She pointed at the neatly folded sheet of paper Clifford produced from his inside pocket. 'The copy of Lieutenant Baxter's letter you gave me. It says I need to find "the proof" to put right this "great injustice". So obviously, the killer needed to get hold of this "proof" to stop this "great injustice" being rectified.'

Sharaf chewed meditatively. 'You are thinking that the killer paid Farah to find this proof as well as hand over the keys to cabin five?'

'Yes. It would have been too risky to search Lieutenant Baxter's cabin himself the night he killed him.'

Sharaf sighed. 'And in the morning, I ordered everyone to leave the boat. But left Farah on board.' He shook his head bitterly. 'This was a terrible mistake.'

'You couldn't possibly have known,' Eleanor said sympathetically. 'I would have done the same. Especially as, like you, I saw Farah in the wheelhouse just before Baxter was shot, so never suspected him of anything. And you did also leave an armed officer with the SS *Cleopatra*.'

Clifford turned his coffee glass on the table.

'I believe Mr Farah's fate was set the moment he agreed to become an accomplice. Had you sent him to the El Asafa with the others, Chief Sharaf, he would merely have been found dead on a hotel bed, rather than a cabin one. His usefulness finished, the poor fellow needed to be eliminated.'

Eleanor pointed at her butler. 'Clifford's right. The last link back to the killer thus dissolved, as it were.' She shuddered. Another thought struck her. 'And the killer may have waited until this morning as it was market day and there would have been far less chance of him being spotted sneaking through the town down to the boat as most of the population were around the market area.'

'Good point, but' – Sharaf refilled their coffees – 'to return to the matter of Lieutenant Baxter.' Over his glass, he held Eleanor's gaze. 'Lady Swift, I may have had a change of heart, but there is still no proper evidence that his death was not suicide. Please,' he said as she went to protest. 'I have sent the gun, the letter and the suicide note together with his passport for fingerprint and handwriting checks as I agreed to. But I have to warn you my superior in Cairo will not be persuaded that it proves the same man killed Farah, whatever the results. It is more likely he will insist I arrest Deckhand Ali for Farah's death because he is the more likely culprit.' He shrugged. 'And easier to put the blame on.'

Eleanor looked pleadingly at Clifford.

'Actually, Chief Sharaf, Mr Ali *could* have killed Mr Farah. But for one element, which regrettably I cannot prove at this juncture. That being my conviction that whoever murdered Lieutenant Baxter, also killed Mr Farah. And Mr Ali cannot have committed the first, because he was in the wheelhouse at the time, as you are aware.'

Sharaf put his hands together. 'I agree to that point. Also, I will say, the murder of Farah is not in the nature of a simple man like Ali. It was too planned. Too clever. A man of no education like Ali would have stabbed Farah and thrown him over the side of the boat for the crocodiles to hide the evidence for him.'

Eleanor groped for some light in the dark. 'I suppose the one positive in all of this is that there's a chance Farah didn't find the proof. Your armed officer would have hampered his efforts at scouring the boat, after all.'

Sharaf clapped his hands together. 'So, what is next for us to do?'

'I've got a different question first,' Eleanor said. 'Which you might not be able to answer, being new to Bawaaba. Who is the uncommonly large Egyptian man who seems to have his office on the second floor of the slightly risqué club at the other end of town, out beyond the market?'

Sharaf frowned deeply. 'A man I cannot begin to think how you even know of him?'

'Ahem! Best not to ask in my experience, Chief Sharaf.' Clifford glanced chidingly at Eleanor. 'The second floor you saw him on? Of an establishment of questionable repute, my lady? Really?' he added in a murmur.

'Chief Sharaf?' she said, studiously ignoring her butler.

He held his hands out. 'This person you ask of is Mahmoud Zaki, an important businessman in Bawaaba. But on the public stage only. Behind the curtains, he is a very dangerous one. A leader of the bandits who smuggle everything and anything across the desert from Cairo to Aswan and back! Including guns. I was warned of him when I accepted my role as the new chief of police here.'

Eleanor considered this information. 'Nevertheless, I think this bandit leader is connected with these murders somehow. And I want to meet him,' she said emphatically.

Sharaf shook his head vehemently. 'That is a terrible idea! He is extremely dangerous. And an introduction from me would not sit well with him at all. It is not that I will not help,' he said firmly. 'I am willing in other ways. But you must understand, I am the chief of police here. Some things I cannot do. But there is one I can.'

'Go on?'

'I can hold the SS *Cleopatra* from leaving until Monday

morning. Because of the murder of Farah, this extension I can order. But no longer.'

She rose as elegantly as she could from the cushion.

'Thank you, Chief Sharaf. For your kind hospitality and for your continued help. But please excuse me. I do not wish to waste one hour of the time now available to catch whoever is responsible for these terrible crimes. Clifford and I will go to the El Asafa Hotel straight from here and find out what we can from Anders and our fellow passengers.'

Sharaf rose too. 'Together, Lady Swift, I hope we can show that cooperation between your country and mine is not only possible, but once set in motion, can be a mighty force for justice!'

24

As Eleanor stepped into the hotel lobby, she hurled her running order for the afternoon's interviews at her butler, who was holding the door open for her. Frederika was striding furiously towards the exit and Eleanor had learned there was no better moment to question a suspect than when they were off balance. She was definitely lying about something. But was it murder?

'He must have done something fearfully wrong this time?' she called, stepping in the woman's way.

Frederika came to a stop with a thin smile. 'I've no idea who you mean.'

Eleanor shrugged. 'It's perfectly natural for a married couple to have a tiff once in a while.'

'And you'd know that how, Lady Swift?' Frederika said coolly. 'Not being married yourself.'

Eleanor tutted. She had no wish to explain that she had been married previously, the marriage ending speedily, and tragically in her husband's death. 'That is a fair point. After all, you know so much about me, don't you?'

She turned to leave, but Frederika tugged her to a stop.

'What... what did you mean by that?'

'Come and have a drink in a quiet corner and I'll tell you.' Eleanor hardened her tone. 'But only if you answer a few things for me.'

Frederika tossed her head like a petulant mare but her eyes darting over Eleanor's face betrayed she was curious.

Or worried, Ellie?

'I suppose a drink won't poison me, so, why not?' Frederika said with unconvincing nonchalance.

In the furthest corner of the empty hotel lounge, she dropped into the nearest cane chair behind one of the lattice screens. 'Isn't it too hot for riddles and games, Lady Swift?'

'So glad you think so too.' Eleanor pushed the bowl of nuts Clifford had placed on the table closer to her companion. 'We're all in a situation we don't want to be in. And, frankly, I'm finding being lied to is too much sour sauce to stomach on top of everything else.'

Frederika looked down at the nut she'd taken. 'I haven't lied to you. Why would I?'

Eleanor sat back in her chair. 'You tell me. And while you're at it, perhaps you'll be good enough to explain why, when you met me, you acted as if you knew nothing about me? Or my past?'

Frederika shook her head emphatically. 'Now I am at a loss. I don't understand how you know that I was familiar with you?'

'Because Ludo told me.'

Frederica's expression blackened. 'Wonderful! Well, he doesn't tell me lots of things,' she added bitterly.

Eleanor tutted. 'It seems both of you omit to tell the other one important details. Like where and when you actually got engaged? And exactly how long you have been married?'

Frederika's face had been growing increasingly tense, but after a moment's silence, she smiled wanly. 'You know, Lady

Swift, I told Ludo you were too sharp not to work it out sooner or later.'

Eleanor leaned forward and patted the other woman's hand. 'I won't breathe a word.'

Frederika sighed. 'The truth is, Ludo and I... well, we're not actually married, as I think you've already guessed.'

Eleanor nodded as Clifford placed two long glasses on the table. 'Then why are you pretending to be husband and wife? Captain Anders doesn't strike me as the type to care one hoot whether you are married or just engaged. All he cares about is filling his cabins. Single, or double.'

Frederika shook her head. 'We aren't even that. Engaged. Or... or friends.' She bit her lip.

'Go on,' Eleanor coaxed.

Frederika sighed deeply. 'It's all the archaeological funding institution's stupid fault. Being married is just a pretence, so we could get a grant to go on a prestigious dig outside Aswan. Without that, neither of us could dream of affording the cost. But because the accommodation at the site is so restricted, the institution would only award the grant to two people of the same sex or a married couple. They're so antiquated in how they view the world. It's ridiculous!'

Eleanor raised her eyebrows. 'From a layman's viewpoint, it strikes me that kind of mentality probably comes with the territory. Given that archaeology is all about the ancient past, that is?'

Frederika shrugged. 'I suppose so. But it left us no choice but to be dishonest because the dig is exactly what we both need at this point.'

'For your careers?'

Frederika nodded again. 'Yes. Although, really Ludo doesn't need the credibility quite so much as I do. He's more experienced, you see. He's taken part in more digs in more countries than I have, including here.'

Eleanor kept her expression neutral.

Didn't Frederika say previously that Ludo had never been to Egypt before, Ellie?

'I appreciate you confessing about your actual relationship, but I'm still confused as to why you both pretended you'd never heard of me?'

'Well, Ludo hadn't. Not before I told him. I hadn't even met him when you cycled near the dig I was on in Turkey. I read about you in the local newspaper.'

'I did wonder,' Eleanor said. 'Because my trip was some years ago, which would mean yours would have been one of the longest courtships in history.'

Clifford discreetly caught her eye with a teasing look. She bit back a smile.

'Followed by mine, I confess.'

'What's he like? Your fiancé?' Frederika said unexpectedly.

Eleanor's shoulders rose as an image swam into her mind. 'The ultimate gentleman. Totally delicious. Divinely built. So opposite to me in lots of ways, it's amazing we fell in love. And he's as brilliant as he is dedicated to his work. For which I admire him more than I think I can ever tell him. But don't ask me what he does.'

'I shan't.' Frederika fiddled with her glass. 'When I noticed your engagement ring, I told Ludo your beau would be that sort of a catch. But he just dismissed the idea. We had yet another row about it, actually.'

Eleanor laughed. 'Probably couldn't imagine anyone respectable proposing to me after the picture you must have painted of my straggling inelegantly across the world on my bicycle.'

Frederika frowned. 'It wasn't that. He seemed... over-interested in your exploits.'

Eleanor looked around. 'Where is Ludo, by the way?'

Frederika shrugged. 'He stomped off this morning after a

disagreement between us. It was lucky, I suppose, he'd finally returned when that policeman came to ask where we had all been.'

Eleanor kept her features neutral but filed that away to check when Sharaf reported on the alibis his men had taken.

Grateful Frederika had steered the conversation in the direction she needed, Eleanor nodded. 'Poor Farah. It's too awful for words.'

'Shot through the chest, apparently. Ludo said he'd managed to get it out of the policeman who questioned him,' she added quickly.

Clifford interrupted them. 'Ahem! Speaking of the gentleman, perhaps it might be more seemly, Mr de Groot, if you were to join the ladies? Any more hovering behind that screen might lead to the erroneous idea you were eavesdropping.'

'Ludo, how long have you been there?' Frederika hissed as his bush of straw-blond hair and unruly beard appeared around the screen.

'Oh, not long, Mrs de Groot,' Clifford said in his ever-measured tone before Ludo could answer. 'Only three minutes by my watch.'

Ludo rubbed his forehead, which had furrowed like a ploughed field at Clifford's words. 'I was not listening. Really.'

As the women shared a disbelieving look, he held his hands up. 'It's not easy for a man to... you know...'

'Be honest?' Eleanor said pointedly. 'Well, Frederika finally has been about the two of you. You should probably know that before you stick your boot any further down your throat.'

He threw Frederika a horrified glance and gruffed something in Dutch as he sat down.

'Ludo!' Eleanor said sharply. 'There's no need to be so cutting to Frederika. Nor to assume I do not have at least a rusty grasp of Afrikaans. It's close enough to your native language to get the gist of what you said.'

Ludo let out a long breath. 'I know that. I simply wasn't aware you spoke it.'

She nodded. 'I worked in South Africa for several years. Mostly in the bush, scouting out safari routes, so I learned more than a reasonable smattering. Now, enough lies. Like you alibiing each other for the time Lieutenant Baxter was found shot,' she bluffed.

The two archaeologists glanced at each other, then quickly back at Eleanor. Ludo leaned forward angrily, then retreated at Clifford's warning growl.

'I tell you. Do not point any fingers at Frederika, Lady Swift!'

Frederika stared at her supposed husband. 'Or at you, Ludo! We had no reason to lie about anything that evening. That I know of?' she ended accusingly.

'I told you the truth,' Ludo said with feeling.

Eleanor leaned forward. 'Then refresh all our memories, please.'

Ludo ran a hand through his nest of hair. 'Alright. I went to the lounge at twenty minutes to midnight to have a cigarette. You asked me before if I saw anyone and I did, as I told you. That man Trott went past in the corridor at a quarter to. Then he came back again ten minutes after that. But on the outside deck. I finished my cigarette at five past midnight and went straight back to our cabin.'

Eleanor see-sawed her head. 'See, that is what you told me before. But why deliberately miss out that you saw someone else?'

He threw up his hands. 'I did not see anyone except Trott, I'm telling you!'

'Well, someone swears otherwise,' she said calmly.

Clifford cleared his throat. 'Mr de Groot. You seem peculiarly precise about the timing of events for a gentleman relaxing over his last cigarette of the evening?'

Ludo sighed. 'I felt bad for something I had said to Frederika, so I could not sleep. And I thought to keep her awake for too long was the opposite of an apology. So, I was looking at my watch all the time.' He tapped the one on his wrist as he spoke. 'Still, I smoked several cigarettes before I had the courage to come back. I'm sorry,' he said to Frederika.

She smiled weakly. 'It doesn't matter now. But thank you.'

'We'd better go.' He stood up. 'Hopefully our next conversation will be easier, Lady Swift.'

'I hope so, too.'

As they passed, Clifford held up a finger. 'Incidentally, Mr de Groot. I noticed just now that your watch is five minutes slow.'

Ludo paused and looked at his wrist. 'Again? I thought I'd corrected it recently.' He shrugged. 'Ancient civilisations' dust in the mechanism trapping me in the past.'

Alone with Clifford, Eleanor turned to her butler. 'Well done for spotting Ludo's timings are probably off as his watch is wrong. It might explain why he didn't see Merrick in the lounge.' She drummed her fingers on the table. 'So they could both be telling the truth?'

Clifford produced her notebook, and she flicked to a crowded page. 'I'll just scribble the alternative timings, if Ludo was out by five minutes, underneath the ones I listed before. Your wizard's memory won't forget a word of what either of the de Groots said, so we can discuss that later. For now, he would have seen Trott pass at ten to midnight, not a quarter to.'

'And return the other way on the side deck at near enough midnight itself, my lady.'

She nodded, crossed out the wrong timings and re-wrote them under the right time.

<u>Baxter's Murder – alibis and timings</u>

11.40
~~Ludo de Groot – in lounge (according to Ludo and Frederika)~~

11.45.
~~Felix Trott – passed in corridor (according to Ludo)~~
Ludo de Groot – in lounge (according to Ludo and Frederika)

11.50
Wesley Merrick – in cabin (according to Merrick BUT left his cabin and went to Baxter's according to Trott)
Felix Trott – passed in corridor (according to Ludo)

11.55.
~~Felix Trott – passed back towards cabins (according to Ludo)~~

12.00
Wesley Merrick – in lounge until gunshot (according to Merrick)
Felix Trott – passed back towards cabins (according to Ludo)

12.05.
~~Ludo de Groot – returned to cabin (according to Ludo and Frederika BUT not seen by Merrick in lounge)~~

12.10
Ludo de Groot – returned to cabin (according to Ludo and Frederika BUT not seen by Merrick in lounge)

Her eyes widened. 'Clifford. I've just realised that means Trott can't have heard Merrick leave his cabin and cross the corridor to Baxter's at ten to midnight. Not if Merrick was in the lounge for fifteen minutes before the shot, as he insisted he was.'

'But what time did Mr Merrick actually leave his cabin, according to him?'

'I didn't ask. But I'm going to now. Or grill Trott again. Whoever I can sink my teeth into first!'

'Beware, gentlemen, there may be a crocodile out for blood in the hotel,' Clifford murmured as he followed her out of the lounge.

25

Eleanor deftly leapt aside as a white ball at knee height hurtled through the air. It shot between the legs of one of the red leather chairs lying on their sides and ricocheted off the wall.

'Howzat!' Trott cried, emerging from behind a stack of more chairs at the far end of the room.

She stared at him in astonishment while Clifford raised an eyebrow disapprovingly. It seemed their next target for questioning had taken leave of his senses.

'Mr Trott, whatever are you doing?'

'Isn't it obvious, Lady Swift? Passing time until I can get back to studying my crocodiles. Which I am sorely missing.'

With a sniff, Clifford held up the ball he had retrieved. 'You only just missed Lady Swift, as it happens, Mr Trott. And by a matter of a few inches!'

Trott shrugged, then turned to her. 'Well dodged, by the way.' He raked back his champagne-fair hair. 'I'll tell you what I'm *not* missing, though. The rest of that rabble from the boat!'

'Not just Mr Merrick, then?' Eleanor said, turning the conversation around to her agenda.

Trott shrugged, but she spotted a fleeting look of unease cross his face. 'Bowl the ball back, friend,' he said to Clifford.

'I have no desire to play wicketkeeper to whatever perversion of cricket this is supposed to be, thank you,' Clifford said tartly.

Eleanor hid a smile as he placed the ball on the floor in front of him and held it there with the toe of his shoe.

'That's not cricket!' Trott huffed.

'No, it isn't,' she said firmly. 'Nor is lying. So, let's put this room to rights and while we do, you can explain what is it about Mr Merrick that causes you to goad him so? Apparently, you only met him three days ago, and yet from the outset you acted as if he were your mortal enemy!'

Trott's panicked look told her she had hit her mark. He hesitated, then nodded contritely. 'Alright. I didn't meet him only three days ago. It has been my unpleasant penance to be stuck with him for half my life. He's... my stepbrother, you see. And the one born on the wealthy side. Father's. My mother was a struggling actress who caught the old man's eye in a show after his first wife died.'

She righted another chair. 'Ah! So you two boys probably didn't have much in common growing up together?'

'Still don't. He looks down on me just the same now as he did from the day Mother and I moved into Merrick Manor, the country seat.' He rolled his eyes. 'At least I don't toady to Father like he does. Not that I'm not grateful Father took me in. But I'm not like him, either. Which he knows, but he still insists I follow in the family business like Wesley. That's my stepbrother's first name, in case you didn't know. Anyway, that's why Father sent us both out here to work in the business. I hacked it for two months but it wasn't my cup of tea and I was damned if I'd give up my dream. So I chucked it and escaped to Morocco.'

She digested the information as she helped set the last

chairs back in place. 'You're not worried he might cut you out of any inheritance, then?'

He shrugged. 'Already has. And good for him. I'm not contributing anything now to the family coffers, so why should I gain anything? You should have heard Wesley going on about what a fool I was, though. And how he'd never leave the business and give up his inheritance.'

'So, you've been in Morocco since you left Egypt?'

He nodded. 'I've been obsessed with reptiles from a boy. And there's plenty in Morocco, like here. The trouble is making enough money. Which is why I've finally returned to Egypt to take up a short post studying the Nile crocodile. It pays awfully, but it pays. And since they built the dam at Aswan, there are more crocs up there than down here. Which is why I am... *was*... on the *Cleopatra* heading up there.'

'So you must have made up with your stepbrother to be travelling together on the same boat?'

He shook his head vigorously. 'Pure coincidence. Neither of us had a clue we were both booked on the *Cleopatra*. We hadn't seen each other, or kept in touch, since the day I left Egypt.'

Coincidence? Or something else, Ellie?

Clifford added the last chair to the neat row he had made. 'I wonder if I may see your passport, Mr Trott? I have never seen a Moroccan stamp.'

Trott scrabbled in his back pocket. 'Well, just have a whizz through that. It's there somewhere. Though it looks the same as all the rest to me.'

Clifford took the passport and pulled out his pince-nez. As he studied it, she moved on to her next line of questioning.

'You said, Mr Trott, that on the night Lieutenant Baxter died, you were woken by the door next to yours opening and footsteps crossing to the lieutenant's cabin. But there is only one door next to yours. Your stepbrother's, as we now know he is.'

Trott held his hands up sheepishly. 'Alright. Another

confession. I didn't hear that at all. I was just having a bit of fun at Wesley's expense.'

'As someone else was at yours.'

His mouth dropped. 'You mean that worm Wesley—'

She shook her head. 'No, it wasn't him.'

Trott frowned as he tapped his forehead as if trying to remember. 'That Dutchman, Ludo de Groot! He was in the lounge when I went for a quick leg stretch at ten to midnight. I didn't think he'd noticed me, he was so busy fiddling with his watch.'

Was he now, Ellie?

'Well, he did notice you.'

His expression fell. 'Sorry for stringing you a line about the night the lieutenant committed suicide. It was only for a bit of fun again. In bad taste, I admit now.' He glanced around the room. 'And, er, thanks for helping tidy up.'

'No problem.'

Eleanor turned to go.

'Your passport, Mr Trott.' Clifford passed it over. 'The Moroccan stamp was quite fascinating. Thank you.'

He closed the door behind them, leaving Trott brooding alone.

Back in the lobby, Clifford whispered to her, 'Mr Trott's passport shows he has indeed been out of Egypt until quite recently.'

'Well done.' She scanned the empty lounge. 'To hang with decorum, Clifford. I'll just have to buttonhole Merrick in his room. I need to speak to him next after what Trott just told us.'

Instead of following her, he waved his pocket watch. She stared at it, mystified.

'What's the significance of three o'clock?'

He held up a finger at the sound of footsteps hurrying down the stairs, then pointed at the hotel's front door. An Egyptian youth of about fifteen scurried in, his blue tunic robe riding up past his scrawny knees as he delved into the bulging canvas bag he carried.

'About time!' Merrick's melancholic grumble reached the lad just before the Welshman himself. Dragging the twine-bound bundle from the boy, he wafted him away. Head bent over, he gruffed at the recalcitrant knot pinched against the newspapers.

'Marvellous! They've arrived,' Eleanor said as she walked over to him.

Clifford tipped the newspaper boy, receiving a delighted smile.

'Allow me, Mr Merrick.' He smoothly inched the bundle from the Welshman's reluctant hands and flicked out the folded scissors of his pocket knife. Heading off across the lobby with the newspapers, he called back, 'Will you be in the lounge, my lady?'

'Yes, Clifford.'

'Now look here. I got them first,' Merrick protested. He jumped as she slipped her arm through his and steered him forwards.

'Yes, you did,' she said airily, trying not to stare at how thickly his hair was slicked down now she was beside him.

In the lounge, the tips of Merrick's ears were as red as his cheeks as he hovered behind Clifford, who was meticulously laying out the newspapers on the coffee table. Eleanor sat in the nearest chair and waved at the two English ones.

'It's very kind of the manager to order them. Which is your favourite one for the crossword puzzles, Mr Merrick? I'm sure you're a whizz at them!' She gestured at the run of pen clips adorning his breast pocket.

He snorted in exasperation. 'Lady Swift. I'm a businessman. I've no time for fruitless diversions.' He glanced at Clifford. 'Nor for having to wait for the latest news!'

Eleanor laughed. 'Oh, let my butler do his thing or he'll be infuriatingly grouchy all afternoon otherwise. Mind, you're very alike in needing things fastidiously neat and ordered. The two of you are almost like... half-brothers, you might say?'

'No, I would not,' Merrick said testily, but his eyes betrayed his unease.

She shrugged. 'Your perfectly aligned pens tell otherwise. It must still rankle that one of the clips got broken.'

'That nonsense again? I told you—'

'A lie,' she said quickly to cover she was bluffing. 'Which wasn't very chivalrous. And has made me wonder what else you lied about, hmm?'

The flush to Merrick's cheeks and ears spread to his neck. He fiddled with the tops of his pens. 'Alright. I was upset about it being broken. But mortally embarrassed that they're important to me... though not as writing implements. It's not very masculine, especially for a businessman.' His Welsh accent seemed even stronger as his expression turned doleful.

Eleanor winced. 'I didn't mean to hit such a raw nerve, apologies. How did you break the clip, incidentally?'

'I didn't! Lieutenant Baxter demanded I lend him a pen after we returned from that awful tomb tour. As good as wrenched it from my pocket.'

'Had he lost his, then?'

'No. Said his had run out of ink. I thought he'd have the decency to bring mine back after he'd jotted down whatever it was he needed to. But no! I had to hound him for it. Despicable manners.' He folded his arms defensively across his breast pocket.

'I hope he at least apologised for breaking the clip when he returned it?'

'That's the worst of it. He didn't return it. Just rounded on me, saying he had no idea what I was on about.' He leaned in close and lowered his voice. 'Not meaning to speak ill of the deceased, but I'm not sure he was all there. Up here, I mean.' He tapped his temple.

'Well, at least you got your pen back?'

He flinched. 'I did. After all, it was mine. And I wasn't going to be bullied by the likes of Baxter. So I took the opportunity when I saw it. Though I'm not proud to admit what I did.'

Having finished arranging the papers, Clifford turned around. 'Repossessing one's own property is hardly the most heinous of crimes.'

Merrick nodded. 'True. But... well, before dinner I think it was, I was about to leave my cabin when I saw someone come out of Baxter's and scarper down the corridor without locking the door behind them. So I slipped in, well trespassed I suppose it was, but I had to have my pen back.' He shook his head in disgust. 'You should have seen the mess, mind. It's disgraceful the way some people live! Like ill-bred swine. And Baxter, a military, or ex-military, man he said. Anyway, I saw my pen on the floor and picked it up. Then I spotted the clip was broken off and was lying under the desk. So I took the pen, but left the clip as a message to him that he owed me an apology!'

'Which you'll never get. Because he's dead now,' Eleanor said, watching carefully for his reaction.

His expression turned to disapproval. 'I'm not one to bear a grudge over another man, living or not, Lady Swift. Now, I must be going.' Spinning around, he swept up a couple of newspapers, frowning as Clifford held fast to the English version of the *Egyptian Gazette* he had been leafing through. Eleanor stood up.

'You said you never bear a grudge, Mr Merrick. Does that extend to your stepbrother?'

With a long-suffering sigh, he turned back to face her. 'Been speaking to Felix, then, I gather?'

She nodded. 'If Felix Trott is your stepbrother?'

He hesitated, then shrugged. 'Yes. And he's hated me from

the day my father married his mother. Jealous, see, because I'm the proper son, in his mind. And he's just the booby one that came with my father's new bride. He's got a nasty streak behind that affable, jokey act he puts on.'

Nasty enough to kill, Ellie?

Merrick's tone turned bitter. 'Father's almost as good at being a bully as he is at making money. I... I can't tell Felix, Lady Swift. But the truth is, I... I admire him. He had the guts to stand up to Father and leave the business, while I just carry on being Father's pawn.' He looked pleadingly at her. 'Please. You won't tell Felix I said that, will you?'

'It's none of my concern,' she said sympathetically.

Unless somehow it's related to a double murder, Ellie?

Merrick's eyes lit up. 'Thank you! Because that would take all the wind out of my sails. You see, I decided last night, I'm done with Father's business too. I'm going to wire and tell him so, the minute I finish the meeting I'm traipsing all the way to Aswan to attend.'

'Mr Merrick.' She stepped in his path as he went to leave. 'That's excellent news. But before you go, you mentioned you saw someone come out of Lieutenant Baxter's cabin the night he died. They left the door unlocked, which meant you could sneak in and get your pen back?'

He stared at her for a moment, as if he had no idea what she was talking about. Then he seemed to register the question. Slowly, he nodded.

'Oh yes. Without a doubt. It was that deckhand the policeman said had been shot. Farah, I think they called him?'

26

Hurrying through the front door of her townhouse, Eleanor threw her hat across the hall onto the side table.

'Oh, my stars!' Mrs Butters flustered up. 'With Mr Clifford right on your skirt tails, m'lady, you'd be in the hot soup if he saw you do that.'

'Not so, Mrs Butters.' Clifford appeared behind Eleanor. 'It is but a minor infringement of etiquette compared to the inelegant charge from the El Asafa Hotel to here fit only for branded livestock and their ilk.'

As her housekeeper hurried off, Eleanor slid the neatly folded copy of the *Egyptian Gazette* from under his arm and waved it at him. 'Well, who knew their ilk included a titled lady lucky enough to have the most brilliant butler ever?'

'Beg pardon, m'lady? Mr Clifford, sir?' Polly's tremulous disembodied voice floated out.

'It's alright now, Polly,' Eleanor called out. 'Clifford's stopped squabbling with me.'

Her youngest maid appeared and curtseyed. Receiving Clifford's permission to speak, she stared up at the ceiling as if trying to remember why she was there. 'Mrs Butters sent me with… 'pologies.' She curtseyed again before turning to scurry away.

'Polly, have you broken something?' Clifford said wearily.

The slip of a maid shook her head, clutching her apron lace. 'No, sir. Honest I haven't. The punchbowl is all cleared up now. But it wasn't my doin'. Not wishin' to tell tales, but Master Tomkins was fishin' all the fruit out like a wild thing. I think he thought it was goldfish and…' She tailed off at Clifford's gently halting hand.

'Then what is the apology for, Polly?'

'Oh yes. Mrs Butters didn't get a chance to say, your ladyship, but your gentleman police visitor is waitin' in the inside out. Only 'tis alright,' she added, clearly misunderstanding Eleanor's concerned look. 'Mrs Trotman's been attendin' to his every fancy.'

Eleanor hastened after her butler as he strode through the room of silk wall hangings and out onto the shady terrace. On catching sight of Sharaf, he stopped and half bowed.

'Chief Sharaf, please excuse any inconvenience incurred through any member of the household.' He shot Mrs Trotman a disapproving look, while trying to coax Eleanor's obstinate ginger tomcat from around Sharaf's neck. 'Her ladyship was unavoidably delayed.'

'Fibber,' she murmured, before greeting her visitor. 'Good afternoon, Chief Sharaf.'

'Good afternoon, Lady Swift.' He tried to rise but was hampered by the weight of her bulldog's portly form lying across his lap.

'Ah, perhaps you've received a slightly overexcited welcome?' she said with an apologetic smile.

He shook his head, deftly dodging Tomkins who was trying to paw his moustache. 'On the contrary, Lady Swift, I have been graciously treated like a pharaoh of ancient times by all the members of your house. Your butler manages a most exemplary staff.'

Mrs Trotman, having finished arranging a three-tiered stand of inviting-looking nibbles, bobbed Eleanor a curtsey and then slid past Clifford with an innocent look. With the terrible two also persuaded to retire to their beds with a selection of treats, Clifford furnished her and Sharaf with long, cool fruit drinks. She took a sip, placed the newspaper beside her and opened her notebook, hoping Sharaf had as much news to share as she did.

'If I might be the first to report?' He opened his notebook. 'The passengers and crew staying at the El Asafa have now been questioned regarding their alibis for the time of Farah's murder.'

'All of whom are also suspects in Lieutenant Baxter's murder, except First Mate Jabir,' she said, tapping her page.

Sharaf's gaze hardened. 'Lady Swift, there is still no evidence it was murder, so the cause of the lieutenant's death is being processed in Cairo as suicide.'

She caught Clifford's cautionary cough and bit her tongue. 'Quite right. So, how do the alibis for Farah's murder hold up?'

Sharaf sighed. 'Unfortunately, like houses built of sand. Not one of them is conclusive. Everyone has a witness for part of this morning, but none cover exactly the time my sergeant on the boat heard the shot and found Farah dead. Except Mr and Mrs de Groot. But they are married and could be lying together.'

'Quite literally.' Eleanor shot Clifford a questioning glance. His hand strayed to his tie, but he gave an imperceptible headshake.

So, he too thinks you needn't betray the Dutch couple's confession they aren't married, Ellie. After all, it doesn't hinder any consideration of them as suspects, either jointly or individually.

'Hmm, that doesn't narrow the field at all then.' She frowned. 'Even Herr Piltz could have reached the *Cleopatra* in time if he left the club straight after me. Dash it! It's a shame I only got to follow him there and not after he left as well.'

Sharaf stared at her. 'This is why you know of the club and Mahmoud Zaki? I thought Mr Clifford had visited to enjoy...' He tailed off, avoiding her butler's stiff gaze.

'I'm afraid I beat him to it.' Eleanor winked at the horrified Clifford. 'Now, what about Ali, Chief Sharaf? Have you interviewed him again?'

He nodded. 'Most certainly. But, as I feared, he said very little. But what he did say, I believe because he is a scared man. He imagines it could easily have been him we found with the bullet in his chest.'

'Poor fellow,' Eleanor said.

Sharaf shrugged. 'I also had my men check passports to see who had been in Egypt during the last two years as you requested. There are four. Captain Anders, obviously, as he runs his boat here. Mr Merrick, who must stay here to conduct his father's business. Mr de Groot, who has been on several dig sites here.'

So Frederika did lie, Ellie, when she said Ludo had never been to Egypt before.

'And Mr Piltz, who runs his art gallery in Cairo.'

'Thank you for looking into that, Chief Sharaf,' she said. 'I don't know if it's relevant yet, but it's good to know.'

'I have another piece of news,' Sharaf said. 'But please, what can you tell me you have discovered?' He sat back, looking hopeful.

She gathered her thoughts. 'A great deal. But I'll stick with what we learned from discreetly questioning the suspects a second time.'

'How did I miss the discreet element?' Clifford muttered as he topped up her drink.

She shrugged innocently and launched into reporting the pertinent facts from the interviews.

As she finished, she noted Sharaf had taken copious notes. And double underlined the very thing she had in her notebook.

'So Mr Merrick was certain he saw Farah leaving Lieutenant Baxter's cabin on the first night,' he said ponderously, tapping his chin.

She nodded vigorously. 'Absolutely. Assuming Merrick is telling the truth, that is. But it makes sense he saw the deckhand. We know Farah had the set of spare keys, so he could easily have entered the lieutenant's cabin. And if our theory that he was in the killer's pay is correct, he probably did so to search for the proof the lieutenant cryptically tasked me with finding. I'm still desperately hoping Farah didn't find it first.'

'Chief Sharaf,' Clifford said. 'Have the results of the items you sent to be analysed come in?'

He nodded. 'They have. The gun taken from the lieutenant's hand, the original letter you found hidden in the statue, and the suicide note itself, plus his passport for handwriting and fingerprints to be checked against.'

Eleanor held her breath, crossing her fingers under the table.

'Fingerprints on all three items match Lieutenant Baxter's,' Sharaf continued. 'There are no others. And the handwriting in the letter is the same as that of the suicide note, although in this second one, it is shaken.' He frowned. 'No, the word I mean is shaky. But this is only to be expected for a man writing his own suicide note.'

Clifford glanced at Eleanor. 'Whether of his own volition—'

'Or at gunpoint,' she said firmly.

Sharaf held up his pen. 'Of that, there is still no evidence.'

'Or is there?' He looked up sharply. She held his gaze. 'Chief Sharaf. I would like to hold the second half of our meeting back on the SS *Cleopatra*. I believe I can show you how Baxter *really* died.'

27

A short while later, Sharaf was standing in the doorway of the fatal fourth cabin on the SS *Cleopatra*, waiting for Eleanor to start her explanation. She opened the copy of the *Egyptian Gazette* she had brought with her to a page she had folded the corner of.

Clifford shuddered. 'May I, my lady?' He leaned forward and smoothed the creases out.

Sharaf stepped into the cabin and she handed it to him. He scanned the page, before looking up, his brow furrowed.

'This is most unusual. Not that a crocodile was shot while trying to attack a goat in one of the villages along the Nile. This is a common occurrence. But that in his stomach was found... a gun!'

She nodded. 'And the remains of a cushion. We have my eagle-eyed butler to thank for spotting the barely three-inch report. And there's more. Clifford checked a map. That village is not that many miles further up the Nile from where we stopped on our tomb tour. In fact, he calculated we would have passed it later that night, just after... midnight!'

'The very hour at which Lieutenant Baxter died,' Sharaf muttered.

She nodded. 'As I said, I'm sure that Clifford and I have worked out how he was murdered.'

Sharaf's dark eyes grew even more animated. 'I am listening.'

'I will need to borrow your gun.' She held out her hand. At his concerned look, she shook her head. 'It's only to make it clearer, visually.'

He hesitated, then passed her his gun, having made sure the safety catch was securely on. She strode to the doorway, imagining the scene. On cue, Clifford sat at the desk and picked up a pen. Eleanor walked back into the room and pointed the gun at him.

She addressed Sharaf. 'The murderer entered Lieutenant Baxter's cabin and forced him to write a suicide note. Then forced Baxter to his bed, where...' Clifford stood up and lay on the bed, Baxter's last resting place. She grabbed the one cushion off the settle. 'Where he shot him using a cushion to deaden the sound. That's why there was only one in his room. All the other cabins have two cushions, I believe, like mine. Oh, and Clifford thinks the murderer possibly also used a silencer.'

Sharaf held up a hand, his eyes betraying his puzzlement. 'Very possible. The use of a cushion to deaden the sound follows the same pattern as Farah's murder. But that time, my sergeant heard the gunshot. And Ali too, from down below the deck. Why?'

'Because,' Clifford said, 'the *Cleopatra*'s engine was not running when Mr Farah was murdered.'

'Ah, of course! And the below pumps failed,' Sharaf said thoughtfully.

Eleanor nodded. 'Just as the murderer had Farah lined up to kill. And too late to not pull the trigger.'

It was Clifford's turn to nod. 'Whereas in the case of Lieutenant Baxter's murder, both the engine and pumps were running. Which, together with the cushion and possible silencer the murderer employed, explains why no one heard the shot, despite being in their cabins.'

Sharaf frowned. 'It was sounding probable, but it is wrong! We three *did* hear the shot which killed the lieutenant. And from further away. Out on the front deck.'

'Actually, we didn't,' Eleanor said. 'The gun we all saw in Lieutenant Baxter's hand is the one that killed him, yes. But it is not the one we heard.' At Sharaf's disbelieving look, she continued. 'You see, having got the suicide note secured, the murderer shot Baxter, wiped the gun and placed it in his hand.' She mimed doing exactly that, placing the gun in Clifford's hand.

'Even attending to the detail of curling the lieutenant's forefinger inside the trigger guard,' Clifford said gravely as Eleanor did so with his.

'I will need the cabin key to demonstrate the next part.' Eleanor held her hand out again. Sharaf dropped the key in her palm and she passed it to Clifford. 'Then' – she strode out of the door, holding the cushion, followed by Sharaf – 'the murderer slipped out of the cabin, taking the scorched cushion with him and leaving the key on the inside of the door. He turned the key from the outside with some kind of... ah!'

Clifford appeared, closed the cabin door and withdrew from his pocket what looked like a particularly long pair of needle-nosed pliers. 'Would you kindly time me, Chief Sharaf?'

Sharaf nodded and stared at his watch. 'Go!'

Clifford knelt at the keyhole, inserted the pliers and with only a little tweaking, gently turned the key on the inside of the door.

'Stop!'

Sharaf's eyebrows rose. 'Fourteen seconds!'

Eleanor nodded. 'Which means not just Piltz, but anyone would have had time to do the same. Anyway, the result was, when we all arrived, the door seemed as though it must have been locked from the inside. With me?'

Sharaf nodded.

'Good. So, having locked the door from the outside as Clifford has just proved, the murderer then played his, or her, masterstroke.' She strode off again. 'By slipping inside the cabin next door, which he had the key from Farah for.'

She stopped in the middle of cabin five, Sharaf next to her. 'The killer then locked the door so as not to be disturbed.'

Clifford stepped in and closed the door behind him as she opened the porthole. She held up the cushion. 'The killer threw the scorched cushion out of the porthole, thinking it would quickly become waterlogged and sink, not eaten by a hungry crocodile! Then' – she withdrew Sharaf's gun from behind her back – 'the killer discharged a *second* gun out of the porthole without a silencer or cushion to deaden the sound. He dropped that into the Nile, too. Again, oblivious to the hungry crocodile outside.' Sharaf hastily reached out as she mimed doing just that. She bit back a smile and returned his gun. '*That* was the shot we heard. A *second* shot from a *second* gun, not silenced. Then the killer slipped out, leaving the door unlocked, and back into their own cabin, or out to the rear deck, or to the lounge, ready to emerge looking confused by all the hullabaloo.'

Sharaf clapped. 'Ingenious! An excellent work of deduction, Lady Swift. And Mr Clifford, also. And an excellent reconstruction of the crime. But' – he held his hands out – 'even if you are correct, sadly, the crocodile cannot give his statement to back up your theory.'

She nodded. 'True. And a great pity. However, it does mean that now we know the murder took place earlier than we thought.'

Sharaf nodded slowly to himself. 'Which means any of the passengers, or Captain Anders, could have killed Lieutenant

Baxter because he was shot some time *before* we thought originally. The preciseness of which we do not know.'

'Quite, Chief Sharaf,' Clifford said. 'However, the barrel of the gun in the lieutenant's hand still smelled strongly of cordite. Which suggests the second shot, which to repeat was the one we all heard, was not fired very long after the first.'

Eleanor pulled out her notebook and added another cross to three names on her suspect list. 'Which means First Mate Jabir and deckhands Ali and our unfortunate Farah remain ruled out because I saw them in the wheelhouse when I stepped out onto the front deck. And that was before I even started chatting with you, Chief Sharaf. But our timings for all the other passengers are out by an undetermined number of minutes.'

He glanced down at his own notebook. 'This I also agree with. But even with all the clever working out you have done, I have to repeat what you do not wish to hear, Lady Swift.'

She felt her insides churn.

He spread his hands apologetically. 'Without firm evidence, I cannot ask my superior to allow me to make a full investigation of Lieutenant Baxter's death, even though I now admit I believe it to be murder. And neither can I detain the SS *Cleopatra* any longer than I have already. I am sorry, but she still sails on Monday.'

Eleanor groaned. 'Which gives us less than seventy-two hours to catch the murderer!'

28

Sharaf broke the uncomfortable silence. 'I have another apology to make to you, Lady Swift. But this one poisons like the bite of our Egyptian cobra.'

She looked at him, mystified. 'Why?'

'You mentioned to me before the man at the dancing club. Mahmoud Zaki.'

'That's right. You said he was the leader of the desert bandits.'

'And I told you he is very dangerous, which is also true. But I told you he would not be involved in the death of Lieutenant Baxter or Farah. I am not a man who likes to be wrong, but maybe I was in that case.'

She frowned. 'Why are you telling me now?'

He smiled thinly. 'You are more... shrewd than I presumed. I would rather work with you, than against you. I was told about Zaki soon after the news I would be sent here to Bawaaba police station. The chief before me had suspicions that the port was being used for illegal operations.'

Eleanor frowned. 'Please don't think it a rude observation,

but isn't "port" a somewhat inflated title for what is really just a single jetty, without even an official customs office?'

Sharaf folded his hands. 'Precisely. This is why it was being used for loading stolen goods and artefacts. A small and unimportant town surrounded by desert is not one to attract the interest of the police superiors in Cairo.'

'I can see that. And the previous chief thought Zaki might be involved?'

'Not only involved, but the head of it all. But Zaki is a very clever man. And a very careful one. Never has it been possible for the police here in Bawaaba to prove anything. Or, at least, they have never dared to do so,' he muttered.

She was still confused. 'Then why do you now think he's connected with the two murders on the boat... oh my, the SS *Cleopatra*! That's the real reason you impounded her, isn't it? You believe Anders is involved with Zaki's illegal business?'

Sharaf nodded. 'This is why I was on the *Cleopatra* from the beginning, Lady Swift. Because I started my investigation before I started my new post. And even before Lieutenant Baxter died, I felt strongly the *Cleopatra* was the boat I sought.'

'What did I miss while we were aboard then?' She glanced at Clifford.

'Most everything, my lady,' he said with a sniff. 'I realise now the inadequacies were because their main focus was on looking after their illegal cargo, not their legitimate passengers!'

Sharaf pointed at him. 'Watching your butler having to fight on your behalf for the most basic of items was one thing that roused my suspicions.'

Despite the situation, Clifford's dedication to her made her smile. 'No wonder Anders was so furious with you for repeatedly making demands, then.' She sobered quickly as her hackles rose. The realisation that in good faith she'd paid passage aboard a boat on which she had been little more than an inconvenience made her cheeks flush with anger. 'The dashed nerve of the man! Anders will be sorry when I see him, I can tell you. But first it's time I paid this Zaki a visit.'

Sharaf's eyebrows shot up in horror. 'This cannot happen!'

She folded her arms. 'We've no time to waste disagreeing. There's a murderer to catch. And only seventy-two hours to do it, if you recall. You want to stop Zaki's illegal activities once and for all. I want justice for Lieutenant Baxter's death. As well as Farah's.'

Sharaf fixed her with a steely gaze. 'I too want justice for the murders, Lady Swift! But I explained before, as the chief of police, he would never agree to see me. Or anyone I sent. Even if I too broke into his dancing club and marched up to him,' he ended pointedly.

'I didn't exactly break...' She tailed off at Clifford's quiet cough.

'Perhaps we might concede Chief Sharaf must adhere to police protocol, my lady? Being the "governor", as it were?'

His coded reference threw her thoughts back to the market.

Hmm, Sharaf can't get us in with Zaki, but maybe we've met a man who can, Ellie?

'You're right, Clifford,' she said contritely. 'My apologies, Chief Sharaf. Can't you work on Anders somehow, though?'

He smiled without humour. 'Not alone. Together would be better.'

'I'm game,' she said determinedly. 'What are we going to do?'

'Apply some pressure to Captain Anders. Of the most unpleasant kind!'

The inside of Bawaaba's police station was even dingier than the many she'd visited before. Beyond the black entrance, the walls were morose grey, the doors reinforced with formidable bars. The air was stale, the weak lighting barely discernible.

'Goodness!' she whispered to Clifford. 'What's that chilling quote I'm suddenly reminded of?'

'"All hope abandon ye who enter here," my lady? Dante's reference to hell in his *Divine Comedy*, in which we could actually be standing at this moment. And, ironically, you are here to play devil's advocate, it seems.'

Sharaf appeared through the barred door behind them. 'I have a lot of changes I wish to make here. If my job lasts long enough.'

Eleanor bit her lip. Had he heard them, or was her face giving her away again?

The room he led her into corrected her initial impression that the police station couldn't feel any more desolate. A battered stool was set below a bare lightbulb which threw out an unforgiving glare. The only other form of seating was a fold-down square of wood on the rear wall, which Sharaf gestured Eleanor towards apologetically.

A barrage of shouting erupted out in the corridor.

'Sit!' Sharaf commanded as the two officers flanking a furious-looking Anders entered the room.

'I won't kowtow to you, Sharaf!' Anders shouted as the door slammed behind the guards.

'I said, sit, Captain Anders,' Sharaf said darkly. 'Having to repeat myself makes me forget the restrictions of being a policeman.'

'What the hell is this?' Anders spat. He seemed to register that Eleanor was there and threw his arms out. 'You, Lady Swift? And your man too. I should have guessed you'd be behind this farce.'

She smiled. 'Actually, I'm behind you. Which is why I suggest you do what Chief Sharaf has asked.'

Anders glared at her in confusion. 'He hasn't "asked" me anything. Yet.' He slumped onto the stool, switching his gaze to Sharaf. 'You've held my boat without good cause. Which you proved yourself by finding nothing. So whatever sham you've pulled me in here on is only going to double how foolish you look.'

Sharaf leaned so menacingly close to Anders' face it made Eleanor flinch.

'I recommend you remember where you are, Captain.'

Anders shifted backwards as far as he could without falling off the stool. 'But why *am* I here, damn it?'

'Because of the deaths of Lieutenant Baxter and Farah,' Eleanor said coolly.

Anders shook his head in confusion. 'Lady Swift, what possible reason is there for you to be interested in my ex-deck-hand and the suicide of a stranger?'

'A very good one. Lieutenant Baxter's death wasn't suicide. He was murdered. Just like poor Farah.'

Anders' jaw hung slack. 'What? Baxter murdered?' His eyes widened. 'You think the two deaths are related, don't you?'

'The two murders, you mean,' she said firmly.

'And, yes, both Lady Swift and I are certain they are,' Sharaf answered for her. 'And you are the number one suspect for both.'

'Now wait there!' Anders leaped up, but Sharaf put his hand on his chest and pushed him back down.

'Kindly stay seated, Captain Anders!'

Anders did as he was told. 'Look, Sharaf. Even if Lieutenant Baxter was murdered, like Farah, just because the two of them were killed on my boat doesn't make me guilty.'

'You're right, it doesn't,' Eleanor said.

Sharaf nodded grimly. 'But the fact you transport stolen goods for Mahmoud Zaki does, in all probability.'

Anders swallowed hard. 'You don't know anything of the kind!'

Eleanor shrugged. 'A foolish reply, Captain Anders. But if

you insist on wanting to talk yourself into a double murder charge, what do I care?'

He threw his head back and groaned.

'Anders!' Sharaf barked.

'What happened to "Captain"?' he said tersely.

Sharaf gave him a knowing look. 'He lost his boat. His livelihood. And then his life!'

Anders groaned again. 'I didn't murder anyone, I tell you.'

Sharaf turned his mouth down. 'Not good enough. I will tell you what happened on your boat. Lieutenant Baxter also worked for Mahmoud Zaki.'

Eleanor winced to herself. Did Sharaf believe that, or was it just to put pressure on Anders?

'But the lieutenant became greedy,' Sharaf continued. 'And kept what he was supposed to have handed over to Zaki for himself. He cleverly made his escape, but then had some bad luck. He chose the *Cleopatra* to continue his getaway. Your boat. Because he had no knowledge that you also worked for Zaki.' He held up a silencing hand as Anders went to speak. 'So, on Zaki's orders, you took the item from Lieutenant Baxter and killed him. But you made the mistake in not realising your deckhand Farah saw you. Or perhaps he worked it out for himself? And then he tried to blackmail you.' He shrugged. 'Either way, you shot him also.'

Anders seemed to have trouble breathing. 'You... you have no direct proof!' he said raggedly. 'Not for one scrap of anything you've accused me of.' His desperate gaze swung to Eleanor. 'Lady Swift. You must realise this is nonsense. Tell him. Please!'

She see-sawed her head. 'You know, I don't believe you either. And Chief Sharaf doesn't really need inconvenient trifles like proof.'

Anders moaned, his expression harried. 'What do you mean?'

'Lady Swift is very smart. And well-travelled,' Sharaf said. 'I think she understands that I have enough evidence of circumstance to be proof for a local court in, what is now, *my* town.'

Anders held up his hands in surrender. 'Alright, alright! I give in!' He took a deep breath. 'I... I might have transported a few... items on the *Cleopatra* for certain people. And maybe Zaki was one of them. But I've no idea what the items were or where they ended up.'

But you do, Ellie.

She held his gaze. 'If you want Chief Sharaf to believe you're actually telling the truth, Captain Anders, then you'd better confess where you really were when Lieutenant Baxter was killed.'

Anders paled. 'I swear, I was out on the lower rear deck, like I told him.'

'And yet the three of us got to the cabins from the front deck before you?'

Anders was visibly sweating. 'I... I didn't come immediately on hearing the shot because I... I was checking that the items I was transporting for Zaki were still there and well hidden.'

She caught Sharaf's eyes lighting up.

Perhaps he may now find whatever he impounded the Cleopatra *for, Ellie?*

Another thought struck her. Had Anders just confessed to transporting stolen goods to deflect a double murder charge?

She glanced at Sharaf, but his expression was as impassive as her butler's.

'Thank you, Captain Anders. My men will revisit your boat shortly, and you will show them exactly where those items are hidden. In the meantime, if you tell anyone about this conversation, you and your boat will never leave this town! Is that clear?'

A defeated man, Anders nodded dejectedly.

'Good,' Sharaf continued. 'Then tell me what you know about Lieutenant Baxter. And no lies. My patience is finished.'

Anders composed himself a little. 'I can't tell you anything much. I'd never seen or heard of him before he boarded the *Cleopatra* in Cairo. Heard him alright once he was onboard. But then he changed. Seemed suddenly on edge and odd. Bizarrely odd.'

Eleanor's ears pricked up. 'How so?'

'Like he'd fallen and hit his head. I found him in weird places, muttering to himself.'

'Places like where?'

'Like below deck the night he died. In the engine room, of all places.'

So that's where he was headed when you saw him going down the crew stairs followed by Piltz, Ellie.

Anders frowned. 'In fact, that was the last time I saw him alive, now I think of it.'

29

The pungent smell of camel wafted up to Eleanor as she testily leaned forward to adjust her seating position yet again. They'd been trekking across endless sands since breakfast that morning, the sun mercilessly stalking them. Despite the blistering heat, she shivered. She had the uncomfortable feeling they were being watched by more than just the vultures circling in the distance.

Clifford's camel let out a bad-tempered bellow.

'Apologies. I might have missed what you said, my lady?'

She laughed. Improbably, he was perched on a saddle between the two humps of his vocal camel wearing a cream linen suit. She gestured at the traditional Egyptian headdress he was sporting against the sun.

'Had I spoken, you terror, I would have said I wish I could take a photograph to tease you with for years to come.'

'Ah, but what better salve for the lady's frustration than the need to employ... patience?' he parried.

She laughed, her good humour fully restored. 'At least squabbling with each other on camels is new. How will we ever top this, do you suppose?'

'I am in no doubt the lady will find a way,' he said in a wry tone.

'Now I know you've both cracked!' Arthur Barr's plaintive London accent called from behind. 'Told you this escapade was unhinged from the start. And that was before you'd caught the blummin' sun.'

'We haven't, Arthur. Though I admit I can almost feel my lungs blistering,' she called, reluctantly easing her camel to an even slower pace so their grumbling guide could draw alongside. 'Ribbing each other is the way Clifford and I let off steam when we're up against it, that's all.'

'Well, you could have fooled me, princess,' he grumbled.

'Nonsense. A shrewd chap like you? I couldn't dream of getting up early enough to get one over on you. Could I, Clifford?'

He nodded. 'That is categorically true. But only because her ladyship has normally only risen in time to devour a late breakfast and segue seamlessly into luncheon.'

Barr looked between them suspiciously, then shook his head. 'I'm tellin' you straight. You're ridin' like trussed-up turkeys into the lion's mouth. This meetin' with Zaki is madness. Any sane person would turn these stinkin' animals around and give it up.'

'You're right, I'm sure.' She had been trying to bury that thought from the outset. 'So, please tell us how to navigate through this featureless ocean of sand to Zaki's place? Then you can hurry back to town. We'll see you later.'

Barr looked affronted. 'Not a hope. You'd never make it there, nor back, without me. Anyways, I can't scarper. Mr Clifford coughed up the readies before we cleared the traps.'

'Paid before we set off,' Clifford translated.

Barr nodded. 'That's what I said. Everyone knows Arthur Barr always delivers on his promises.'

'For a king's ransom,' Clifford murmured to Eleanor with a tut.

'You're invaluable, Arthur.' She was still quietly burning to ask how he had secured her this meeting at all.

'Well, none of us'll be anything 'cept gonners if we ain't safely back in town by dusk. It's way too dangerous to be out here in the desert at night.' He pointed to their left. 'Zaki's men are watching us already.'

So that's why you felt unnerved, Ellie.

Two men in white robes on tall, cream horses had appeared over one of the ridge-baked dunes. The rifles slung over their shoulders left little doubt in her mind they were the same pair who had watched her from afar a few days earlier.

'I hear you,' she said earnestly to Arthur. 'And we'll be in and out with Zaki before you'll have a chance to worry.'

He laughed mirthlessly. 'You really think you'll have any say in how it goes? Stone me, you are in for a nasty surprise.'

They fell into an uneasy silence until Barr pointed ahead to where the dunes seemed to rise sharply. 'There it is. Zaki's country residence.'

'That? Am I seeing a mirage because' – she lifted her sunglasses to focus through the shimmering heat haze, hastily shielding her eyes against the sun's blinding glare – 'it looks like an old walled sandstone fort?'

'Cor lummy, catch up, princess. Where else would the most dangerous man from Cairo to Aswan live?'

He indicated they needed to stop before they reached the formidably barred metal gates. Eleanor estimated they were at least twenty feet high. As Barr dismounted and approached them cautiously, the slotted grille in one of them slid back.

Barr slapped both his hands to his chest and lowered his head, saying something in Arabic to whoever was on the other side. The only thing she understood amongst it all was her name. The gate swung open, revealing a high-walled courtyard of bare sand across the centre of which a line of armed men like the ones on horseback were waiting, save these men were swathed head to toe in black. At Barr's beckoning, she swallowed hard and coaxed her camel forward.

For Lieutenant Baxter, Ellie. And Deckhand Farah.

That none of the black-robed and long leather-booted men spoke felt all the more intimidating. And confusing, given their respectful attention in taking command of her camel and assisting her to step off. Barr offered her a grimace as he leaned against the wall and pulled out his cigarettes. The tallest of the guards clapped his hands, which made ten of the men close ranks around her and Clifford, while the remaining two stood guard on Barr. Eleanor and Clifford were escorted through another set of smaller gates and up steep, sand-strewn steps into the interior of the fort.

Inside it was blissfully cool compared to the searing heat of the sun. And blindingly dark, until her eyes adjusted to the weak light. They were in a lavishly appointed hall hung with opulent silk hangings, all depicting a rearing ivory stallion ridden by what could have passed for a king in various triumphant poses. The richly patterned tiled floor was peppered with luxurious turquoise and gold upholstered ottoman seats and low tables. Two tall and intricately carved screens stood on either side of the ornate double doors at the far end.

Two men stepped across her path, arms folded. 'Welcome to Sayyid Mahmoud's home, Lady Swift and Mr Clifford,' one of them said. 'You will take refreshments.'

She shook her head politely. 'No, thank you. I'm sure Mr Zaki is very busy. I'll just—'

'Take refreshments,' the man repeated slowly, with a thin smile.

. . .

She couldn't deny the pale amber mint-infused tea was soothing to her parched throat. But her insides knotted in frustration as an hour passed with nothing more than another pot arriving.

She paced the room, smiling wryly to herself.

Barr did warn you, Ellie.

Finally, her patience gave way. She spun around to Clifford.

'You know, I think this is all an elaborate joke. I think this Zaki character is nowhere—'

'Nowhere? The mighty Zaki is everywhere!' a booming voice declared.

30

Eleanor jumped like a scalded cat.

'Mr Zaki, or Sayyid Mahmoud as I would suggest addressing him, my lady, has been watching us for some time, as I was trying to discreetly point out,' Clifford said under his breath.

The lengthy pause before the owner of the voice appeared she thought unnecessarily theatrical. Finally, however, the doors opened and his imposing form loomed.

'Mr... Sayyid Mahmoud, it's very good of you to see me,' she said brightly, trying not to feel intimidated by his giant stature and hard ebony-eyed glare as he approached.

'I know this,' he said in a bear-like growl. 'Nevertheless, do not think it is with the wish to make friends, Lady Swift.'

Strangely, she found there was something more menacing about him being dressed in a fine-tailored crimson silk suit than the traditional robe his guards wore. The fringing of his white scarf swung with the pound of his heavy footsteps as if marking time. Hopefully not the end of hers, she thought. It was then that she became aware Clifford was standing unusually close.

But even his six-foot frame was dwarfed by the mountain of a man now bearing down on her.

'You should not have come.' Zaki stood in front of her, his stare seeming to bore into her very soul as if wanting to pluck it out.

She shook away the unsettling notion. This was no time to lose her composure.

'That's rather immaterial, isn't it, Sayyid Mahmoud? Seeing as I have?'

He raised his bushy eyebrows. 'You have the stubborn temperament of a donkey. And an entirely wrong idea that you and I can have any business together.'

She nodded her head. 'I'll just about concede your first point, although it isn't very gentlemanly of you. However, I shall let that slight slip of etiquette pass, as I believe we do have business together.'

His thick black brows met. 'Why did you ask to see me?'

'Because I am told you are the most powerful man in this area. Which means you know almost everything that goes on here.'

'Not almost! I know everything. Sit!'

'Even better.' She settled herself comfortably on the nearest ottoman seat, then looked pointedly at the opposite one. 'It's alright, you won't look any less fierce or formidable if you join me,' she said in a stage whisper.

Looking fleetingly bemused, he lowered himself regally. 'I do not sell information, if that is what has brought you here?'

She smiled. 'That's a relief, because I wasn't offering to buy. The thing is, I've landed in something of a sticky situation. And my butler here is driving me to distraction, nagging me. Because, you see, I'm supposed to be on holiday.'

Zaki glanced at Clifford, receiving only an impassive look in reply.

'The problems of a disappointed tourist do not concern me,

Lady Swift. You have two more minutes,' he said coolly, but she spotted a glint of interest in his eyes.

'Thank you. Well, take all the rumours wafting around Bawaaba about stolen goods. How can I blithely spend all my tourist money on souvenirs and presents, if I don't know what's legitimate and what isn't?'

Zaki's eyes narrowed. 'Why should I know the answer?'

'Because if anyone knows about what passes through the town, it's you. You said yourself you know everything.'

He shrugged. 'True. But I do not trade in goods of any kind.'

'Shame. Because to be truthful, I don't care one fig how anyone comes into possession of something. If I want it, I shall have it. That's what comes of being brought up a spoilt princess, you see.'

'And what is it exactly you wish to take home to your fairy-tale English castle, Lady Swift?' he said in a curious tone.

'Well, that's where I need your expert opinion, Mr Zaki. Something rare and precious. So sought after people would be willing to risk... murder to obtain it? What would you suggest?'

His laughter bellowed around the room. 'A case of good judgement. Because you are lacking in this completely. Now, your two minutes are finished. I cannot help you.'

She kept her expression neutral. 'That's a shame. However, I heard there was someone who can help me if you can't. A German chap named Herr Piltz, I think it is?'

Zaki shrugged. 'Never have I heard of this man.'

She had to hand it to him, he sounded disarmingly convincing.

She phrased her next question carefully. Sharaf had warned any hint that Anders had confessed to transporting stolen goods for Zaki would almost certainly see him as dead as Baxter and Farah.

'The other person I was told might be of use to my penchant for a special something to purchase was a boat chap.

Admiral... no... Captain, Captain Anders, that's it! Is he trustworthy?'

'He is English too, I think. So most likely not,' Zaki said coldly.

'Ouch!' she said with feigned offence. 'But you have heard of him?'

He nodded. 'He operates a Nile cruise boat, I believe. What of it?'

'Oh, nothing,' she said lightly. 'Only that I heard a man committed suicide on his boat. And that his deckhand was shot.'

'I do not know anything of this,' Zaki said blandly.

'Gracious! You told me that you knew everything that went on around these parts. It seems not.'

'I will tell you something I do know,' Zaki said darkly. 'You, Lady Swift, deal with the police. And I do not!' He halted her reply with a low growl. 'I also do not like uninvited guests!'

'You might not have invited me, per se, but you agreed to see me.'

'I was not speaking of today. Or here. But your previous uninvited visit to my club.'

She kept her features neutral. 'Your club? Which one is that then?'

'You know very well which it is!'

'Yes, I do,' she said in a steely tone. 'It's the one in which you were talking to Herr Piltz. The man you've just sworn you've never met!'

He frowned. 'Because I have not. The meeting you spied on was with a man I had also not met before. And he did not call himself "Piltz". Now, we are done. And I warn you this once only, Lady Swift. Stay out of my affairs or you will be very sorry!'

As she climbed back onto her camel out in the courtyard, Barr tipped his cigarette packet upside down to highlight it was empty.

'Nice to see you were in charge enough to nip in and out quick like. Blummin' dusk'll be right on our tail now,' he grumbled.

Even the stiff desert wind couldn't cool the frustrated flush of her cheeks as they set off back to Bawaaba. Zaki clearly knew more than he had said. But about what? Which of his answers had been bluff or lies? And who was Piltz, if Zaki had told the truth about him? The murderer, perhaps?

Beside her, Clifford let out a sigh. 'More to the point, my lady, as Mr Zaki knew you were "spying" on him in his club, what else does he know of which you are unaware?'

'Dash it! I hadn't thought of that.'

It had been a hideously long day by the time they reached the outskirts of the town. But they made it just before nightfall and returned the camels to the dubious character who Barr insisted it was best she forget ever seeing. They trudged through the dark of the unlit streets until they arrived at the steps to her townhouse. Eager to curl up with Gladstone and Tomkins, she hurried up them, only to be met by Mrs Butters at the door.

'Evening, m'lady. Waiting for you in the silk room. 'Tis your visitor again.'

She jumped at the apologetic cough behind her. Sharaf stepped forward.

'Lady Swift, please forgive me for coming straight to the point, but I had a telephone call from my superior in Cairo.'

'Ah, some news then?' About to lead him back to the comfort of the sitting room, she froze at his words.

'Yes. But news you will not welcome hearing.' Sharaf nodded as she turned back to him. 'I have been ordered to let the SS *Cleopatra* sail. First thing in the morning.'

31

'In the morning?' Eleanor repeated in horror. She sank down onto the nearest settee and stared up at Sharaf. 'As in *tomorrow* morning? Only what, fourteen hours away?'

'Likely less than twelve, I would conjecture, my lady. Given the lateness of the hour,' Clifford said soberly, having joined her. The snap of his pocket watch closing didn't cover Sharaf's sigh.

'Unfortunately correct, Mr Clifford. The boat, passengers and remaining crew will depart at ten o'clock tomorrow.'

Eleanor lurched forward in her seat. 'But it can't! If the *Cleopatra* sails, the murderer of Baxter and Farah will...' She bit her hand, the truth too awful to finish articulating.

'Will sail away with her. For good,' Clifford said gravely.

Sharaf nodded grimly. 'The investigation into Farah's death is to be officially closed. I will arrest Deckhand Ali for his murder before the *Cleopatra* sails in the morning.' He held up his hand. 'I have no choice, but I do not intend that he shall ever be tried. And Lieutenant Baxter's death has been recorded as suicide.'

'There must be something you can do to buy us some more time?' she pleaded.

Sharaf sat on the seat opposite hers, his expression earnest. 'I wish with all my heart that there was. But I am truly sorry. Even with all my yearning for justice, an order from the head of the Cairo police cannot be disobeyed.'

'But—'

'Lady Swift, if I had sent immediately to him my badge with a letter of resignation at the end of his telephone call, it would make not a single difference.'

'Another officer would simply be dispatched to ensure the *Cleopatra* sails as ordered, I imagine?' Clifford said.

Sharaf shook his head. 'No. *All* the officers from my police station would be sent. To make sure there would be no delay in its departure.'

Eleanor groaned. 'Who could have put enough pressure on your superior, though? Oh gracious, unless, of course, he's a... you know, thoroughly rotten egg himself?'

'Absolutely, he is not,' Sharaf said ardently. 'Please, you must not think this. He is an honest man. But, in certain circumstances, even the hands at the top are tied, so they have no choice. I do not like this truth either, but it happens here. As elsewhere.'

'A universal and regrettable condition of the invincible influence of power, Chief Sharaf,' Clifford said, nodding.

'But whose power?' Eleanor said.

Sharaf shrugged. 'I can think of only one. Zaki.'

'That wretch? Well, it's time he learned even he can be toppled!' She steamrollered Sharaf's protestations. 'I understand your position. Really. But I can't let a double murderer go free. Nor can I fail Lieutenant Baxter after he put his trust in me, however misguidedly. I'd never forgive myself.'

'And I understand your position also.' Sharaf's tone hardened. 'But you gave your word you would stop investigating once the *Cleopatra* sailed.'

She threw her arms out. 'And I would never go back on my word. But that was when you promised us we had until Monday. Heaven knows, the investigation was near enough impossible when we thought we had seventy-two hours. And now we've only, eleven or twelve!'

'Yes, that is so,' Sharaf said flatly.

'Clifford!' She leapt up. 'Back to the El Asafa and hurl anything to hand into our cases. We'll sail on the *Cleopatra*, too!'

He stayed where he was, only a slight flicker crossing his face. She frowned in confusion. Sharaf nodded slowly.

'Mr Clifford has realised the full power of Zaki, I think. The order from my superior states that neither you, Lady Swift, nor Mr Clifford, are to be permitted to sail with the *Cleopatra*. On threat of immediate arrest if you try.'

She slumped back down onto the settee. 'But that's a disaster!'

Clifford arched a brow. 'But not so surprising a one, perhaps, my lady? Given the vehemence of Mr Zaki's warning to stay out of his affairs.'

'Ah!' Sharaf shook his head disapprovingly. 'So you did visit Zaki, Lady Swift? Against my most clear advice.'

She shrugged defensively. 'I had to do something.'

'You did plenty. This is the result,' Sharaf said reproachfully. 'I see now, always you act as you believe is best, not as any other tells you. Even when that other is the chief of police in an Egyptian town you have never before visited.'

Too honest to argue, she looked contrite, only to spot a glint of something in his dark eyes she couldn't quite place. Was it annoyance, or maybe a flicker of... admiration?

Clearly you don't know him at all, Ellie.

'One last point I should mention.' Sharaf rose briskly. 'Now that Farah's death is closed, the investigation into the smuggling of stolen goods I was holding the *Cleopatra* for has also been closed. By order from Cairo again.'

She thought that an odd bit of information given it hardly compared with the unthinkable matter of two murders going unpunished. However, she waved a hand in acknowledgement out of politeness.

Sharaf continued. 'I have forbidden anyone to return to the *Cleopatra* until nine o'clock tomorrow morning. An hour before she sails. Also, I have called back all my men guarding the boat as I will need them for other duties.' There was that puzzling glint in his eyes again. He shrugged. 'I may not have mentioned this to Captain Anders.'

She raised her eyebrows. 'But that leaves Ali as the only person on board?'

'Lady Swift, I will say goodnight,' Sharaf said. 'But I will borrow your question to me of some days before. We are "on the same page", I hope?'

Not waiting for her answer, he strode from the room.

'Clifford! Quick. What do we need?' she hissed, tugging on his cream linen jacket sleeve.

'To temporarily abandon our standards of decency, regrettably.'

'Only in the very best cause, though.'

'Most assuredly, my lady. Thus we need something impossible to source in an unknown Egyptian desert town at almost midnight. Impossible, perhaps, that is, without the assistance of a certain disreputable gentleman we have just left...'

The outer reaches of Bawaaba were deserted, which, given it was now three in the morning, was not surprising. With the lack of any street lighting, it was also a great deal darker than was helpful. However, torches weren't yet an option if they were to stay undetected.

As Clifford paused to question his mental compass, she murmured, 'Lucky we both inadvertently packed some dark clothing suitable for a spot of burglary!'

He pointed forward. 'Burglary? Tsk!'

'What would you call what we're planning, then?'

'A soupçon of subversion, followed by an interlude of incidental vandalism.'

Despite the gravity of the situation, she bit back a laugh. 'I didn't know one could be an "incidental" vandal?'

'Neither did I, my lady,' he whispered, gesturing at the coded flash of a torch off to the right. 'So, let's see if one can.'

'Crikey, you've definitely lost it this time,' Barr hissed, clicking off his torch as they joined him. The moonlight was just strong enough for him to count the bundle of notes Clifford held out, then pass him a sturdy holdall. 'Blummin' good job I don't ask no questions. But in your case, it's mostly 'cos I don't want to hear the answers!'

Clifford inspected the contents, then closed the bag and offered their unwilling accomplice his hand to shake. 'Perfect. Good man.'

'You know I said you're invaluable, Arthur?' Eleanor whispered. 'I was wrong. You're something else altogether.'

'What am I then?' Barr said guardedly.

'A hero if we manage to pull this off!'

She turned and sprinted across the open ground towards the boat jetty.

32

The SS *Cleopatra* cut a brooding silhouette as they reached the now unguarded jetty and crouched behind an old barrel. Eleanor pointed at the wheelhouse.

'Look!' she whispered. 'I can just make out Ali up there. With the way the glow of his cigarette is dropping, I think he's definitely falling asleep. At worst, though, we'll have to overpower him.'

Even as the words left her lips, she shook her head, then realised Clifford was too.

'In good conscience, my lady, neither of us could countenance instilling more fear into the poor man. Not after the way Chief Sharaf said he reacted to his colleague Farah being shot.'

'Then extra stealth is needed.'

Holding her breath, she darted along the jetty to where—

'Clifford,' she hissed. 'There's no gangway!'

'Naturally, Ali would have had the good sense to remove it so no unwanted visitors could get aboard, my lady. I had anticipated such. Hence this.'

He opened the holdall Barr had supplied and, to her amazement, pulled out a rope ladder. With a deft flick of his wrists, he adjusted the knots at the top to form a lasso. She watched the loop fly, only releasing her breath as it slipped over one of the mushroom-shaped bollards on the side deck, then drop to hold fast. He made two more loops at the other end of the ladder and secured them to the iron rings on the jetty.

'An unpredictable gangway,' he whispered. 'But for a lady raised on a sailboat, eminently doable.'

"Unpredictable" was an understatement, she thought as she crept up the first swinging rungs, the whole thing threatening to twist over on itself and drop her into the Nile. Not relishing the idea of being a crocodile's supper, she reached the deck and risked bobbing her head over the gunwale. Deserted. She slid aboard, Clifford stepping noiselessly up beside her only a second later.

'The furthest lounge door,' she mouthed, nodding as Clifford produced his trusty roll of picklocks.

Inside the boat, she shivered at the eerie feeling that wrapped around her. Two men had been murdered only thirty or so feet from where she was standing. Rolling her shoulders back, she crept towards the hatchway which led to below deck. She breathed a sigh of relief. At least that wasn't locked. Clifford tapped her wrist firmly and mimed he'd go first. The hatch creaked ominously as he eased it up just enough to duck onto the top step of the short, steep flight down.

As she followed and let the hatch close behind her, they were plunged into ink-black darkness. After a beat, Clifford clicked on his torch and shone it around the small corridor that led off into the engine room.

'No one, thankfully.'

A few steps in and the stench of engine oil and diesel was making her empty stomach roil. And that was before Clifford risked lighting one of the oil lanterns.

She dropped to the floor beside him and yanked out the roll of tools from the holdall. Already on his knees, he wrenched his jacket and shirtsleeves up past his elbows without a hint of his usual methodical neatness. Or horror at his lack of decorum in doing so in her presence.

'Forgive the deplorable presumption,' he whispered. 'But I will require your assistance as second mechanic, my lady.' He took the first two spanners. 'Now we shall temporarily disable only. Not permanently ruin.'

'How long will it take?'

'Depending on the severity of the corrosion on the bolts of the engine casing, among others, anything from twenty minutes to lunchtime tomorrow,' he said soberly.

'Then let's hope Anders is more thorough at routine maintenance than he is at customer service.' She picked up the spanner he motioned for her to hand him. 'You've never failed us before.'

'There is always a first time,' he muttered as the spanner's head sheared off. 'Although, a poor workman blames his tools...'

How long they had been unbolting, wrenching, and grinding their teeth while trying to rush their work of sabotage with insufficient light and even less accessibility, she couldn't say. Her sore knees had a good idea, however; too long.

'Smaller fingers needed again,' Clifford murmured from where he was now lying on his back.

She slid her hand into the cramped space. 'If ever there was a time expletives would be acceptable—'

Just as her arm threatened to give out, she felt the bolt move a fraction. Then some more. A few minutes later and Clifford was holding up their prize.

'Excellent! Well done.' She shrugged. 'But what exactly is it?'

'It is an assurance that the murderer of Lieutenant Baxter and Deckhand Farah will not sail away to safety today as planned. For this, my lady, is one fuel valve removed. Bravo, second mechanic, bravo!'

She nodded, but her brow furrowed. 'Are you sure Anders can't get a replacement easily?'

'The likelihood of one being available except in Cairo is next to nil, I would estimate. Particularly given the age of the boat. Which means, as it would have to come by river and then be fitted, I cannot see a circumstance where the SS *Cleopatra* could sail this weekend. Especially as we are going to rebuild the engine to disguise our act of sabotage, so it should not be discovered until they try to start it.'

'So we'll have at least until Monday morning, as per Sharaf's original extension?'

He nodded confidently. 'Excluding hell or high water, I believe so.'

The engine rebuilt in less time than she'd thought possible, they snuffed out the lantern and groped their way back up the stairs by the beam of Clifford's torch. There they crept to the rear deck, where Clifford dropped the fuel valve into the Nile. They'd discussed hiding or keeping it, but if it was recovered, then all their efforts at sabotage would have been in vain.

As he turned back from the rail, he paused. 'The tool bag, my lady?'

She clapped her hand over her mouth. 'I thought you had it!'

He shook his head. 'It is too risky to leave. It is unlikely, but it could be traced to Mr Barr. And then maybe even us.'

They crept back down to the engine room, Eleanor fretting over the extra time they were spending on the boat. What if Ali—

'Got the tools,' Clifford murmured.

Before they could start back up the steep steps, she noticed a faint glow of light around the hatchway. Clifford immediately switched off the torch. Instinctively, they both felt their way into the engine room and squeezed themselves into a corner as they heard footsteps descending. As the beam of a torch swung about in the corridor, they slunk further into the shadows behind a stack of oil drums.

Eleanor tried to quieten the treacherously loud beating of her heart. Just as she thought it might give out, the light and footsteps receded.

They waited silently, neither daring to move until the sound of the hatch dropping closed.

'Time to go, my lady!' Clifford said urgently, clicking on his torch. 'Before we end our days here!'

'Wait!' she gasped. 'End our days... like Baxter. Clifford! Anders said he found him down here in the engine room. And that was the last time he saw him alive!'

'True. But we cannot risk searching—'

'No need,' she said breathlessly. 'In your torch beam. I saw...' She slid her arm into the narrow gap between a large tank and the rear wall, her trembling fingers reaching out. 'This!'

33

'Clifford, what on earth are the ladies doing up at this hour!' Eleanor paused mid-tiptoe into the hallway of the townhouse.

He gestured past her housekeeper, cook and second maid, who were shuffling into a bleary-eyed line.

'Hmm, "up" being debatable in Polly's case,' he murmured.

The sight of her youngest maid, curled up fast asleep around her loudly snoring bulldog, made Eleanor's heart skip with affection. She semaphored to Mrs Butters not to wake the girl and beckoned the three of them forward. Tomkins beat them with a flying leap into her arms, his soft pussycat paws cradling her neck.

'Lawks, m'lady, we've all been frettin' buckets with worry,' Mrs Trotman said, hurrying up.

Eleanor looked at her staff in puzzlement. 'Gracious, what's happened?'

'Ahem,' Clifford said. 'I conjecture the ladies' consternation has been concerning your safety, my lady.'

The three tired and pale faces nodded in unison, which made Eleanor want to pull them into a hug.

'Goodness, I'm fine. Why did you think I might be in trouble?'

Mrs Butters scanned her face with a motherly look of concern. 'Beg pardon for saying so, m'lady, but 'twouldn't be the first time by a mighty long chalk. Not after so many nasty happenings afore.'

She couldn't deny that. Before she could offer any more reassurance, Mrs Trotman clucked her tongue.

'Butters is right, m'lady. That's why we were concerned, like, when that Mr Barr called around to check an hour back.'

'Arthur Barr? Who we met in the market?'

Mrs Trotman nodded. 'That's him. Right rascal of a gentleman,' she said, patting her hair.

Clifford's brow flinched. 'The contradiction therein notwithstanding, Mr Barr was not asked to call. Particularly at such an inappropriate time of night.'

Eleanor's confusion turned to surprise. 'But it seems he did to make sure we had made it back here alright.'

Clifford tutted. 'More likely to request additional remuneration if we had, as you described it, "pulled it off", my lady.'

He darted forward and held the sleepy bulldog as Polly stirred and almost fell off the chair.

'So sorry, Mr Clifford, sir,' she stuttered, blinking rapidly in horror as she caught sight of Eleanor. 'Didn't mean to be sleepin' in front of the mistress.'

'It's alright this time, Polly,' he said gently. He turned to the other staff. 'Ladies, your commendable dedication to duty has been duly noted. Now, bedtime, all of you. I will attend to her ladyship.'

As they trooped off, Clifford led Eleanor to the kitchen without a word, despite normally declaring it not a place for a titled lady. From the day she had inherited Henley Hall, whenever life had run off the rails, she'd gravitated to the heart of the house.

Before she had even settled, the smell of strong coffee filled the room. He set the envelope they had found on the SS *Cleopatra* and a letter opener in front of her. Then placed his emergency hip flask by the two.

'Here goes.' She ran the letter opener slowly along the seal.

Tentatively, she unfolded the paper inside and spread it out for them to read together, her breath catching.

Testimonial, and Confession, of Lieutenant Alton Baxter.

I had hoped to never have to write this document. But, fate having decreed it so, I have no choice, so I shall start at the beginning...

One evening, a long-standing army mate asked if I was up for 'a bit of a lark' and some easy money into the bargain? He told me all I'd need to do was take part in a fake raid on a nearby archaeologist camp at an ancient tomb. To my shame, I admit we used to play similar 'tricks' on local settlements, to liven up the gruelling monotony when stationed for months in the desert. My mate assured me no one would get hurt. None of the archaeologists were armed. We'd simply dress as Arab bandits and secure the camp. No one would recognise us. Then the anonymous man who was paying for the job, the 'boss' as my mate referred to him, would grab whatever he was after and we'd all hightail out of there.

I admit I agreed to the plan. Partly because I needed the money, but also because I confess over the last year I missed the excitement of active service. And I had no conscience over the idea of the 'theft'. After all, whatever it was this 'boss' wanted, the archaeologists had only stolen it from the tomb. It hardly belonged to them! It felt no crime to rob a grave robber.

Unfortunately, things did not work out the way my mate had promised. Contrary to what I had been told, when we rode in, we found the camp guarded by two young, and obviously inexperienced, British soldiers. I later found out their names were Private Gareth Morgan and Private Wilfred Allen. I assumed we would beat an instant retreat, but instead we were ordered to subdue the soldiers and tie them up. I should have left then. But my military training took over, and I found myself unable to disobey orders in the field. The soldiers were disarmed and tied up on one side by my mate and I. While we guarded them, others bound and restrained the archaeologists in their quarters. That's when the 'boss' arrived and disappeared into the tomb. On a signal, I presume. I never saw his face. Or learned his name. He was disguised exactly like the rest of us.

Eleanor gasped, her thoughts racing. 'Clifford. That's the murderer! The "boss" of that fake raid.'

'My lady?'

'Think about it. That's why Baxter had no idea who on the SS *Cleopatra* was trying to kill him.'

He nodded slowly. 'Of course. Because he never saw the "boss" that night, except swathed in disguise. I believe you are right.' He frowned. 'But that does not explain why he did not recognise the killer's voice? Unless it was disguised?'

He added a dash of fortification to her coffee as she returned to the testimonial...

As the 'boss' emerged with his sidekicks I noticed he was carrying what looked like a bejewelled death mask as might have been made for a pharaoh or prince. My attention being distracted by its sheer beauty, one of the soldiers, Private Morgan, broke free and grabbed his rifle back. I could have disarmed him without too much trouble, as the young man was inexperienced. But he was also clearly terrified. Unfortunately, he was determined to prove fit to wear his soldier's uniform and be a hero. Before I could reason with him, the 'boss' grabbed

Private Allen's rifle and shot poor Private Morgan dead. I rounded on the 'boss', but was told unless I got back on my horse and rode out of there immediately, he would put a bullet in me too. Arguing seemed no option, so I left the camp with the others, feeling a traitorous coward. At the first crossroads, we dispersed, each back to where we'd come from.

Then, a few weeks later, I learned Private Allen had been put on trial by his garrison commander and found guilty of aiding the 'bandits' who raided the camp and shooting his colleague, Private Morgan. His sentence; death.

'The "great injustice"!' Eleanor cried, instantly lowering her voice as Clifford glanced towards the servants' quarters. 'This must be what Lieutenant Baxter was trying to put right. Gracious, that poor young man!'

Clifford's eyes gave away how troubled he felt. 'The gravest offence in the army. Erroneously levied against an innocent cadet.'

She swallowed hard. 'Maybe there's a light at the end of this tale's tunnel?'

They both held up crossed fingers and turned back to the testimonial.

I fought with my conscience for weeks, but was too cowardly to act, fearing I would not be listened to, but instead accused of contributing to Private Morgan's death and executed alongside. Then I learned an appeal had been lodged by the soldier's parents. I prayed with all my heart that it would be successful. As weeks turned into months, my hope vanished. Alas, in the end, the appeal was dismissed.

Eleanor fought a prick of hot tears. 'The "miracle" Baxter mentioned in his letter.'

Clifford nodded sadly. 'That never happened. Indeed.'

'All I can think of is how desolate and abandoned young Wilfred Allen must have felt when he heard his only hope had failed.'

Clifford scanned her face, his own etched with concern. 'Upsetting yourself by dwelling on such matters cannot turn back the clock, my lady.'

She sighed. 'You're right. Let's finish this…'

So I finally gave in to my conscience and set out to stop Private Allen being executed for crimes he did not commit. I had relinquished my army life and was living in Alexandria at the time, as far from the scene of that terrible event as I could. So, I travelled to Cairo and from there booked on to the SS Cleopatra.

But the first night I found my cabin ransacked. There was no way a thief would leave a cabin so obviously disturbed. Not when there was no way of leaving the boat until it docked. It was plain to me that someone knew of my plan and had been searching for any evidence I might have had. How they knew I have yet to find out!

It also seemed clear to me that the man who had ransacked my cabin was most likely the 'boss' who had killed Private Morgan. And that I was marked for death myself.

I made a hasty plan to disembark at the first town and try to carry on overland. But as I had no idea who, among the passengers, or perhaps crew, my would-be killer was, I knew there was a strong chance I might not survive that long.

Then suddenly, fortune smiled on me, and I found a young lady of such remarkable resolve and ingenuity, I was sure she could finish my mission for me.

If you are reading this, then the young lady who handed this testimonial to you is she, Lady Swift.

And I am dead.

Please, I implore you to accept this testimonial as definite proof that Private Wilfred Allen, who is currently incarcerated for aiding the 'bandits' and killing his colleague, Private Gareth Morgan, was completely blameless.

Signed: Lieutenant Alton Baxter

Dated: Tuesday 1st July 1924

She folded the testimonial carefully and slid it back into the envelope. 'Well, we have Baxter's "proof". But still no idea where, or who to present it to in order to save young Wilfred as Baxter never finished the letter we found in the statue in his cabin. And the British Army must still have hundreds of men here in Egypt, stationed all over the country.'

'Thousands, my lady. If you will forgive the sobering observation.'

'I've another,' she said grimly. 'We still have absolutely no idea who the murderer is!'

34

Back out in the unlit streets of Bawaaba, Eleanor's yawn turned into a groan. Their supposed shortcut had ended in another dead end.

'Dash it, Clifford! Why is it so wretchedly difficult for us to find the El Asafa?'

'I stand to be corrected, of course, my lady.' He peered sideways at her. 'But perhaps because neither of us can read the Arabic scripted street names, it is as good as pitch-black and we have not slept. Oh, and the only form of sustenance in even distant memory has been of the liquid variety. Or maybe it is because this entire Nile sojourn has descended into yet another regrettably unsavoury business!'

'Feel better?' she said affectionately, knowing his uncharacteristic outburst was borne entirely out of his dismay she was caught up in such events again.

He nodded contritely. 'My abject apologies.'

'Are not needed. Unlike a route to this wretched hotel before everyone there wakes up. Otherwise, the whole point of sneaking in, freshening up, and then emerging as if we've been there all night will have been for nothing.'

'Noted.' He turned in a slow circle, tapping his forehead.

She tutted. 'Come on. Maybe— Aagh!'

She felt a hand around her throat and another over her mouth. From the scuffling of feet and incensed growls, she realised Clifford had been set upon as well.

'Do not fight. It will be the worse for you,' a thick Arabic voice gruffed as the harsh white-orange flame of a petrol lighter swung threateningly between her face and her butler's.

Too tired to put up with being manhandled, she bit down hard on the hand still smothering her mouth while kicking her assailant sharply in the shins. Not pausing to enjoy the yelp of pain this drew, she pushed herself away and spun around to see Clifford doing the same, minus the biting.

'Whatever it is you want, there's no need to be barbarian about it,' she said tartly.

The man with the lighter looked confused. 'Us? We want nothing. But if you do not come with us, we will be forced to be very rough!'

Their other assailants withdrew what she had to admit were very barbaric-looking cudgels. She glanced at Clifford, who nodded in agreement. This was a fight they couldn't win.

With men in front and behind, they were propelled through a formidable barred door into a storeroom of some kind. It was filled with a vast number of crates, bottles, and a few broken chairs. They were then marched to the far corner, where a short flight of steps led steeply up.

As she reached the middle step, a disembodied voice hailed her from above, the owner obscured by the honeycombed stone balustrade. 'Being infuriatingly tiresome is not enough for you, I see?'

Now she knew where she was. Though eerily silent, the colourfully tiled floor she stepped onto confirmed she was right. Clifford appeared beside her, catching her eye questioningly.

She raised her voice. 'It appears Sayyid Mahmoud has

opened his exotic dancing club just for us, labouring under the misguided impression it holds an allure at this time of the morning. Business must be scarce.'

The disembodied voice barked something in Arabic and they were marched up the ornate staircase she had seen Piltz emerge from onto the second floor.

Zaki sat behind his vast desk on one side of the viewing gallery. Resplendent in a burnished bronze silk suit on a throne-like chair, he scowled at her, cracking his knuckles threateningly. The tassel of his fez hat swung as he rose, towering over her.

'I warned you not to get involved in my business, Lady Swift. And never to spy on me again!'

'I'm not,' she shot back, exhaustion making her too testy to mince her words. 'I'm only here because your thugs dragged me in on my way past. And my butler, too.'

'Lies!' Zaki slapped his bear paw of a hand on his desk. 'I do not believe you. You insult my intelligence. You expect me to imagine you just happened to be passing my club at this time in the morning? And I am also insulted that you doubted me when I told you I had nothing to do with the two deaths you accused me of at my fort.'

'There was no accusation. Genuinely,' she said. 'Not then. But after this overtly heavy-handed show of yours, it's going to be harder to believe you.'

He leaned forward, his tone darkening. 'Tell me the real truth about what you are doing in Bawaaba, or I will make sure neither of you can ever bother me again!'

There was no missing the malevolent intent in his voice. And yet, her doubts whispered, if he was behind the murders of Baxter and Farah, why hadn't he killed her and Clifford at his fort? And thrown their bodies to the vultures to dispose of? But if she was wrong, and he carried out his threat, she would never catch the murderer. And she would have failed Baxter. Worse still, she would not be able to present the testimonial in time to save young Wilfred Allen, wherever he was. Her thoughts whirled. Then they calmed as her intuition spoke to her. Whatever Zaki was, despite his formidable form and threatening demeanour, his black eyes boring into hers held something else. Reason? She glanced at Clifford, who shrugged.

'My only certainty is you have never failed us yet, my lady.'

Trusting his confidence in her, she turned around.

'Alright, Sayyid Mahmoud, I will tell you the truth. But it's a torturous tale, so for goodness' sake, can't we sit like civilised people?'

With a bemused look, he nodded at one of her recent assailants. He brought a chair, and she gratefully collapsed onto it. Clifford remained standing as Zaki sat back down behind the desk.

'Right, here's the truth. The whole truth,' she said firmly, making a mental note to leave out their sabotaging efforts only. 'It all began the day we boarded the SS *Cleopatra*...'

Zaki listened intently as she relayed the tumultuous events of the last few days, not interrupting even once. Neither did he look disbelieving as she ended with, 'Hand on heart, I don't want to make any trouble for you. I only want justice. And to somehow put right the great injustice Lieutenant Baxter charged me with.'

For a few moments, he sat silently, his dark eyes brooding. Then he clapped his hands above his head smartly. Within a trice, they were alone. He held her gaze. 'I believe you have been truthful with me. So, I shall show you the same honour.'

She felt a frisson of hope. 'Thank you.'

He waved her thanks away. 'Lady Swift. I too must place my hand on my heart. You see... I am not who you think I am.'

35

Zaki rose, his goliath form obscuring the light from the lamp behind him. 'I am not a killer, despite the rumours. Neither am I a gunrunner.'

Eleanor's brain whirled. That couldn't have been further from what she imagined he was going to say. Too intrigued to trust her face not to give her away, she leaned forward again.

'You've got the whole area fooled you're both of those things, though. So there must be a good reason?'

'It suits my purpose to let everyone think this.' He held his giant hands wide. 'Since you are a lady, for the nicety of words, I shall find a polite way to explain what I do.'

'Consideration of my delicate sensibilities appreciated,' she said demurely.

Zaki waved a thick finger of disagreement. 'The man whose hand still shows the marks of your angry teeth and, on other parts of him, the mark of your furious boot, is certain you have no delicacy.'

'Not true, Sayyid Mahmoud,' Clifford said. 'It is merely that it is often comparable to the delicacy of a rhinoceros.'

Zaki snorted with laughter. 'And one who has seen and

done many things even a lady rhinoceros is not supposed to! So, you will not be overcome with a faint if I say I am primarily a' – he spread his huge hands wide – 're-distributor of items liberated from their previous owners.'

She nodded sagely. 'Ah, I understand! You know, we have a term for that in England. But I'm sure none of your counterparts there can claim the glamorous mystique of receiving their "liberated items" at a desert fort. Nor of having them sold on from a modern art gallery in Cairo. But you can, of course?'

'Very clever of you to work out how my enterprise operates,' Zaki said. 'But I expected little less from you.'

She avoided pointing out that was partly due to her having spied on Piltz on the very landing they were now sitting on. Finally, she'd understood why Piltz had been following Baxter. Piltz may not have known exactly where Anders and his crew had secreted the SS *Cleopatra*'s illicit cargo, much of it bound for his art gallery. But he did know that he didn't want one of the passengers snooping around below decks!

'But why go to such lengths to be seen as someone involved in far more illegal activities?'

Zaki shrugged. 'Simple. When I started my... endeavour, my shipments were regularly attacked by bandits. So, to stop this, I had to become more feared than those doing the attacking. And also become feared enough that the police kept their distance. My desert fort, for instance, is useful for my business, but also as part of that image. As are my vultures.'

'Your *vultures*?'

His dark eyes lit up. 'Aren't they perfect? And so loyal. But only because I feed them all the raw meat they want, so they stay so menacingly circling above!'

She couldn't help smiling at the wiliness of his ruse. 'They're very unnerving, I agree.'

He nodded. 'My whole plan was successful. I started to gain

a lot of respect. And fear. Which stopped the attacks. And' – he shrugged – 'I admit, I rather liked the notoriety.'

'I appreciate your honesty. Genuinely,' she said. 'But it's eating me up not to ask. Why on earth have you told me all this?'

He leaned back and regarded her. 'Because I was wrong before when you came to my fort. And when I think this morning, you slunk around here to make more trouble.' He put his hand over his heart. 'I am, I hope, still humble enough to admit when I have made a mistake. And to right that mistake. So' – his manner became brisk – 'I will help you. What is it you need to know?'

Her breath caught. 'Have you heard of any incidents near a British garrison over the past year which could have ended in the "great injustice" I mentioned?'

He shrugged. 'In the last few years, what great injustice has not happened near a British garrison? My country and yours have had many violent disagreements in that time.'

'I realise that. But something not political. Remember what I told you Lieutenant Baxter confessed to in his testimonial?'

He nodded. 'This is really why I have told you everything. Because when you started telling your story, I thought I would know nothing. But at the end, I am thinking, ah, maybe I know a small part! But, then again, maybe it is nothing.'

'Oh, please go on. Anything, no matter how small, could be vital.'

'Archaeologists,' he said disparagingly, missing the meaningful glance she shared with Clifford. 'These people I do not like, Lady Swift. Not because they dig only to take what they find back to their own countries, robbing mine, but because they have no respect for the dead.' He thumped his chest. 'I do not wish to be pulled from my grave in a thousand years' time and my bones put on display!' He shrugged again. 'But sometimes, I have to confess, they find something, an "artefact" you

English call it, that is so rare. So pure. So beautiful, even I am tempted.'

'So *priceless*, perhaps?' she said in a non-judgemental tone.

He nodded emphatically. 'This particularly. I was offered one of these artefacts. Discovered by a group of archaeologists who were German, I believe, from the accent of the man who called on me. He said they had told no one about their discovery and he had come with the permission of all the group. But I did not believe this. He was working only for his own pockets, I think.'

'What was the artefact?'

'You have heard of the mask of King Tutankhamun?'

Clifford put his hands together. 'An ancient masterpiece of gold, carnelian, obsidian, lapis lazuli, turquoise, and glass paste. Discovered by Howard Carter only a couple of years ago with a chisel given to him by his grandmother for his seventeenth birthday by some accounts.'

Eleanor flapped a hand. 'The encyclopaedic in Clifford is really very endearing when you get to know him. But suffice to say, yes, its fame has spread to all of Europe. But surely you weren't offered something like that?'

'I was. Smaller, but similar enough to be worth a fortune. Created of gold and several of the other precious gems you mentioned, Mr Clifford. A veritable death mask for a young pharaoh!'

The mask Baxter saw the 'boss' taking from the archaeologists' camp, Ellie.

Zaki's expression darkened. 'But I threw him from my club like the rat with disease! I do not buy items that have had the blood of men spilled for them!'

She leaned forward eagerly. 'The man who was killed when that mask was taken. His murder was wrongly blamed on a young British soldier who was sentenced to death for the crime.'

Zaki nodded. 'I know this.'

She swallowed hard. 'Do you know then where the soldier is to be executed?'

'Yes. At the British garrison stationed to the south of Aswan. Just outside as you approach on the main highway.' He rose, straightened his burnished bronze jacket, then clapped his hands above his head. 'Now, Lady Swift, we are done. I have other business to attend to.'

The thickly bearded leader of the men who had abducted them from the street was noticeably more courteous as he led Eleanor and Clifford from Zaki's presence. As they descended the dog-legged staircase and crossed the tiled floor below, a muffled voice on the other side of a latticed screen made her start. She'd heard that voice before somewhere. But where? That almost familiar accent?

As the door out to the still dark streets closed behind them, it hit her.

'Of course!'

Clifford arched a mystified brow.

'No time to explain. We need to get to the hotel as quickly as possible. The last piece of the puzzle just fell into place!'

36

'Thank goodness!' Eleanor never thought she would be so glad to see Bawaaba's police station, but it was the first landmark she recognised. 'At least we're almost at the hotel.'

Her joy was short-lived, however, as she spotted Anders outside standing toe-to-toe with Sharaf. She ducked out of sight, Clifford following her.

'What can have upset Anders so much that he'd risk challenging Sharaf so soon?' she whispered.

Creeping closer, Eleanor caught the captain's tense-jawed words.

'I heard all your threats to arrest me before, Sharaf. Which is why I followed your ridiculous orders. And why I'm doing my damnedest to control my temper. But having called off your armed guards and without telling me, it makes you responsible for someone having vandalised my boat engine!'

Eleanor and Clifford shared a horrified look.

Sharaf regarded Anders coolly. 'I have no knowledge of this, Captain Anders. I removed my men because they were needed for other duties. However, I allowed Deckhand Ali to remain on board. So the security of your boat was entirely your responsibility.'

'Ali was nothing like enough security, as I tried to tell you at the time. He's—'

Sharaf interrupted with a dismissive shrug. 'If, as the captain, you cannot even employ a proper crew, that is your failing, not mine.' His voice hardened. 'However, it is clear you have not followed my orders. Otherwise you would not know there is a problem with your engine, would you?'

Anders scoffed. 'The SS *Cleopatra* is an excellent workhorse of a boat, but she is an old lady. The single hour your orders permitted me to board in advance of her sailing at ten o'clock this morning was preposterous!'

Sharaf looked unmoved. 'I am not interested in your difficulties, Captain Anders. Only how long it will take you to fix whatever you are saying has been vandalised?'

Anders glared at Sharaf. 'No thanks to you, but I have a replacement part on its way already.'

From Cairo, Ellie. It will take days as Clifford—

'Four hours and it will be here,' Anders said in a jubilant tone.

Clifford let out a soft groan.

Anders folded his arms. 'Having cruised the Nile for fifteen years, I know enough other men who operate vintage boats on this river and radioed them. One cruiser is laid up for repairs, so her owner was happy to remove the part I need and send it down on another boat in exchange for a new replacement later.' He jabbed an irate finger at the police chief. 'The *Cleopatra* will depart first thing this afternoon. With no thanks to you, again!' Anders turned on his heel and strode away.

'My sincere apologies, my lady,' Clifford murmured as Sharaf returned to the police station. 'I involved you in a disgracefully unlawful act for nothing.'

His deep dismay made her hide her own. 'Chin up. It

wasn't for nothing. Without it, we'd never have found Baxter's testimonial. And it's still earned us' – she winced – 'a few extra hours.'

But surely not enough, Ellie?

'Well, there's no point in speaking to Sharaf,' she said determinedly. 'He could never do what we need now in order to root out our murderer in the little time remaining.'

'True, my lady. Chief Sharaf is a good man, but like your fiancé, bound by orders from his superiors.'

Forcing down her rising panic at the ticking clock in her mind, she managed a wan smile. 'So, let's go and unmask a killer!'

The El Asafa reception was in shadows as they stole into the hotel through the service entrance. Clifford repocketed his picklocks as the night porter, dozing behind the front desk, snored noisily.

'It appears, my lady, none of the guests have risen yet.'

Her empty stomach clenched at the smell of spice, musk and jasmine overlaid with cheap—

'Where have I smelled that tobacco before, Clifford?'

He nodded towards the lounge.

Of course, Ellie.

Hurrying up to the only occupied armchair, she stood in front of it and hissed, 'Ludo!'

'Ach! *Verdomd!*' The Dutch archaeologist's eyes shot open, his shock of blond hair bouncing as he clasped his hands to his chest. Next to the chair was a half-finished cigarette in an already overflowing ashtray.

'Lady Swift, you nearly stopped my heart!'

'Like someone did to poor Farah when they shot him,' she said grimly. 'Or rather murdered him, I should say. And like Lieutenant Baxter.'

Ludo blanched. Untangling his tall frame from the chair, he rose hesitantly to face her. 'Baxter? But he... he committed suicide?'

She dropped into the armchair opposite with a disbelieving tut. 'Oh please! That's the worst of all the pretences you've tried to pull.'

'I don't understand.' He stepped closer, which made him loom over her, his bird's nest beard almost brushing her forehead.

'Mr de Groot. You will sit to hear what her ladyship has to say,' Clifford commanded, pointing at the other armchair.

Reluctantly perching on the edge, Ludo stared at her. 'What is it you are trying to say, Lady Swift?'

'There's no "trying" about it, Ludo,' she said impatiently, glancing quickly at the still snoring porter. 'Two men were murdered aboard the *Cleopatra* and I know who's responsible. Someone who is not who they are pretending to be.'

He swallowed hard. 'I see. And you think you know who?'

'No, I'm certain who. It's you, Ludo.'

Lips flapping, he shook his head. 'Me! Why the hell would you imagine me guilty?'

'Firstly, because you aren't who you say you are.' She counted off on her fingers. 'You lied about never having been to Egypt before this trip. You lied about being married. You lied about your alibi for the time of Baxter's death, then cleverly kept your watch running five minutes slow in case the suicide was realised to be fake. Which meant all the timings you'd given would still proclaim you innocent.'

Ludo was sweating visibly. 'Now, look—'

'I haven't finished,' she snapped. 'You also had the cabin next to Baxter's, so the timing was still tight, but easier for you. And, of course, you used a disguise.'

'I haven't, I didn't... what disguise?' he said guardedly, both hands fiddling with his untamed beard.

She tutted. 'Really, Ludo. I'm not referring to you disguising your physical appearance.'

Ludo's lips twitched. 'Then what?'

She held his gaze. 'Your accent. Dutch. Which is so close to German, to many people it's indistinguishable. Especially to anyone who rarely comes across it. Like, say, an Egyptian bandit and smuggler? You certainly played the convincing German archaeologist there.'

She caught Clifford's glance of comprehension.

Thank God you heard Piltz at the club again this morning, Ellie.

At first, she'd thought the man she couldn't see had been speaking Dutch. But then realised it was German, and Piltz the one talking. Which in turn made her realise Zaki had been wrong when he'd said they were German and British archaeologists at the camp that had been raided. They'd been Dutch and British!

'That's not true!' Ludo blustered.

She waved a dismissive hand. 'Fine. But that horribly full ashtray is shouting that you're getting very nervous about something.' She rose and strode towards the archway with Clifford only half a step behind. 'And I should think it's about to get a whole lot worse as we're just off to see Chief Sharaf. He's waiting to hear from me.'

'Stop!' Ludo hissed. 'Lady Swift. Please!'

The porter grunted, opened his eyes, then promptly closed them and started snoring again.

'I'll confess,' Ludo said quietly. 'The full truth this time, I swear.' He crossed his heart. 'On my life.'

37

With Eleanor seated once more, Ludo sank onto the edge of the coffee table. He swallowed hard, nodding slowly.

'You are correct about some things. I have been to Egypt before. On a series of digs with a small group of other Dutch archaeologists. But we were running out of money. The grants we were given shrank dramatically every time. We had to accept whatever dig we were offered next. The last one was in Aswan. And we even had to share it with British archaeologists.'

Eleanor looked sceptical. 'Odd? After the Tutankhamun tomb and all its spoils were found, I would have thought money was hurled at archaeologists here in Egypt?'

He laughed without humour. 'It was. But only on "celebrity" digs. Ones led by a prestigious professor. Or any Englishman with a trowel and a title.' He shrugged. 'All we knew in my group was that we had barely enough to live on. Especially with the locals pilfering our equipment whenever possible. Yet collectors around the world were paying mind-blowing fortunes for any artefact unearthed with even a hint of a gem in it. Or a fabulous tale attached to it. And the teams who found them became famous.'

Eleanor stared pointedly at the wall clock. 'I didn't agree to listen to your sob story, Ludo. Get to the point.'

'Alright,' he said defensively. 'It was on the last dig. The one we were forced to share with the British. Beyond the outer empty tomb, we hit upon a passageway which turned in two directions to what we all hoped would be inner tombs. The two groups agreed to toss a coin for who got which direction.'

She frowned. 'You weren't working as one team, then?'

'Not a chance! Think of what was at stake, Lady Swift. If one group unearthed something collectable, money and fame would be theirs. Who would want to share that?' His eyes lit up. 'Certainly not us, not after what we found in our inner tomb.'

She tried to keep her expression neutral. 'A bit of a trinket, was it?'

'No. A death mask, among other, lesser finds,' he said breathlessly. 'Smaller, but enough like Tutankhamun's to be worth an unimaginable fortune. And fame, of course,' he added with a dismissive toss of his head.

She shared a glance with Clifford. 'You didn't fancy fame then?'

He laughed scornfully. 'I wanted the money. I grew up hungry. And ashamed of how poor my family was.' His jaw tightened. 'But the others in my group wanted the fame, the fools! The only thing we agreed on was to keep it a secret from the British. Well, it was our find.'

'What happened then?'

Ludo opened his mouth hesitantly, then sighed. 'I admit, I decided to take my chance. Alone.'

'To smuggle the mask out of Egypt?'

He looked aghast. 'Absolutely not! After the Tutankhamun find, the Egyptian authorities tightened security on searching the luggage of foreigners leaving the country. Especially any that had a connection with ancient sites. Have you any idea what they would have done to me if I'd got caught? Which I would have on the spot. I'm no smuggler. Just an archaeologist.'

'A thieving one, though. Since you obviously planned to steal it away from your Dutch colleagues?'

He held his hands up. 'Yes. The amount it was worth would have made even the guilt of tricking them worthwhile. And the week before, I'd been approached by a man after he overheard me tell someone else I was on an archaeological dig. He told me he was a "go-between" and offered to buy anything we found on behalf of the man he represented. My split would be fifty per cent of the price his boss got.'

That being Zaki, I bet, Ellie.

'But my first problem was to sneak the mask out of the tomb itself. The British knew nothing of our find, and the local petty thieves never dared venture inside the digs themselves. But the rest of my group were guarding the mask like rabid desert dogs. This go-between had a simple solution, however. An old trick he said never failed.'

She interrupted him impatiently. 'We know what that "trick" was. Just tell me, why were there two British soldiers guarding the camp?'

He stared at her in disbelief. 'The... the British archaeologists had lost equipment to local thieves and decided enough was enough. So they asked the commander of a small British fort only half a mile from the dig for help. And he grudgingly sent two young soldiers back with them to guard the camp.' He ran a disconsolate hand through his hair. 'The raid party captured the soldiers and marched them off somewhere. The others tied us archaeologists up in our camp area.'

Which ties in with what Baxter wrote, Ellie. And why Ludo and Baxter didn't recognise each other on the SS Cleopatra.

'What about the man the go-between represented?'

'I never saw him. But he definitely came and took the mask himself.'

Eleanor leaned forward. 'How can you be sure?'

'I found out later,' he said bitterly, shifting awkwardly on the corner of the table. 'Well, back to the raid. Once they'd gone, we managed to free ourselves. Then, I waited the one week I'd agreed with the go-between and went to collect my fifty per cent at our meeting point. But...' He shook his head.

'He never showed up.' Eleanor felt her hopes dwindling she would learn anything more of use.

Ludo's fists clenched. 'No, he didn't! But I wasn't going to be tricked so easily. So I searched the town high and low for days. One thing archaeology teaches you is to be patient. And it worked. I spotted the go-between one night and trailed him to a club where he met the boss, I presume. I never saw the boss, though. I couldn't get inside, so I listened through a grating out in the street as best I could. It was really late and there was no one else around.' At her impatient look, he hurried on. 'To cut the story short, I heard the boss tell the go-between the prize would be hidden deep in the old catacombs for three months.'

Eleanor was flummoxed. 'Why wait three months?'

'Because the others in my group told the British archaeologists what was stolen the night of the raid. And they told the British authorities who realised that Tutankhamun's tomb was obviously not a one-off. So every ancient site of any sort which had a British link was immediately sent guards while they still could. I don't think the Egyptians liked it, but...' He shrugged.

Eleanor nodded slowly. It made sense. The mask would have been too hot to sell immediately. Probably only Zaki would have bought it, and he'd refused. But there was something else about what Ludo had just told her that bothered her. Unable to pinpoint it, she concentrated on finding out more.

'What did you do then?'

'I decided to wait for two and a half months in Cairo before I would search those catacombs myself. Then I had a piece of luck.'

'Go on.' She glanced at the clock again.

'The Aswan catacombs were granted the licence to an archaeological dig.'

Eleanor's eyes widened. 'The catacombs in Aswan are the dig that you and Frederika are going to! Because you can search for the stolen mask without being questioned. That's why you were on the *Cleopatra* bound for there. And why you went to all the trouble of pretending to be married to secure yourselves the places on the dig.' Before he could expand on his nodded reply, she grimaced. 'Ludo, surely you knew you'd be recognised? You're quite distinctive-looking, you know?'

He held up a finger. 'I've changed my appearance as much as possible in case the go-between or his boss also decided to try and get the mask early.' He gestured at his head. 'I looked completely different before, without this hair and beard.'

She rose briskly and studied him with a disgusted expression. 'I don't believe you, Ludo. None of your story, actually.'

He leaped up. 'But it's true! Every word. Why do you think I am lying? Because I didn't tell you the whole truth before?'

'No. Because you're not telling me the whole truth now! You know one of those two young soldiers was shot dead during the raid. Private Morgan, actually. And the other soldier, Private Allen, wrongly blamed for his death.'

He shook his head in confusion. 'But they were part of it too, don't you see? Both soldiers had to be! One of them must have tried to double-cross his partner and been shot by him. That's why the group pretending to be bandits didn't cry off when they arrived and found the soldiers. And why the soldiers didn't run off when the bandits charged in, waving guns.'

'No, Ludo.' She fought the wave of sadness chilling her from head to toe. 'They were just two innocent young cadets who had no idea what was going on. Your go-between's boss shot Private Morgan who tried to bravely do the right thing.

And now Private Allen will be unjustly executed for it very soon.'

Hand over his mouth, Ludo collapsed back into his chair. 'Then... then I've as good as condemned that young soldier to death by starting the whole plan to steal the mask. I... I killed him through my greed.' He looked up, eyes swimming. 'But it's not too late! You said "soon" he'll be executed. I will confess now to Chief Sharaf and take the blame!'

She shook her head sadly. 'It will do no good. They'll see through your lies, anyway. And it won't help catch the real killer.'

'Frederika had nothing to do with any of this,' he murmured. 'If you only believe one thing I've said, let it be that. She wasn't even with me in Aswan.'

Eleanor shook her head again. 'I can't, Ludo. As the dominant one between you, I'm convinced you're covering for her.'

He jumped up. 'But you must believe me! Frederika isn't—'

'Isn't what?' Frederika's icy tone cut across the rest of his words.

Eleanor flinched. Had she been eavesdropping?

'Isn't good enough to even be your pretend wife?' Frederika strode forward and slapped Ludo's cheek as if making up for every woman scorned. 'Or isn't smart enough to realise she's just being used?' Tears spilled down her face. 'Forget it,' she said numbly, suddenly looking embarrassed in front of Eleanor and Clifford. 'This has all been too much, that's all. I'd better go back and apologise.'

Ludo gave her a wan smile and pointed at his cheek. 'No need. I'm sure I deserved this.'

'Not you,' she said scathingly. 'The man who did this.' She gestured at her dress.

Eleanor craned forward, but couldn't see— Ah! a faint streak of what? *Oil, Ellie?* Her brow furrowed.

Frederika nodded, wiping her eyes with a handkerchief from her bag. 'I shouldn't have been so rude when he bumped into me like that, but it's a new dress and I was—'

But Eleanor didn't hear the end of Frederika's sentence as she was already running for the door with Clifford in startled pursuit.

38

Eleanor wondered if there could be a more desolate spot in all of Egypt as she gazed around at the crumbling walls of the surrounding roofless buildings. Coupled with the once colourfully tiled floors losing the battle with the encroaching desert, they merely emphasised the bleakness of Bawaaba's 'empty quarter'. Whatever the town leaders may have hoped, it was clear the expected rush of tourists to Bawaaba's answer to Rome and Paris' catacombs had never materialised as Sharaf had said.

She pulled on her warmest cashmere jacket over the wool layer she already wore, barely noticing the prickly heat blistering her skin. Her thoughts were too full. She shielded her eyes, imploring the dancing orange spots from the blinding midday sun to stop blurring her vision. Beside her, Clifford was also squinting as he rose from lighting the two oil lanterns standing ready on the nearby rock. At their feet, a narrow opening descended into blackness.

If you're wrong, Ellie...

She crossed her fingers and started descending, feeling her way onto each of the crumbling spiral stone steps below as her eyes failed to adjust quickly enough to the feeble lantern light.

Despite her layers, she felt a chill take hold of her. But it was one of unease, not cold, even though the temperature was dropping rapidly as she corkscrewed downwards.

The increasingly stale air, laced with centuries-old dust, settled on her lungs, causing her to clear her throat. She paused, gesturing for Clifford to do likewise as she tied her scarf around her nose and mouth. This was no time to alert the enemy to their approach, especially with a fit of coughing or sneezing. Soon, even the lamps would need to be extinguished.

She stumbled off the last step onto the loose dirt and sand that made up the floor of the underground passages and caverns dug out centuries ago. Holding up her lantern, she noted the ancient scars of picks and chisels on the walls and ceiling.

Concentrate, Ellie. There's no time for sightseeing. The Cleopatra *sails in less than two hours.*

Hurrying forward, however, she silently groaned. Even in the inadequate light, she could see the start of at least three more passageways. Drawing level with them, it was obvious they too split in myriad directions. The whole place was an underground maze with no map to help retrace one's steps when, not if, one got lost.

For once, all Clifford could offer was the bemused shrug of a brow. She opted for the largest fork on the right, assuming the person they were tracking didn't know this labyrinth much better than they did, so would stick to the main tunnels. And her intuition also told her no sane person would have hidden a prize within easy reach of the entrance if it was worth killing an innocent man in cold blood for.

They pushed on, every few steps bringing them level with another cell-like chamber, accessible only to the most undernourished frame. The enormity of the task hit home; the murderer had a hundred places to hide themselves and to have hidden their spoils.

Straightening up too quickly after exploring yet one more of these chambers, she cracked her head on the rough stone. The shock made her stumble and close her eyes, stars shooting across them. Silently cursing, she pressed on, the creeping worry she was leading them further and further into the unknown becoming harder to shrug off.

Then, as she so often did at the most troubling times in her life, she felt her mother's presence at her side, whispering in her ear the same comforting words she used to offer before she vanished without a trace one night: "Follow your heart, darling girl. That alone can steer your feet best."

She nodded and blew a kiss heavenward. Beckoning to Clifford, she moved forward stealthily, with renewed confidence. A moment later, the tunnel ended in a cavern shaped like a giant bell. Three low openings led off.

But which one is the killer in, Ellie?

She strained for any sound. Nothing. Yet she had the creeping feeling they were no longer alone. And it wasn't a benign spirit this time. Risking a glance through the first opening, she could make out the start of an enormous cavern beyond. But to reach it, they'd have to walk through what looked like a graveyard of bones.

'They are animal bones, my lady,' Clifford whispered as he joined her. He advanced a few steps into the tunnel, holding his lantern out before recoiling. 'And some I'm almost sure are... human!'

She pointed back the way they'd come. He nodded, but before she could move, a sound came from somewhere—

In front, Ellie?

It was difficult to tell with the acoustics in the bell-shaped cavern. She stiffened as the sound echoed almost imperceptibly around the walls again.

She held her breath. Silence. Then a muffled cry of triumph filtered out from the furthest opening. They both extinguished their lanterns and flattened themselves against the far wall, Clifford slowly withdrawing his service revolver.

After what seemed minutes, but must have been seconds, a figure appeared carrying a lantern in one hand and a cloth-wrapped bundle held tightly in the other. As the figure hurried into the cavern, Eleanor swiftly stuck her foot out, sending it tumbling.

She clicked on her torch as the figure scrambled to its knees. 'Not the most elegant entrance, Mr Merrick,' she said grimly. 'But then slithering about in the dirt is where your kind belongs.'

She flinched as he pulled a gun from the bundle he carried, but Clifford had already fired... only he hadn't!

She gasped

It's jammed, Ellie!

Without hesitation, she hurled her lantern at Merrick and covered her face with her hands just before he fired. Shattered glass sprayed spitefully as the bullet buried itself into the wall behind her. She glanced at Clifford, who was pulling violently on his revolver.

Scrabbling to his feet, Merrick kept his gun aimed directly at her chest.

She turned back to him. 'Actually, I was wrong,' she said calmly. 'Where you belong is dangling from a noose.'

Clifford nodded emphatically. 'I heartily agree, my lady.'

Merrick waved his gun. 'Drop your revolver. Now! It's no use to you anyway,' he said smugly. 'It seems rather to have let you down at a critical moment!'

Clifford shrugged. 'This is the first time I can recall such an event occurring. Which is a shame as it has temporarily rendered me unable to deal with vermin like you as I would see fit.'

Merrick's face reddened. He swung his gun towards Clifford's chest. 'You sound just like Father! Well, I'm the one in charge now!'

Eleanor's mocking laugh echoed around the cavern. 'Really? You? In charge? After the catalogue of mistakes you have made?'

His face contorted with rage. 'I do not make mistakes! My plan has worked perfectly. Even with you and your butler sticking your noses into things that don't concern you.'

Don't overdo it, Ellie. He's getting too off-balance.

'I take your point, Merrick,' she said, keeping a tremble from her voice. 'After all, you've been meticulous about your plan. Yet, somehow you've still been found out.'

His tongue flicked over his bottom lip. 'So tell me, before I get bored and put a bullet in you and your butler, what "mistakes" have I made exactly? Because from where I'm standing' – he raised the gun further – 'I'd say the mistakes are all on your part...'

39

Eleanor took a deep breath, aware of Clifford's eyes checking out any opportunity to turn the tables. She shifted slightly to the right to give him a little more cover.

'Actually, Merrick, let me correct you on that. Mistake number one on your part; thinking no one would guess where you'd hidden the mask. Wrong! You see, Bawaaba has been the gateway to this puzzle all along. Not Aswan as, I admit, I thought for so long. It was the inexplicable fact that the *Cleopatra* docked in Bawaaba as part of her itinerary that finally gave the game away. It's a tiny town on the edge of the desert with nothing at all attractive to the type of tourist who typically takes a Nile cruise. Or even those working or researching. No, something else was obviously making it worthwhile for the *Cleopatra* to stop here. The same thing, in fact, which made it worthwhile for the Cairo authorities to send Chief Sharaf here. And also why Chief Sharaf planned to impound the *Cleopatra* before Lieutenant Baxter had even died. You see, I learned "Bawaaba" means "gateway". Fitting, as Mahmoud Zaki used it as the gateway for his operations. And you used it to hide the mask here after you tried to sell it to him and he refused. Which makes you, without a doubt, the "boss" mentioned in Baxter's testimonial who arranged the raid on the Dutch and British archaeologists. And the man Ludo called the go-between was one of your men, I take it?'

'My right-hand man, if we're being accurate, Lady Swift.' He waved his gun threateningly for her to continue.

'Mistake number two. During the raid, you killed a young soldier, Private Gareth Morgan. In cold blood,' she said with disgust. 'Which made the mask too hot to buy. Added to that, the British authorities had been told about the mask. And they wanted it. So you were forced to hide it. Which is where Ludo comes in again. You see, he told me he was just a "Dutch archaeologist". Not a thief. Or a bandit. So when he overheard you telling the go-between that the mask was going to be hidden in the catacombs until the fuss died down, he assumed you meant the Aswan catacombs.' She shook her head disparagingly. 'Whereas a seasoned thief like yourself, Merrick, would never have risked hiding the mask in the same town it was stolen from when you knew there was a safer option. Bawaaba's own, much less well known, catacombs, underneath the empty quarter. All you needed to do was wait, then collect the mask and sail down the Nile to sell it yourself in Cairo, or maybe even Alexandria. Or perhaps you hoped Zaki might have changed his tune by then and you could sell it directly to him?'

She flicked out her curls, discreetly directing the shower of glass shards at his feet. His hand gripped the gun tighter.

'Very clever, Lady Swift! But none of this could have led you to guess I killed Baxter. Or that useless deckhand!'

She gritted her teeth, but then forced herself to relax. 'You're right. It didn't. What did was, number one.' She ticked the points off on her fingers. 'Only you, Ludo, Piltz and Anders spent most of the last two years or more here in Egypt. And therefore could have set up a criminal organisation with the contacts to arrange the raid on the camp and sell the mask. We checked Trott's passport and then got Sharaf to check the rest when we realised how important it was to identifying the killer.'

Clifford tutted. 'Then you made the error of mimicking me.'

Eleanor nodded. 'Big mistake, Merrick. When you did so in the games room at the El Asafa Hotel, it was such a remarkable likeness, it proved you're an incomparable mimic. And that answered perhaps the most perplexing of all the questions. Why hadn't Lieutenant Baxter recognised the killer's voice on the SS *Cleopatra*? We know why he never recognised the killer's features, because he never saw them. But he heard the killer. He threatened to shoot Baxter. The only answer could be because the killer cleverly disguised his voice!'

'Anything else?' Merrick said, his eyes narrowing.

She winced exaggeratedly. 'Plenty. The broken pen clip I found in Baxter's cabin? When I taxed you the second time about it, you confessed it was yours but you'd lent it to him unwillingly. And I admit, it was almost convincing. Until I ran back over your story. A fastidious man so desperately in need of his pens as a crutch for his anxiety as you'd portrayed yourself, could never have left that broken clip on the floor.' She fought the wave of nausea that rose in her throat. 'You made Lieutenant Baxter write his own fake suicide note with that very pen. Then shot him. And dashed out to let off the second shot through the porthole of the empty cabin, too preoccupied to even notice the pen clip you'd stamped on. Sloppy, Merrick. Very sloppy.' She grimaced. 'But there's worse.'

A muscle in Merrick's jaw pulsed. 'My plan still worked. I have the mask and you two fools at gunpoint. Who's the sloppy one, eh?'

'We shall have to find out, Mr Merrick.' Clifford pulled a handkerchief slowly out of his top pocket. 'I believe you have a splinter of glass near your eye, my lady.' Keeping eye contact with Merrick, he passed it over to her. As she took it, he met her gaze. She dabbed at her eye, then laughed raucously.

Caught unawares, Merrick scowled. 'What the hell are you laughing at?'

She carried on dabbing her eye while still laughing. 'Your vanity! It was your fourth and greatest mistake.' Clifford's handkerchief slipped from her fingers as she switched her expression to one of disgust and folded her arms. 'That hair oil you wear. You inadvertently smeared some on Frederika's dress this morning when you collided with her. I recognised it instantly as being the same oil smeared on poor Farah's robe. I assume you got the oil on his robe while you were searching him to make sure he didn't have Lieutenant Baxter's testimonial? I don't know if Farah told you he hadn't, and you didn't believe him, or what. But I do know that's when you condemned yourself to death!'

'Your handkerchief, my lady,' Clifford said just before she'd finished speaking. With Merrick's eyes still on her, he'd knelt down to pick it up. As he did, Merrick noticed the movement and swung around to face him. Too late. Like a magician, Clifford hurled the sand and glass shard filled handkerchief into Merrick's eyes.

Merrick yelled out as he clawed at his face with one hand while firing off two shaky shots with the other. Clifford, however, had already rolled to the right and Eleanor to the left. Springing up, Clifford headbutted him in the stomach, knocking him to the ground. Not with quite enough force to loosen his grip on the gun, though. Scrabbling up, she thought for a moment Merrick was going to stand and fight. But then he let off another random shot that whipped past her ear and ran.

'He's making for the entrance!' Eleanor yelled as loud as she could, for Merrick's benefit, not Clifford's. Her butler was running by her side, but Merrick probably still had more bullets, and they needed him to panic and waste them. It was a dangerous gambit, but with Clifford's revolver jammed solid, they needed to even up the odds.

Trusting her intuition that Merrick knew the catacombs slightly better than she did, as he'd been there at least once before, she followed him. It was too risky to try to cut him off by taking a different route through the maze of passageways. Just before they turned a corner, Clifford hurled the lantern he was still carrying at Merrick's back, immediately pressing himself and Eleanor against the wall. Merrick yelped and, half turning, fired off another two poorly aimed shots which sailed harmlessly past them.

Ahead of them, Merrick's footsteps echoed on the stone steps as he started up the spiral stairs to the entrance.

'He's getting away, Clifford!' she yelled, calling on her last ounce of reserve as she sped up.

'My lady! He still has a bullet, remember!' Clifford shouted in warning.

Her lungs burning, her breath ragged, she slowed to keep one twist of the staircase between her and Merrick's remaining bullet.

It's too dangerous to try and catch him on the stairs, Ellie. And once he's out in the open, he can pick you off as soon as your head appears.

Groaning silently, she slowed to a stop as she reached the top, only to hear the smack of a fist and Merrick cry out. Leaping out of the catacombs entrance into the blinding light, she shielded her eyes with her hands as a coarse London voice gruffed, 'I don't like you, pal!'

'Arthur?' she gasped, staring from the staggering Merrick clutching his face to the angry cockney. Barr winked.

'No charge. This one's on me, princess.'

As he lunged to punch Merrick again, she cried, 'Stop, Arthur! He's got one bullet left!'

'That's right,' Merrick smirked, removing his hand from his bleeding jaw and waving his gun.

She shrugged as Clifford joined her. 'You're still outnumbered, Merrick. One bullet. But three of us.'

Facing them, with his gun swinging wildly between them, Merrick retreated, stumbling backwards. 'If any of you move, I'll—'

'Snake!' she cried. 'On that rock. Behind you!'

'Haven't you tried enough pantomime, Lady Swift?' Merrick scoffed and, to her horror, took another step backwards. 'I've won. And you've lo—' Merrick's last bullet flew out across the desert as he fell sideways over the rock, then screamed.

Eleanor instinctively went to rush forward, but Clifford and Barr restrained her. The snake had reared up again at her approach, its hood inflated. For a moment, it swung from one to the other of them, then dropped to the ground and slithered away.

'Egyptian cobra that. Deadly,' Barr said matter-of-factly as the three of them reached the sprawled figure of Merrick, who was clutching his neck, lips flapping, eyes filled with horror. 'You, mate, are done for.'

Clifford nodded. 'It is generally believed the asp Cleopatra used to kill herself was an Egyptian cobra.'

Eleanor's heart faltered as she remembered Trott's words at the first dinner aboard the *Cleopatra*; 'Its venom can kill an adult elephant in only three hours.'

'Hurry!' she said determinedly. 'We need to get him to a doctor as quickly as possible!' She darted to his side and rallied her nurse's training and experience in the South African bush to the fore.

Barr shook his head. 'Fifteen minutes tops for a big strong ox of a bloke to die from a bite in the neck like that. This runt is not even a bantam. I'm tellin' you it's hopeless.'

'And I'm telling you we try anyway!' she shot back. She felt for Merrick's pulse while trying to swallow her horror at the rate of swelling on his neck, where the cobra's puncture wounds were clearly visible. 'But he has to be carried.'

'And carefully,' Clifford added, holding a handkerchief under Merrick's lips as he began to drool.

Barr rolled his eyes. 'Or we could use my horse and trap instead? It's over there behind that wall. It's slow, but it'll still be faster than carrying him.'

'Get it, man!' Clifford commanded.

'We'll do our best, Merrick,' Eleanor said as Barr hurried off. 'The doctors will have an anti-venom in the hospital,' she added soothingly, hoping desperately that was the case, but doubting it at the same time.

Merrick blinked rapidly back at her, the muscles of his heavily sweating face twitching feverishly. 'Too late,' he slurred through his lips, which were swelling alarmingly. 'Arms feeling quite numb already. But I'll... I'll tell you everything.' An unnerving flicker of malevolence streaked through his glassy-eyed look as he held her gaze. 'Then you'll know why... why you've still lost. And I've won!'

40

Propped up on Eleanor's jacket, his top half swathed in Clifford's, Merrick lay in the back of Barr's horse and trap. His breathing sounded increasingly laboured as she huddled next to him. Clifford deftly slid his tall, slim frame on the other side of the sick man as Barr started the horse off at a steady trot.

'Don't trust me with your mistress?' Merrick wheezed at Clifford.

'Not an inch, Mr Merrick, but you wanted to have your moment.'

'While you still can!' Eleanor caught Barr mutter up front.

She checked Merrick's pulse. It was weakening by the minute. 'I'm listening,' she said, releasing his wrist.

'Good,' he breathed raggedly. 'Father is a self-made man. Rich. And a rotten bully. Made my life hell as a boy. I learned early to shut up and play the submissive son. "Yes, Father, this. No, Father, that". I...' He strained against the floor of the trap but was too weak to sit up. He groaned, obviously now in serious pain.

Eleanor gently applied another of Clifford's handkerchiefs

to the stream of blood still trickling from the snake bite as the horse and cart turned onto the road into town.

'That must have made working in his business difficult?' she said, to keep him talking. And conscious.

Merrick's swollen mauve lips twisted into a sneer, making his already contorted face even more ghoulish. 'No. It was my plan from the start! Make Father think he could pull my strings. Then I could use him. And beat him. Was never going to get rich on the crumbs he threw my way. Always knew I was better than him, anyway. And Felix too, my stupid stepbrother. He showed his hand. Refused to stay working for Father because he's too moral, the prig.'

Something in his tone made Eleanor break her intention to just let him speak. 'You never did tell me what line of business your father is in?'

His eyes rolled towards her, his pupils dilated. 'Arms, Lady Swift. Lovely, lovely guns.'

She focused on refreshing the now blood-soaked handkerchief. Out of the corner of her eye, she saw they were nearing the centre of town. Clifford pointed over her shoulder. She turned to see Sharaf hurrying up the street towards the police station from the direction of the El Asafa. She mopped Merrick's brow and raised her voice.

'It's going to be fine, Merrick. We'll be at the hospital in minutes.'

The policeman jerked around, then, having spotted her, nodded and broke into a sprint back the way he'd come.

'You were saying about your father?' she coaxed.

It was all Merrick could do to nod. She leaned closer to catch his words.

'He'll cut me out of my inheritance when I leave. He's no idea,' Merrick continued. 'I've been using his expenses to make my own successful business. In crime.' He tried to laugh, but was caught in a paroxysm of coughing which sprayed more blood onto the handkerchief. The fact he was talking as if he still had the upper hand disturbed her. But more so that he didn't seem to have any remorse. Even now, in the throes of—

Death, Ellie.

'Nearly there.' Barr steered them off the main street.

'Living and travelling in Egypt allowed you to make some useful, if dubious, contacts, I imagine,' she said, giving Merrick a moment to catch his breath.

He nodded weakly again. 'I was in prime position after the Tutankhamun tomb finds made the market explode. That's why I jumped on the chance to get that mask. And you know the rest.' His legs convulsed as he tried to sit up. 'The mask! Where's the mask?'

'It's here,' Eleanor said, far more calmly than she felt. She could now see a brick two-storeyed building that had the hallmarks of a small-town hospital. They swung through the gates onto the driveway. A group of chattering white-aproned women stood around a row of wooden trolleys waiting outside a set of open double doors.

Barr jerked the horse to a stop and leapt out, semaphoring to the women and calling out urgently in Arabic.

A puffing Sharaf appeared from around the corner of the building. He shot up to the trap and stared at Merrick, then Eleanor, with an enquiring look.

She lowered her voice. 'Snake bite. Cobra.'

Sharaf nodded matter-of-factly. She could see the unspoken words in his eyes. Just a matter of time. She winced and nodded back, patting Merrick's hand, which drew no response, telling her he had now lost all feeling in it.

'You haven't said how you knew Lieutenant Baxter was planning to come clean about who really killed Private Morgan? Which was who, by the way?'

Merrick seemed oblivious that Sharaf had arrived, his eyes

heavily glazed and fixed on his feet. 'Me. I shot him. Idiot boy was trying to be a hero!'

Eleanor's stomach roiled with nausea at his black-hearted callousness. 'And you killed Lieutenant Baxter to stop him telling the authorities in the Aswan barracks the truth, didn't you? And you killed Farah because you had no more use for him after he got you the keys to cabin five and couldn't find Baxter's testimonial?'

Merrick's laugh turned to a gurgle. 'Yes.'

She glanced up at Sharaf, who nodded back in acknowledgement.

'And you knew Baxter was travelling on the *Cleopatra* how?' she said evenly.

Merrick managed a twisted smirk. 'He told his old and trusted... army friend. The fool!'

'The one who encouraged him to join your raid where you stole the mask?'

'That's the one. The joke is he... he works for me,' Merrick said with a sudden trickle of renewed vigour. 'Lady Swift, here's another lesson for you. Never trust your friends!'

A doctor ran out of the hospital, with a nurse in tow carrying a silver kidney-dish. Eleanor jumped out, along with Clifford, to give the doctor room.

Merrick groaned as a convulsion took hold of him. The doctor peeled back both of the dying man's eyelids with a swift hand. He lifted the handkerchief covering the now sickening black fist-sized swelling around the bite and frowned.

'Hurry, Doctor, the anti-venom, please,' Eleanor begged, pointing at the syringes in the kidney-dish.

So they did have some, Ellie.

The doctor shook his head pragmatically and selected the smaller syringe.

'This one only.' He plunged it without ceremony into

Merrick. 'To lessen the pain. Nothing can save him now. He has two, three minutes to live at the very most.'

Merrick's ragged breathing was drowned out by Sharaf's second in command panting up to them.

'Urgent message, Chief!'

Eleanor shook her head. Nothing could be urgent enough to interrupt the last moments of a dying man. No matter who that man was.

'The British soldier to be executed in Aswan.'

She spun around, hopeful of some good news.

'The execution. It's been moved forward to this afternoon!'

41

'This afternoon?' Eleanor murmured, her legs threatening to buckle.

Clifford stepped close to her side, his face filled with concern. 'My lady, you tried everything.'

'I won, Lady Swift!' Merrick's tremulous voice called up to her.

She turned slowly back to see Merrick gazing triumphantly up at her through yellowing eyes.

'You... you arranged for the execution date to be changed?' she gasped.

'Yes! Just as I got Sharaf's orders over... overruled so the *Cleopatra* could leave. Zaki isn't the only one with influence,' he wheezed gloatingly.

'What gives you that influence, Mr Merrick?' Sharaf said grimly.

'All the guns I sell, of course.' He coughed so hard she thought it was the end. But he recovered enough to continue, although she had to lean close to his mouth to catch his fading words. 'Zaki isn't your gunrunner. I am! I took a leaf out of Father's book and sold to both sides. And many guns found their way into the hands of desert bandits, not soldiers, for a price. So I had dirt on British and Egyptian officials.' His whole body shook as he laughed maniacally. 'Now Baxter and Farah are dead, that soldier is the only one who can point the finger at me. Who can have me convicted for killing his colleague the night of the raid.' His words became fainter and more slurred. 'I realised you were shrewd enough to work it out in the end, Lady Swift. So I had his execution brought forward.' For a moment, his eyes glowed evilly. 'You see. I was right. You still lose. And I still w—' The light in his eyes faded as he convulsed violently.

Eleanor's hand flew to her mouth as the doctor leaned over him.

'He is dead.'

Clifford took her gently by the arm and steered her away from the pitiful image now lying motionless. 'My lady, you did so much more for him than that monster deserved.'

She shook her head. 'Hideous though it feels to say it, I'm not upset for Merrick. He died as he lived. Violently. It's Private Allen I'm thinking of!' She turned to Sharaf. 'There must be something you can do? You heard Merrick's confession...'

She broke off at the policeman's emphatic headshake. 'I am sorry, Lady Swift. But the Egyptian police have no influence on the British Army. Not even now my country is supposedly independent. They are the ones who have sentenced him.'

Clifford also shook his head. 'And regrettably, his lordship, your late uncle, held no sway in this part of the world, so invoking his name with the British authorities in Aswan will do no good either.'

Sharaf nodded. 'Aswan is hundreds of miles down the Nile from here.' He gestured at Anders, who was striding towards them. 'You would never reach there in time, Lady Swift. Even with the SS *Cleopatra* being repaired and ready to sail, which I assume is what you have come to tell me,' he added, turning to Anders.

'No, Sharaf. It isn't,' Anders said forcefully. 'I'm here to speak to Lady Swift, who I've just found out was responsible for sabotaging my boat.'

'Not now, Anders!' Clifford growled.

'Yes, now!' the captain shot back. He unexpectedly smiled at Eleanor. 'I have just spoken to the doctor who heard you talking. You may have sabotaged my boat, Lady Swift, but by catching Baxter and Farah's killer, you've saved me from the double murder charge Sharaf had me fitted up for.'

'You're welcome.' She smiled weakly. 'But in Chief Sharaf's defence, I might have had something to do with that as well.'

He smiled ruefully. 'It doesn't matter now. But the life of that young soldier does. Lady Swift, you stopped that cur Merrick getting away with murder when he was alive. And I'd bet the SS *Cleopatra* herself that you're not going to let him get away with murder now he's dead!'

Her eyes flashed. 'You're dead right!' She flinched. 'Bad choice of words.'

'But excellent choice of sentiment,' Clifford muttered.

'It's a long shot, but meet me at the jetty in one hour,' Anders called over his shoulder as he sprinted away.

An hour later, Eleanor stood on the jetty next to the SS *Cleopatra* with an equally confused butler and chief of police. Barr joined them, shaking his head.

'What's his game? That old heap won't get you to Aswan by next week, let alone by this afternoon!'

Sharaf nodded. 'Even if Captain Anders were to sail her at full steam all the way, there is no chance you would arrive in time. I have no idea what—'

'Lady Swift!' Anders appeared at the other end on the jetty, waving his hands.

She hurried to meet him, followed by the others.

'What's the plan?' she said, still frowning in puzzlement.

His reply was lost in the loud throbbing overhead. Her fiery curls were whipped out sideways in the wind that had sprung from nowhere. He pointed upwards. 'That's the plan!'

She stared into the sky, shielding her eyes from not only the sun, but the rush of air from the wings of a seaplane.

'A... plane?' she was still repeating in disbelief as the pilot motored back and brought it to a graceful halt alongside the end of the pier not occupied by the *Cleopatra*.

'Courtesy of Mr Zaki!' the pilot said with a salute as he stepped out onto the float.

Sharaf whistled. 'Lady Swift, my second in command told me it was Mahmoud Zaki who sent the message about the change of date of the execution to my police station. And now he has sent this here. I believe you have found the heart in him he himself never knew he had.'

She smiled. 'Perhaps. But maybe also there's a little bit of him that likes the idea of being the saviour of the day.' She shrugged. 'But a plane has to be our only hope.'

Clifford slid the cloth-wrapped bundle Merrick had retrieved from the catacombs out from under his jacket.

'Gracious, I nearly forgot.'

She handed it reverently to Sharaf, who swiftly, but carefully, unwrapped it. His breath caught as he gazed in wonder at the treasure in his hands. She gasped as he held up the gold headpiece, perfectly encapsulating the face of a young boy picked out in gems of mesmerising blue lapis lazuli and raven-black obsidian. The gold and carnelian on the back reflected the sun, making it seem as if it was actually in flames. He offered it out for her to hold.

'No, thank you,' she said quietly. 'There's a spirit searching for that. And I'm sure you know what best to do with it.'

Sharaf nodded, smiling broadly. 'Good luck, Lady Swift.'

'Oi?' Arthur yelled as she stepped into the plane, followed by Clifford. 'Well?'

'Yes, Arthur,' she called back, nodding. 'Whatever happens now, you're still an absolute hero, my friend.'

As the pilot revved the engine, and her fingers fumbled to buckle her lap harness, she bit her lip anxiously. 'Clifford? Tell me we won't be too late?'

He hesitated. 'Would that I could promise such, my lady. However, if it is not to be, you will have done Private Allen the greatest honour possible. By clearing his name. Even...' he faltered, 'even if posthumously.'

EPILOGUE

ENGLAND 26 JULY 1924 (A MONTH LATER)

The drizzle accompanied them as they left Southampton and, under leaden skies, headed out into the waterlogged English countryside. They drove for hours in virtual silence, the only sound being the rumble of the Rolls and the splattering of the rain.

Eventually, the village of Lower Mundy, nestled in the rolling folds of the Quantock Hills, greeted them listlessly as they turned off onto what passed for a main road, leaving the car no choice but to splash down the rutted byway.

As Clifford finally steered them onto the cobbled high street, Eleanor glanced around. Normally, even in the rain, she'd have smiled at the whitewashed cottages and thatched roofs lining the way, but today her mind and heart were too full. Then, just as the Rolls turned into a small cul-de-sac and eased to a stop, the sunless sky seemed to relent, the drizzle slowing.

In front of them crouched a sleepy cottage. But in the parlour window, she could see a thick candle burning brightly. And behind it, a middle-aged couple who jumped up and hurried to the window at the sound of a car stopping, their faces pressed anxiously against the glass.

'Please, just hurry to them,' she whispered, her overspilling emotions having taken all but the last of her voice. Her eyes welled up as the young man beside her reached forward to shake Clifford's hand, before turning back and squeezing hers without a word.

'Goodbye, Wilfred,' she managed through a stifled sob as the young soldier climbed out and saluted her and Clifford.

His hasty stride up the tiled path turned into a euphoric sprint as the front door flew open and the couple ran out to meet him. The young man was swamped in a heartfelt hug as his mother and father encircled him.

Without Eleanor needing to ask, Clifford quietly drove away. She looked back through a cascade of happy tears to see him still wrapped in his parents' arms. Their three heads were pressed together, a ray of sunlight beaming down on them from the heavens as the sun broke through the clouds.

'Oh, Clifford,' she said breathlessly. 'There's a faint rainbow arcing over the cottage.' She choked.

Miracles do happen, Ellie. And dreams do come true.

She was overcome with the need to hug her loved ones. Having to content herself with those nearby, she squeezed Gladstone and Tomkins as hard as she dared. And if she couldn't hug her fiancé or ladies...

Letting go of her bulldog and tomcat, she scrambled into the front seat. Clifford opened his mouth, but she silenced him with a pleading hand. 'This is not the time for a lecture in—'

'No lecture forthcoming, my lady. I was merely going to ask if you had made a wish on seeing the rainbow?'

She nodded. 'And I just saw it come true on the garden path of a tiny cottage.'

He peered sideways at her. 'I rather believed you were supposed to make a wish for a *future* event coming true?'

She shrugged. 'I don't think I could be that greedy, Clifford.

Not after witnessing...' She broke off to dab her eyes with the handkerchief he passed her.

'I thoroughly agree, my lady. And it would have been a wasted wish to hope my mistress might—'

'Ever become a decorous lady?' She laughed, failing to dodge Gladstone's slobbery kisses.

'Oh, how the dream fades! Thankfully,' he added, to her amazement.

She gaped at him. 'Clifford?'

He slowed the Rolls and turned to her. 'My lady. Young Private Allen's circumstances would have ended tragically but for your irrepressible selflessness, fortitude and courage.'

'By which, beneath your respectful dressing up of words, you mean maddening obstinacy, impatience and impetuousness? As well as my total disregard for propriety and decorum?'

'Most assuredly,' he said with a wink, which made her roar with laughter.

'You are a terrible man, Clifford. But one I can't imagine life without.'

'No escape for me then, gentlemen!' he stage whispered to Gladstone and Tomkins.

She was too filled with affection not to squeeze his arm just this once. Evidently harder than she'd intended as the Rolls veered wildly left.

'Sorry!' she said, catching herself yawning. 'I admit I'm rather wrung out with all the emotion.'

He reached under his seat. She took the petite leather case he passed her with a shrug.

'Lovely thought, Clifford. Bit small for a picnic though, isn't it? You said Henley Hall is at least three hours away from here?'

He tapped it in enigmatic reply.

Unbuckling it, she gently pushed her bulldog and tomcat's greedy faces away as they snuck up front, scenting treats. Inside was a brandy miniature, diminutive balloon glass and a bar of chocolate. And, folded meticulously, a newspaper.

'The English edition of the *Egyptian Gazette*? But how?'

'Alas, discretion forbids, my lady. However, page three.'

She turned to the page, struggling with Tomkins' excited flurry of paws batting at the paper. There was no need to scan the print. The headline leaped out at her.

She read aloud, '*Double killer captured.*' Wait, there's more below the headline. '*Within his first week of being appointed the new chief of police in Bawaaba, Yakub Sharaf captured the murderer of an English army veteran and an Egyptian sailor.*' She sighed. 'What a relief. I thought he'd never agree to take the credit. He's a very fine policeman.'

'The gentleman was most reluctant, my lady. Though I noted a quoted line wherein he wholeheartedly acknowledged anonymous help of an unorthodox nature.'

'I wonder where he got that phrase from, hmm? However, I'm just relieved it's all over.'

'Perhaps, then, it is better not to relive the events by reading on down, but turn to pages four and five instead?'

Having won the battle with Tomkins a second time, she gasped. 'A double-page spread with a photograph! *Yakub Sharaf, the new chief of police of Bawaaba with the mask he recovered from the murderer.*' She read on: '*This priceless artefact which the murderer was attempting to smuggle out of the country will now be displayed in perpetuum for all to revere in Cairo's Museum.*' She stared at Clifford. 'It says it's to be transported there under heavy guard, including, by special request, a small British Army presence.'

He nodded. 'Chief Sharaf's way of immortalising the cooperation between an Egyptian policeman and an English titled lady, which, as he'd hoped, proved to be a mighty force for justice. Also, at his insistence, your name will be included on the plaque which will accompany the mask once on display.'

She winced with embarrassment. 'Gracious, I didn't expect that. And I thought I was done with emotion for today.'

'Not a chance, my lady. Hence the fortification of the brandy and chocolate.'

She looked at him suspiciously. 'What ruse have you got up your butlering sleeves now? I thought we were just going home to Henley Hall to collapse?' She took a sip of the brandy and savoured a mouthful of the delectable chocolate.

'Indeed we are, my lady. However, via the railway station at Oxford to collect your reprobate ladies. For comestible shopping of a most irregular nature, I fear. RSVP has yet to be received from one party, mind you.' He pointed at her.

She laughed. 'Stop teasing and tell me!'

'Your ladyship, you are formally invited by your staff, and Masters Gladstone and Tomkins, of course, to join them for a disgraceful breaking of all known rules of etiquette and decorum.'

Her hand flew to her mouth. 'A party!'

'Indeed. Into the small hours, no doubt, in Henley Hall's kitchen with unwise amounts of your cook's home-made fayre, and home-brewed concoctions. "And platter-loads of all the best fancies to put some meat on the longest, finest set of bones I did ever see in Buckinghamshire",' he added in a flawless imitation of her cook, Mrs Trotman.

Eleanor clapped her hands with glee. 'You mean Hugh's coming too?'

He nodded. 'Chief Inspector Seldon, as your betrothed, might as well find out in advance just how beleaguered your poor butler is. Certainly, in trying to restrain the five reprehensibly behaved women whom he will be shackled with permanently at some point. Whenever that may be?' He glanced at her, eyes bright.

'We agreed on a long engagement, you know that.' She settled back in her seat, cuddling Tomkins curled up in her lap with one hand, and Gladstone in the footwell with the other. 'But we'll just have to wait and see if he survives tonight's party!'

A LETTER FROM VERITY

Dear reader,

I want to say a huge thank you for choosing to read *Murder on the Nile*. If you did enjoy it, and want to keep up to date with all my latest releases, just sign up at the following link. Your email address will never be shared and you can unsubscribe at any time.

www.bookouture.com/verity-bright

I hope you loved *Murder on the Nile* and if you did I would be very grateful if you could write a review. I'd love to hear what you think, and it makes such a difference helping new readers to discover one of my books for the first time.

I love hearing from my readers – you can get in touch through social media or my website.

Thanks,

Verity

www.veritybright.com

HISTORICAL NOTES

ANGLO-EGYPTIAN WAR

Egypt was mostly under the rule of the Ottoman Empire until 1882, when Britain went to war with Egypt over protection of its interests in the country. From that point, even though Egypt wasn't officially part of the British Empire, Britain controlled it. And Clifford, as ever, was quite right. Even after Egyptian independence in 1922, British troops didn't leave the country in any number until thirty-four years later, in 1956.

SUEZ CANAL

Clifford tells Eleanor that one of the British interests the army is there to protect is the Suez Canal. An amazing feat of engineering, the canal connects the Mediterranean Sea with the Red Sea. Built in 1869, the canal was officially owned by Egypt, but Britain and France had, in reality, controlling shares. Interestingly, the Suez Canal was the inspiration for the Statue of Liberty that features in another Lady Swift mystery, *Murder in Manhattan.* The idea for the statue was originally to have it cast as an Egyptian woman in traditional costume with a torch, but the French sculptor couldn't find any interest in Egypt. So he tried selling the idea elsewhere, until New York decided they couldn't do without it. And the rest is history.

THE NILE

Often referred to as the longest river in the world (although some claim the Amazon is longer!), the Nile runs the full length of Egypt. But it also travels through ten other countries during its four-thousand-mile journey. It is still a vitally important asset to Egypt, with over ninety-five per cent of its population living in, or around the river. And if you fancy it, you can still take the same boat up the Nile that a famous crime writer took a hundred years ago, before penning a rather well-known novel. And, as Clifford would tell you, it's definitely more luxurious than the SS *Cleopatra*!

THE ASWAN DAM(S)

You may notice that Clifford only refers to one Aswan Dam in the book. Is this finally a chink in his encyclopaedic knowledge? Actually, no. In 1924, there was only one dam. Built between 1899 and 1902 by the British and known as the 'low' dam, it was the largest masonry dam in the world at the time. The second dam, the 'high' dam, was built between 1960 and 1970 and was the tallest earthen dam in the world. As my knowledge of dam construction is quite limited, I think I'll stop here before Clifford witters my ears off, as Eleanor knows all too well. :)

TUTANKHAMUN

Tutankhamun's tomb was discovered in 1922 by the British archaeologist, Howard Carter. The discovery sparked a huge worldwide interest in Egyptian relics which many people, including Merrick, tried to take advantage of. What is not so widely known is that as well as the gold funeral mask, Carter also found over five thousand other items in the tomb. Including a vast array of shoes, some of which might have appealed to Zaki's sense of theatre as they had images of Tutankhamun's enemies on the soles so he could crush them whenever he walked.

NILE CROCODILE

Trott may be trying to goad his stepbrother, Merrick, by quoting facts about the Nile crocodile, but he's not lying. The Nile crocodile is reckoned to kill hundreds (or even thousands) of people a year. To put that in perspective, that is more than all the other crocodile species put together. Over sixty per cent of all attacks by the Nile crocodile are fatal. Trott was also right about the Egyptians mummifying crocodiles and worshipping them. One such croc, known as 'Sharp Teeth' or 'Lord of Fear', was worshipped as the embodiment of Sobek, a half man, half-crocodile god.

EGYPTIAN COBRA

Just like the Nile crocodile, the Egyptian cobra is a deadly animal. As Arthur Barr rightly says, its venom can kill an adult elephant in three hours. However, unlike the Nile crocodile, it does not attack people unless provoked. (And yes, falling on one as Merrick does while it's sunbathing on a rock constitutes provoking in the extreme!) Like the Nile crocodile, however, it had great significance to the ancient Egyptians, often appearing on pharaohs' headdresses as a symbol of power, or protection. Perhaps the Egyptian cobra's greatest claim to fame, as Clifford states, is that it is believed it was the snake referred to as an 'asp' that Cleopatra apparently used to commit suicide.

SILENCERS

It is never established whether Merrick did use a silencer (or suppressor as they were known then as well) to kill Baxter and Farah. The American inventor, Hiram Percy Maxim, is credited with inventing the first usable silencer around 1902 and patenting it in 1909. By 1920, there were various models available, so it was perfectly feasible Merrick, who was in the gun trade, may have used one.

ACKNOWLEDGEMENTS

A huge thanks to all at Bookouture for their part in making *Murder on the Nile* so much fun to work on.

PUBLISHING TEAM

Turning a manuscript into a book requires the efforts of many people. The publishing team at Bookouture would like to acknowledge everyone who contributed to this publication.

Audio
Alba Proko
Sinead O'Connor
Melissa Tran

Commercial
Lauren Morrissette
Hannah Richmond
Imogen Allport

Cover design
Tash Webber

Data and analysis
Mark Alder
Mohamed Bussuri

Editorial
Kelsie Marsden
Nadia Michael

Copyeditor
Jane Eastgate

Proofreader
Liz Hatherell

Marketing
Alex Crow
Melanie Price
Occy Carr
Cíara Rosney
Martyna Młynarska

Operations and distribution
Marina Valles
Stephanie Straub

Production
Hannah Snetsinger
Mandy Kullar
Jen Shannon
Ria Clare

Publicity
Kim Nash
Noelle Holten
Jess Readett
Sarah Hardy

Rights and contracts
Peta Nightingale
Richard King
Saidah Graham

Milton Keynes UK
Ingram Content Group UK Ltd.
UKHW040224210924
448566UK00004B/272